PRAISE FOR *The Tomorrow Code*

A Junior Library Guild Selection

A Kids' Indie Next List Pick

"Readers are swept into visions of ecological
disaster and a planet fighting back. With puzzles aplenty,
codes, computers and a submarine called Mobius, this
technothriller offers gearhead ecowarriors everything,
including a hugely satisfying ending. Exciting and
thought-provoking, it will raise awareness
of serious issues as it entertains."
—*Kirkus Reviews*

"Falkner crafts a solid thriller for his U.S. debut,
in which immunology, ecological depredation, and
Maori culture all play significant roles."
—*Booklist*

"[Brian Falkner] is one of New Zealand's
most popular authors of fiction
for young readers."
—US Federal News

THE TOMORROW

CODE

BRIAN FALKNER

RANDOM HOUSE ⌂ NEW YORK

Grateful acknowledgment is made to the following
for permission to reprint previously published material:

Alfred Publishing Company, Inc.: Lyrics from "Big Yellow Taxi," words and music by Joni Mitchell,
copyright © 1970 (renewed) by Crazy Crow Music. All rights reserved by Sony/ATV Music Publishing.
Lyrics from "Santa Claus Is Comin' to Town," words by Haven Gillespie and music by J. Fred Coots,
copyright © 1934 (renewed) by EMI Feist Catalog, Inc. Rights for the extended renewal term in the
United States are controlled by Haven Gillespie Music and EMI Feist Catalog, Inc. Exclusive
worldwide print rights administered by Alfred Publishing Company, Inc. All rights reserved.

Sony/ATV Music Publishing: Lyrics from "Yellow Submarine," words and music
by John Lennon and Paul McCartney, copyright © 1966. All rights reserved.

Visit us on the Web! www.randomhouse.com/teens

Educators and librarians, for a variety of teaching tools, visit us at www.randomhouse.com/teachers

Crack the code, or tomorrow is history! www.tomorrowcode.com

The Library of Congress has cataloged the hardcover edition of this work as follows:
Falkner, Brian.
The tomorrow code / Brian Falkner.
p. cm.
Summary: Two New Zealand teenagers receive a desperate SOS from their future selves and set out
on a quest to stop an impending ecological disaster that could mean the end of humanity.
ISBN 978-0-375-84364-8 (trade) — ISBN 978-0-375-93923-5 (lib. bdg.)
— ISBN 978-0-375-84365-5 (tr. pbk.) — ISBN 978-0-375-89233-2 (e-book)
[1. Science fiction. 2. Environmental disasters—Fiction. 3. New Zealand—Fiction.] I. Title.
PZ7.F1947To 2008
[Fic]—dc22
2007036607

Printed in the United States of America
10 9 8 7 6 5 4 3 2 1
First Trade Paperback Edition

For
Rachel,
Nicki,
Frances,
Ray,
and Nancy,
my team of secret agents,
without whom nothing would have happened.

And for Claire B.,
who was right.

CONTENTS

She yearns for things that once were.
He dreams of things that might be.

They must learn from the past
to change the future.

But they are running out of time.

BOOK 1

THE CHIMERA PROJECT

THE END

The end of the world started quietly enough for Tane Williams and Rebecca Richards, lying on their backs on a wooden platform on Lake Sunnyvale. Which wasn't really a lake at all.

Sunnyvale School was set in a small valley. A nice little suburban valley. A hundred years ago, it had been a nice little swamp where Pukeko and Black Stilts had competed for the best nesting positions, and croakless native frogs had snared insects with their flicking tongues. But now it was a nice little suburban valley, surrounded by nice little homes belonging to nice little homeowners who painted their fences and paid their taxes and never gave any thought to the fact that when it rained, all the water that ran through their properties also ran through the properties below, and the properties below those, and so on until it reached the lowest point of the valley floor. Which happened to be Sunnyvale School.

As a consequence, Sunnyvale School had to have very good drainage. When it rained hard, as it often did in Auckland in the spring, an awful lot of that rain made its way down from the hillsides and ended up on the playing fields and courts of the small but cheerful school.

And sometimes the water, sauntering its way down the slopes with a mind and a mischievous personality of its own, would playfully pick up odds and ends along the way with a view to blocking those very good drains that the council had put in many years ago after the first and second (and possibly the third) time the school had flooded.

Sometimes it worked, and sometimes it didn't. It depended on what the water happened to find in its path. Little sticks and paper food wrappings washed right through the big metal grills of the drains. Small branches, stones, and other large objects generally just ended up at the bottom of the homeowners' nice little properties.

But light twigs and pieces of plastic sailed merrily down the surface of the water and blocked the drains beautifully.

That was what had happened this particular time, and the sports fields of Sunnyvale School were covered in at least four inches of water, high enough to lap at the doorsteps of the cheerful little classrooms across the way, but fortunately not quite high enough to get inside.

Tane and Rebecca lay on their backs on the small wooden viewing platform in the center of the two main playing fields and looked up at the stars, for the rain had stopped many hours ago, and the night was clear and beautiful.

Neither of them were pupils of Sunnyvale School; in fact, both of them were far too old to attend the school, and for another fact, both of them were in their second year at West Auckland High School.

However, when they were younger, they had both gone to Sunnyvale School, which was why they knew that when it rained really hard during the day and stopped at night, it became a magical, wonderful place to be.

The stars above shone down with a piercing intensity that penetrated the haze of lights from the suburban homes around the valley. The moon, too, was lurking about, turning the weathered wood of the small platform to silver. All around them, the lights from the sky above reflected in the inky blackness that was Lake Sunnyvale. The lake that sometimes appeared on the playing fields after a particularly heavy rainstorm.

There were stars above and stars below, rippling slowly in the light breeze, and it was like being out in the center of the universe, floating through space on your back.

Tane and Rebecca thought it was the coolest place to be. On Lake Sunnyvale. After the rain.

Tane tossed a pebble into the air, and there was a satisfying *plop* a few seconds later as it landed. They both raised their heads to see the widening circles of ripples, shaking the foundations of the stars around them. Then, as if controlled by the same puppeteer, they put their heads back down together.

Tane's feet were pointing one way, and Rebecca's were pointing the other, so the tops of their heads were just about touching. If they had been boyfriend and girlfriend, they might have lain down side by side, but they weren't, so they didn't.

From an open window in a house somewhere on the surrounding slopes, an old Joni Mitchell folk song reached out plaintively across the water to them.

Rebecca said again, "Time travel is impossible." She said

it more firmly this time, as if that were simply the end of the discussion, and the judge's decision was final, and no correspondence would be entered into.

Now, ordinarily Tane would have given up at that point, because Rebecca was almost certainly right. After all, it was Rebecca, and not Tane, who had aced her Level One Physics exams the previous year, the top student in the entire country, at the age of just thirteen! Which had been no real surprise to Tane, who had been in the same classes as his friend as she had confounded science teacher after science teacher and math teacher after math teacher by somehow, instinctively, knowing as much about the subject they were teaching as they did.

Some teachers enjoyed having Rebecca in their class because she was very, very clever, if a little rebellious and uncontrollable at times. But other teachers found it stressful to have a girl amongst their students who took great delight in correcting them whenever they made mistakes.

So if Rebecca said that time travel was impossible, then time travel was impossible. But there was something about the stars that night. Something about their slow drift through the heavens above and below them, something about the beautifully random and randomly beautiful patterns they made.

Or then again, it might just have been that Tane liked to argue, and he especially liked to argue with Rebecca.

"I read a book once," Tane said. "I can't remember what it was called, but it was about these grad students who go back in time to medieval days to rescue a missing historian, and they fight—"

"*Timeline*," interrupted Rebecca, who also loved a good

argument and especially enjoyed showing that she knew more than Tane. "Michael Crichton, 1999."

"Yeah, that's it. But anyway, they manage to create this . . . like . . . pinprick in the fabric of time somehow, and then they kind of transmit themselves through it."

"I know. I read it," said Rebecca. And then, perhaps because she realized that she was sounding a bit negative, she said, "I mean, the science was quite good in it, about the fabric of space-time, and the quantum foam, all the way up to the part where they transmit themselves through this tiny hole into the past."

Tane twisted his head around to look at her, but it hurt, and all he could see were her shoes, so he twisted back again. He thought for a moment. True, he wasn't as good at math and science as she was. Tane's strengths were in art and music, and he was a school legend on the harmonica, but even so, the time-travel thing sounded at least feasible to him.

"Why?" he asked eventually. "Why couldn't they transmit themselves?"

"Try to think logically," Rebecca said firmly but not unkindly. "How could you transport a live human being through a pinhole of any kind?"

"What about a fax machine!" Tane said suddenly. "You put a piece of paper in at one place, and it gets sent along a telephone wire and comes out in another place."

"No, it doesn't."

"Yes, it does," said Tane, starting to get into the argument, even though he knew she was going to turn out to be right.

"No, it doesn't," repeated Rebecca. "A copy of the piece of

paper comes out. The actual piece of paper you sent stays right where it was. All you are sending is an electronic image of the paper, just like a digital photograph of it. *Fax* is short for *facsimile*, which means 'copy.'"

"So . . . um . . ." Tane was losing and he knew it.

"We can transmit pictures, sound, even movies, through wires, or through the air in radio waves. But we can't transmit a solid object. Not even a piece of paper."

And that was pretty much the end of the conversation for the moment. They stayed on the platform for a while longer. Neither of them really wanted to go home, for reasons of their own. They talked about school a bit and made some jokes about some of the people in their classes. It was about ten o'clock, after they had sloshed their way through Lake Sunnyvale back to the road, when Tane resumed the argument, as if they had never left off. Which just showed that he had been quietly thinking about it the whole time.

"Well, if we can't transmit people through time, what about sounds, pictures, and movies, like you said?"

Rebecca had to actually think about that for a moment, which was a small victory for Tane. He pulled out his harmonica and played a slow blues riff as they walked. "Nope," she said at last. "If I understand the science right"—and Tane thought she probably did—"then you could only send stuff backward. You couldn't transmit to the future because that hasn't happened yet."

"But you could send it to the past?!"

"Well . . . theoretically. But let's say we invented some kind of radio transmitter that could broadcast through time. Something that could transmit messages through the quantum foam. Nobody could listen to the messages we were sending, because in the past they wouldn't have invented a radio receiver that could pick up the transmission."

"Oh," said Tane, thinking that Rebecca, as usual, made perfect sense.

They reached Rebecca's house and stopped.

All the lights were off, but one of the windows flickered with the blue glow of a television. Her mum was watching TV, which was no great surprise, because that was pretty much all her mum did all day and all night. At least since Rebecca's dad had died.

"Oh," said Tane again pointlessly, and glanced up at the sky just in time to catch the brief flash of a shooting star.

That was when the inspiration struck him. That was the moment when it all seemed so clear.

"So what if someone in the future had already invented a time radio transmitter and was sending messages back to the past, waiting for someone to invent a receiver?"

He wasn't sure if that sounded silly or not, so he just waited for the usual rebuff from his friend.

It didn't come.

"What's that again?"

"Well, let's just say that some time in the future, someone invents one of those transmitters you were talking about. And just say they are sending out messages, through that foamy stuff, just waiting for someone in the past to invent a receiver."

"Well, I . . . um . . ."

"What if we built a receiver and just listened. Just waited for a signal from the future."

"Well, the whole concept of quantum foam is not even proven. And I wouldn't have the slightest idea how to build a receiver," Rebecca mused. "But it's an interesting idea."

That may not have sounded like much, but it wasn't very often that Rebecca thought that Tane had an interesting idea, so it was kind of an important day, if only for that reason.

Although, in hindsight, it was actually an important day for much bigger reasons than that.

"You want to come on another march with me?" Rebecca asked, walking slowly backward up the driveway toward her darkened house.

"Of course," Tane said automatically. "What are we protesting about this time?"

"Whales," Rebecca said.

Tane shook his head. "I've got no problems with whales. They've never bothered me."

Rebecca laughed. "It's a couple of weeks away. I'll remind you."

She turned and disappeared into the carport and inside her home.

FATBOY AND HIS MOKO

It was a couple of weeks before the subject of the quantum foam came up again, and in all that time, Rebecca never mentioned it once, which made Tane think she had forgotten about it.

However, a lot of other things happened during those weeks, some of which were to have far-reaching and long-lasting effects, such as Tane's older brother asking Rebecca out to the movies or Rebecca getting arrested. Another thing that happened was that Rebecca and her mother were kicked out of their home.

Tane's older brother's name was Harley. Harley had been a chubby kid, and with a name like that, he quickly picked up the nickname Fatboy, as in the classic Harley-Davidson motorcycle. He hated the name when he was ten, but by the age of fifteen, thanks to years of rugby, the weight had turned into muscle; yet the name had stuck, and Fatboy—Fats to his friends—kinda liked it. It was no coincidence that when he got his full motorcycle license, he came home the same day with a genuine Harley-Davidson Fat Boy.

Fatboy was a musician. The kind with dreadlocks and a leather jacket, not the kind who played in a symphony orchestra. And he wasn't a rock star about to be discovered and have number-one hit singles around the world. At least Tane didn't think so.

Fatboy was a session musician. He played guitar and he was pretty good at it. Good enough that he had dropped out of school before his sixteenth birthday to pursue it. ("Over my dead body," their mother had said, but somehow she had survived.) Fatboy had a kind of natural affinity for music, which must have run in the family because the same aptitude flowed through Tane's veins.

Fatboy was seventeen, and although he wasn't particularly good-looking, he always seemed to have at least two girlfriends on the go at any one time, which seemed a bit excessive to Tane, who (in his opinion) was much better-looking but didn't have a girlfriend at all.

Rebecca, on the other hand, had had a couple of boyfriends, but they hadn't lasted long. She was quite nice to look at, quite pretty in fact, in her rebellious, punky way. But some boys were afraid of her intelligence and thought she was a bit of a know-it-all, which in fact she was. Other boys thought she was going out with Tane, which in fact she wasn't.

The day that Fatboy asked Rebecca out, she was at Tane's house playing chess. It was Sunday. The day after Lake Sunnyvale.

The lounge of Tane's house was huge and split over three levels, so it was almost three lounges connected into one. Up through the center of the three levels grew the massive trunk of a hundred-and-fifty-year-old tree. It wasn't technically inside the house. It was more like there was a hole up through the center of the house in which the tree grew, with huge plate-glass windows on all four sides.

They were on the lower of the three lounges, nestled into the embrace of the native bush that surrounded the home. From the middle lounge, the house had million-dollar views out across the valley to the lights of the city, and from the uppermost lounge, a long balcony led off to a series of treetop-level rope walkways. This high in the mountains, you could walk out amongst the trees and surround yourself with birdsong on a warm summer's evening.

It was a very expensive house that Tane's father was able to afford because of his very successful career as an artist. Rangi Williams painted animals, usually New Zealand native animals, in their own environment. He often disappeared into the bush for days at a time, armed only with his sketch pads. His paintings sold all around the world. There was something especially appealing, apparently, about paintings of New Zealand's native creatures painted by a descendant of the Maori, New Zealand's native people.

The architecturally designed house was a stark contrast to Rebecca's home, which was old brick and tile and was nestled on the hillside that encircled Sunnyvale School.

Tane advanced his knight to attack Rebecca's rook. He liked to attack his opponents' rooks early in the game, as it weakened their attack later on.

"Are you sure you want to do that?" Rebecca asked.

Tane considered the move. And he considered Rebecca. Sometimes she would say that because he had just made a really dumb move. But other times she would say that to make him think that he had just made a really dumb move when really he hadn't.

He examined the board once again and removed his hand from his piece.

"I'm sure."

Rebecca shrugged and moved her rook. On her next turn, she captured his queen.

"Bum," Tane said quietly. It *had* been a really dumb move.

The throaty roar of an engine was followed by a spray of gravel from the driveway as Fatboy spun his motorcycle around and flicked down the stand. He always parked like that, roaring up at high speed and spinning the back wheel around on the gravel. He said he liked to leave the bike facing the way he was going, not where he had been, but Tane thought he did it just to show off. It annoyed their mother to distraction, as she had to spend hours picking pieces of gravel out of her prizewinning flowerbeds.

Still, he knew she was always secretly pleased when Fatboy came to visit, which wasn't all that often now that he had his own flat in the city.

He left his motorcycle boots at the door. Not even Fatboy was brave enough to tramp all over their still-new-looking carpets wearing outside footwear. He left his jacket on, though, as he swaggered inside and was just taking off his helmet when he noticed Tane and Rebecca lying on the floor with the chessboard.

"*Kia Ora*, Rebecca. *Kia Ora*, little bro," Fatboy greeted them in Maori.

"*Kia Ora*, Fats," Rebecca replied.

Tane just said, "Whatever."

Fatboy changed his culture like other people changed their clothes. A couple of years ago, he had been totally into his "homeboy" phase, walking around with an outsized baseball cap and calling everyone "m'homey." Now he was into this Maori heritage phase. Tane couldn't help wondering what was next.

Rebecca glanced up as Fatboy took off his helmet. "Cool!" she said.

Tane looked to see what she was talking about. Fatboy was grinning at them through a brand-new *moko,* a Maori face tattoo. The left half of his face was inscribed with a fern-like design that seemed to swirl and dance with a life of its own.

Tane turned back to the game, shaking his head. "Mum is going to kill you."

Fatboy laughed. "No, she won't. It's cultural."

Tane ignored him and launched a vengeful, ill-considered attack on Rebecca's queen.

"What are you doing?" Rebecca asked slowly.

"Revenge," Tane said with a mock sneer. "Teach you to take my queen!"

Rebecca shook her head and studied the board. "You can't play chess like that."

Tane looked up. Fatboy was watching the game with interest.

"You look like a gang member," Tane muttered.

Rebecca said, "I think it looks great. Really suits you."

She smiled at Fatboy, which annoyed Tane more than a little. She had known Fatboy almost as long as he had, and she was the last person he would have expected to be taken in by the whole dreadlocks, leather jacket, rock-star-in-the-making persona. And now that Fatboy had a face tattoo, he was "cultural" as well. Tane thought things couldn't get a whole lot worse.

Things got much worse, very quickly.

Fatboy stopped at Rebecca's smile. Whatever he had come home for, he seemed to forget about it. It might have been to get their mum to do his washing or ask to borrow the Jeep (because as cool as it was, sometimes a motorcycle could be a little inconvenient); but whatever it was, he forgot it and stopped, looking at Rebecca as if seeing her for the very first time.

Tane looked at Rebecca, who had already turned her attention back to the board, and he thought he understood why. The short, spiky haircut with the blond tips. The pierced nose and the determinedly unfashionable clothes. Her eyes were too big for her face, but that with her fine cheekbones gave her a slightly elfish appearance (in a rebellious, punky kind of way!). The slightly awkward girl he had grown up with was blossoming into the kind of lovely young lady who would attract the attention of people like his older brother.

Get lost, he willed Fatboy. *Go and show Mum your* moko, *or whatever you came here for.*

"Are you winning?" Fatboy asked, turning on his false rock-star charm for the first time with Rebecca. *Surely* Rebecca would see through that in a second.

"I'm doing all right," Rebecca said, glancing up. Tane gave Fatboy a dirty look.

"What are you doing on Saturday night?" Fatboy asked.

Tane glared at Fatboy and bit his lip. It started bleeding.

"Nothing," Rebecca said cautiously.

"I'm recording with Blind Dog Biscuit all this week," Fatboy said, name-dropping with relish, "but I'm free on Saturday. How would you like to go to the movies? On the Harley," he added for good measure.

"I, um . . ." She looked at Tane for inspiration, but he just shrugged.

"It'd be fun," Fatboy said.

"Okay. That'd be okay," Rebecca said after a moment, trying unsuccessfully to act cool.

"I'll pick you up at seven," Fatboy said. "Blind Dog Biscuit might be having a wrap party later on for their new album. We can go to that too, if you want."

Rebecca shrugged. "Okay."

Fatboy disappeared into the depths of the house, leaving Tane staring after him, trying not to show his annoyance.

Rebecca moved her queen to the end of the board. "Check-mate," she said with a smile, and looked up at him. "Your lip is bleeding," she noted with some concern.

"It's nothing," Tane said.

She looked at him closely. "Tane, you don't mind if I go to the movies with Fatboy, do you?"

He shook his head quickly and said with just a trace of irritation, "No, why would I?"

Just then, there was a scream from the kitchen.

The week passed surprisingly quickly. In fact, when he looked back on it the next weekend, Tane felt as if time had somehow compressed itself, and they had somehow time-slipped from one weekend straight to the next and missed the five days of school in between. Which made him think idly about his time-radio-transmitter idea.

On the Saturday night when Rebecca was out with Fatboy, he spent a lot of time thinking about his time-radio-transmitter idea. But she hadn't mentioned it at all, so he felt he was probably just wasting his time and brain cells.

On Sunday morning, Tane arrived at Rebecca's house just after eight, the panicky phone call from Rebecca ringing in his ears the whole way. He'd cycled the few miles between their houses at a breakneck pace.

It was drizzling, which made cycling dangerous and not much fun, but he made it without incident. He left his bike lying in the carport next to the old two-door sedan with the missing front bumper and raced up the cold concrete steps.

Rebecca met him at the front door, crying. She was trying to hold it back but was failing, so her words came out in muffled lumps between the sobs. She put her arms around Tane's neck, and he hugged her.

"Is this something to do with Fatboy?" he asked. "Last night . . ."

She shook her head. "No. No. He was nice. It's this."

She uncurled from around his neck and showed him a piece of paper she was clutching. He read it quickly. It was a notice from their bank of the mortgagee sale of their house.

"I got home really late after the party last night. I had such a good time, and Fatboy was such a gentleman. And I got to meet the band, and they weren't like I thought they'd be; they were just regular guys. But the party went on all night, and I didn't get home till four this morning."

Tane thought that was far too late for a fourteen-year-old girl to be out at night. Especially with *his* older brother.

Rebecca continued, "I was tired, but really happy. I'd had such a great time. Then a man came to the door this morning, at seven-thirty; he got me out of bed. I was barely awake. He wouldn't talk to me and insisted that I wake Mum up. When she came down, in her dressing gown, he asked her for her name, and when she told him, he just handed her this envelope, and said, 'You have been served,' and walked away. Just like that. He didn't say anything else."

"Oh, Rebecca," Tane said, feeling useless.

"Mum just threw the envelope in a drawer and went to watch TV. She didn't even open it."

Judging by the sounds from the other room, it sounded like Mum was still watching the show.

"So I opened the drawer, and look!"

Rebecca took Tane into the small dining room of the house. On the old glass and metal dining table were piles of envelopes and pieces of paper.

"They're bills and mortgage demands; they go back months."

Tane picked up an electricity account. "This one's up-to-date," he noted.

Rebecca nodded. "Dad had set up most of them to be paid by automatic payment. Things like the power and the phone. But others have just been accumulating. And it looks like the mortgage hasn't been paid for months!"

It took Rebecca three or four days after school to straighten out the accounts.

Tane helped as much as he could, which mostly consisted of opening the envelopes for her and sorting out bills into piles from the same company, and also by date.

It wasn't good news at the end, though. The house was definitely going to have to be sold, and with all the unpaid bills, Rebecca and her mum would have nothing. No house and the only money they'd have to live on was the small allowance her mum got from the government as a widow with a dependent.

"What will you do?" Tane asked when they finally worked out all the numbers and realized just how dire the situation was.

Rebecca shrugged. "I tried to talk to Mum, but she was watching *The Beautiful Years,* and Dr. Messenger was just about to poison his wife's sister, so she wouldn't listen to me." There was the faintest trace of bitterness in her voice.

"So what will you do?"

Rebecca sighed. "I think we're going to have to move to Masterton, to live with Grandma."

Tane caught his breath and held it for a moment before releasing it. Masterton was a six-hour drive away. That meant he would hardly ever see her. If ever.

"When?" he asked.

"The lady at the bank said we have about a month, until the house sells."

Tane nodded. He looked at Rebecca, head in her hands, leaning forward over the lined pad she'd used for her final calculations. The light from the single bulb above the table made little shadows around her eyes. He thought she suddenly looked a lot older.

He wished there was something he could do. But there wasn't.

"Just a month," she said slowly, shaking her head. "It's not much time."

"No," Tane agreed, trying to think of a way to take her mind off her problems.

To his surprise, though, her mind was somewhere else entirely.

She said absently, "So we'd better go and see Professor Barnes as soon as possible."

Tane raised an eyebrow. "Professor Barnes?"

"As soon as possible."

THE BURST AND TRANSIENT SOURCE EXPERIMENT

The university corridors were long and winding. The high arched walls of the outside quickly disappeared to high, polished wood panels, which in turn gave way to white-paneled walls, white-paneled floors, and white-paneled ceilings.

This deep inside the university, the corridors branched frequently and unexpectedly.

The maze of corridors would have stymied Tane, but Rebecca had been there a few times to visit her dad, when he'd worked there, before the accident.

Rebecca's father had been one of the brightest minds in the Earth Science department at the university. Some said the only brighter mind was that of his wife. Rebecca's mother.

His car had been crushed by a furniture truck that had failed to take a bend. The truck driver was a sensible, experienced, and sober driver. He just took a bend a fraction too fast one day and killed Rebecca's father.

Rebecca was familiar enough with the layout to understand

the rather confusing array of small blue signs posted on the walls at corners as they hurried down the long passageways to a pair of white-paneled double doors marked GEO-PHYSICS LAB.

Rebecca caught Tane by the arm. "Let me do the talking, and agree with everything I say," she said.

"Are you sure you should be doing this?" Tane asked. He'd asked the same question a couple of times at school that day and had gotten pretty much the same answer, but he asked it again anyway. "I mean, with the house and everything."

It was Friday, and after spending most of the week straightening out her family's bills, it did seem a little odd that she was now spending energy on what was really nothing more than a whimsical conversation they'd had while lying on a platform at night on Lake Sunnyvale.

Then again, he thought, maybe it took her mind off her worries.

"I already told you," Rebecca said. "After we move to Masterton, I won't have the opportunity to do this. This is the only lab in the entire country that has access to live feeds from BATSE."

Tane still had no idea why they needed live feeds from BATSE, or even what on earth BATSE was, and he wasn't even really sure he wanted to know; but Rebecca had promised to explain it all in very simple terms, "terms that even an artist can understand," she'd said, after they had the data. Which was what they were here for.

She pushed open the doors, and they stepped into the lab, which didn't look like a lab at all. Whatever Tane had been expecting, it was not simply a row of desks with a computer on each one.

A balding man with gray hair and beard and narrow, wire-framed glasses looked up from his desk and rose to greet them. He looked very much the image of a university scientist, which of course he was.

"Rebecca," he said warmly. "You've grown." He looked as though he didn't know whether to hug her or shake her hand, so ended up doing neither.

"This is my good friend Tane," Rebecca said, and the man shook Tane's hand; then, as if that had made his mind up, he shook Rebecca's as well. She continued, "Tane, this is Professor Barnes. He used to work with my dad."

"How's your mum?" Barnes asked.

"She's . . . okay. She's fine."

"So, Rebecca, how can I help you?" the professor asked after a moment or two longer of meaningless small talk. "You said something about a piece of art? But I couldn't work out what that has to do with geophysics."

Rebecca smiled. "Tane is an artist, and a very good one, and he has this great idea of creating a piece of art from transmissions from the depths of space. Sort of an 'art of the universe' thing. It's kind of hard to explain." She gave Barnes a look as if to say, "Artists, you know."

"I see. I think," Barnes mused, and turned to Tane. "Any particular kind of transmissions you had in mind? There are a lot of them, you know."

Rebecca cut in before Tane would feel that he had to answer. "I was telling him about BATSE and the gamma-ray bursts. Tane felt that we could use the raw data from one of those bursts and model it digitally to create visual patterns in the computer."

Barnes looked confused. "Well, I suppose that could be considered as art. Actually, I paint a little myself. Landscapes, still lifes, that sort of thing. I have quite an original technique using flat knives. Maybe that would be of use to you, too. I could take some photographs and e-mail them to you. There is one painting in particular—"

"That would be great." Rebecca cut him off with such a wide smile that it didn't seem at all rude. "And the BATSE data?"

Barnes considered for a moment, then said, "Well, I don't suppose it would do any harm. As long as you're only using it for artistic purposes. We're the only lab in the country that has access to live feeds of this data, you know."

"Really?" Rebecca said, wide-eyed. "I didn't know that."

"There was a burst this morning. I downloaded the data a few moments ago. It's all just bits and bytes, though. Raw numbers, if you know what I mean. Are you sure that will be of any use to you?"

"Oh yes. We'll put it into some imaging software that will create representations of it, no problem," Rebecca said.

"Very well, then, I'll write it onto a disk for you." He disappeared through an unmarked door at the back of the lab and reappeared a few moments later with a CD.

"You promise you won't let anyone else have a copy of this? It's not top secret, but the data is copyrighted; it belongs to NASA."

Rebecca said sweetly, "Who on earth would I give it to?" She took the CD from Barnes's outstretched hand and passed it straight to Tane.

The data made no sense to Tane at all. It was as Barnes had described, just long strings of ones and zeros. Raw computer data. But he also didn't understand Rebecca's explanation of what this was all about.

He lay on his bed, watching her tap carefully at the keyboard on his study desk. They were at Tane's house because he had a new and powerful computer. Tane knew Rebecca envied his computer and resented a bit the fact that he mainly used it to play games. Rebecca didn't have a computer at all.

"Okay, try and stay with me on this," she said, adding a line of code to the computer program she was working on. Tane concentrated furiously on her face, in the hope that by doing so, he might somehow "stay with her on this."

"I did some reading about quantum foam, and I found out that scientists think it may be possible to detect the stuff, if it exists, by looking for fluctuations in these gamma-ray bursts."

She stopped, staring at her code for a moment, then added a pair of brackets around part of an equation.

"Go back a bit," Tane said. "What are gamma-ray bursts, and where do they come from?

"Okay. They are explosions of a type of radiation called gamma rays, which are a bit like X-rays or radio waves but with an extremely short wavelength."

That didn't help Tane a bit, but he nodded as if it did.

Rebecca continued, "Nobody knows what causes them, but they seem to come from all over the galaxy. In 1991, NASA sent up a satellite called the Compton Gamma Ray Observatory. It has an instrument on it called the Burst and Transient Source Experiment."

"BATSE!" Tane exclaimed.

"Right, BATSE. It's the most sensitive detector of gamma rays in the world. What we have on this disk is data from a burst of gamma rays that was received by BATSE this morning. It's probably just random data from random gamma waves. But if the quantum foam scientists are correct, then the gamma rays could be affected by the quantum foam, and therefore, theoretically, and don't ask me how, it could be possible for someone in the future to transmit a message using these fluctuations in the gamma rays."

"Nope," Tane said. "You lost me at BATSE."

"Doesn't matter. We'll analyze the data and look for patterns. That's what this program is for. If we find them, great. If not, well, it was a wild idea to start with."

She pressed a couple of keys on the keyboard and said, "Hold your breath."

Tane looked at the screen and waited, but apart from a single, flashing cursor, nothing was happening.

"What's it doing?" he asked.

"My program looks for patterns. It could take a while, though; there is a lot of data to look through, and the patterns could be quite complex. But if it finds a series of numbers that form a definable pattern, it will stop and we'll be able to look at it."

"Okay, cool," Tane said, although he had really been hoping that it would have been flashing colors and weird patterns on the screen as it worked, a bit like the ambience patterns you got on Windows Media Player.

They watched the flashing cursor for a bit, but it got very boring very quickly.

"Why wouldn't NASA have found these patterns?" he asked after a while.

"They're not looking for them," she said. "They're trying to find out what causes the bursts. They think it might be two neutron stars colliding, or maybe a neutron star being swallowed by a black hole."

"Really," Tane said, nodding his head and wondering what on earth she was talking about.

"There are some scientists from Texas who are looking for fluctuations, but they're trying to prove the existence of quantum foam, and they're still trying to work out what a quantum gravity signature would look like. Nobody is looking for messages in the rays."

"Just us."

"As far as I know."

Tane watched the cursor for a while longer, then turned and looked at his friend, looking at the cursor. Her eyes never left the computer screen.

He had known Rebecca all of his life. A lot of people said things like that, but in their case it was true. They shared the same birthday, and their mothers had shared a maternity ward at the hospital. They had even lived close to each other in those very early years, before Tane's father's career had taken off and he and Tane's mum had built the big house amongst the trees up in the mountains. Tane and Rebecca had played together in kindergarten and now went to the same high school. For nearly fifteen years, there had never been a time when he had not known the spiky-haired girl sitting next to him.

"I'm going to miss you when you go to Masterton," he said.

Rebecca said quickly, "Don't forget the march tomorrow. We need to get down to the station before nine to catch the bus into the city."

"I'll set my alarm clock," Tane promised.

SAVE THE WHALES

On the day of the big march, Rebecca got arrested. The Japanese prime minister was visiting Auckland. What he was doing there, Tane wasn't sure. Some trade summit or international congress of some kind; he didn't really know or care.

The protest march was set to start at the same time as the prime minister's flight arrived at the airport, which was mid-morning on Saturday. It would wend its way up through the central city, arriving at the prime minister's hotel just about the same time he would be.

Tane gripped his placard with both hands and held it high. Just to show his support for the cause. The cause was something to do with whales and saving them from Japanese whaling boats, but it was actually more complicated than that and had something to do with fishing quotas and scientific whaling and all sorts of other things that he was sure were worth fighting for, or against. Whichever it was.

Rebecca certainly believed so, and Tane couldn't let her march by herself. He hadn't let her march by herself on the anti-nuclear march or the anti-GE (genetic engineering) march, although he'd had the flu on the day of the climate-change march, so she had done that one by herself.

There had probably been a time when Rebecca didn't feel strongly enough about some issue to want to march in protest about it, but that was probably when she was in preschool, and Tane couldn't remember it.

He thought most people in the difficult situation that Rebecca now found herself in would have lost interest in protest marches. It was she who needed saving at the moment, not the whales. It could have been another excuse to take her mind off her problems, but Tane thought it was rather more than that. He'd known Rebecca a long time, and he knew that when she committed to something, she always saw it through.

Which was why they were both there at the very front of the marchers. On the front line of the battle, as it were.

A long swelling chant began at the back of the line of marchers: "*Ichi, ni, san, shi* . . . don't kill whales, leave them be. *Ichi, ni, san, shi* . . .*"

"What's this itchy knee business?" he asked Rebecca in a quiet moment between chants.

She rolled her eyes. "It's 'one, two, three, four' in Japanese. It's because the—"

"Yeah, yeah, I get it now," Tane said as the chant began again.

"*Ichi, ni, san, shi* . . . don't kill whales, leave them be!"

"Thanks for coming, Tane," Rebecca said after a while.

"Gotta save those whales!" Tane said enthusiastically, waving the banner around and accidentally clouting a large man with a shaved head who was wearing a leather jacket and marching next to them.

"Sorry," Tane said.

The man grinned and nodded to show that no harm was done.

It was an officially sanctioned, organized march, which meant that the road was blocked off by police cars with flashing lights at each intersection along the route.

Another police car preceded them, rolling slowly forward just a few yards in front of Tane and Rebecca.

Along the way, early morning shoppers either raised their arms in the air and shouted in solidarity or just stared curiously at the throng, which was wide enough to completely cover the roadway and stretched away behind them. There had to be a thousand marchers, Tane thought, although he wasn't much good at estimating the size of crowds.

The march started down on the Auckland waterfront and proceeded straight up Albert Street to the huge Sky City casino complex, with its massive three-hundred-sixty-yard-high Skytower.

They turned right just before the casino onto Victoria Street, then stopped at the entrance to Federal Street, where the Japanese delegation's hotel was.

Wooden barricades prevented the marchers from entering the street, so they had to wait, milling and chanting, completely blocking the road.

It didn't take long for the prime minister's motorcade to arrive. First came a police car, then a large black van that had to be filled with security guards. Then a long black Mercedes limousine.

The chanting rose to a crescendo as a line of police

officers formed a human barricade behind the wooden one. Behind the blue line of police, Tane could see the slender figure of the Japanese prime minister emerge as a large man in a dark suit opened the door of the limousine and stood to attention.

Several New Zealand dignitaries that Tane didn't recognize stood in front of the hotel, waiting to greet the man.

And that might have been the relatively peaceful end of it, if it hadn't been for the prime minister stopping as he got out of the car, turning to the protestors, and waving cheerily.

Maybe he was just being friendly. Maybe he was waving to someone he knew. But it was the worst thing to do to a crowd that had been winding itself up, chanting and shouting over the past twenty minutes while marching. It was like pouring gasoline onto a barbecue.

There was an angry roar from the crowd, like that of a wounded animal; then suddenly the wooden barricades were down, toppling under an onrush of protestors. The police linked arms and stepped forward to meet the onslaught. Behind them, more police officers drew batons and waited.

The Japanese prime minister and the other dignitaries scurried toward the hotel, all thoughts of ceremony vanishing in the face of the wild beast that lunged toward them.

Tane tried to push himself backward, but it was impossible with the press of the crowd behind him, and he found himself crushed up against a huge policeman with a beard and bad breath. The air squeezed out of his lungs with the pressure from behind, and an overwhelming feeling of claustrophobia enveloped him.

The thin blue line held, though, the storm of protestors safely contained on the outside. All except one, Tane saw through a thin gap in the blue uniforms. A small, quick shape, a blur of movement, and Rebecca was halfway toward the Japanese delegation, dodging around the larger, slower policemen like a rugby player evading tacklers.

She almost made it, shouting and screaming something about whales and murder, when one of the large, dark-suited men grabbed her by the arms, pinning her and forcing her to the ground.

At that point, the line fractured and split apart in a dozen places, the fury of the crowd intensifying as one of their own was attacked. Suddenly there were protestors running everywhere, some battling police batons with their makeshift placards.

The bearded policeman whirled away from Tane, and he managed to fight his way sideways, unable to see Rebecca, unable to do anything but try to claw breath back into his lungs and get out of the running, crushing crowd.

He found a small oasis amongst the huge concrete pillars at the base of the Skytower and slumped to the ground, exhausted.

In the end, they had to call in the riot police to clear Federal Street. Over a hundred people were arrested, but most were released without charge after being processed at the Auckland Central police station, just a few blocks away.

Tane waited outside for four hours until Rebecca finally emerged, bruised and disheveled but defiant.

"That was awful," she said. "They photographed us, took our fingerprints, and jammed us all into these tiny cells while someone decided what to do with us."

"I tried to get to you," Tane said, which wasn't really true but seemed like the right thing to say.

"You couldn't have done anything," Rebecca said. "They had me into the police van in three seconds flat. In handcuffs!"

She rubbed her wrists, and Tane could see red marks where the cuffs had been.

"It's so unfair," she raged quietly. "They're the criminals, killing whales and calling it research, but we're the ones who end up with a criminal record!"

"Don't worry about it," Tane said. "You're still a kid. They have to erase all record of the arrest the day you turn eighteen. I read that somewhere."

She was silent.

"Really," he insisted, trying to make her feel better. "It's nothing. It won't matter at all."

He was wrong, though—as it turned out, Rebecca getting arrested mattered quite a lot.

11100111

Tane's computer was very new and very powerful. It had a shiny silver case and a flat nineteen-inch screen, with a cordless mouse and keyboard. It was very expensive. He'd gotten it for his fourteenth birthday, so it was pretty much the latest processor, and it had a lot of memory, a fast hard drive, and a high-powered graphics processor, and it was generally really quick at anything, especially games.

So it was a little bit hard for Tane to understand why it was taking so long for it to run Rebecca's program. She started to explain it to him once or twice, but her explanation about the program code made no more sense to him than the code itself.

The only good thing was that once it was running, it kept running all by itself, without needing assistance from anyone. Not that Tane felt he would be able to give it any kind of assistance anyway.

They had started it running on Friday night, the day

before the protest march, and it was still running the next Sunday. And Monday.

More days passed. A week. Then another. Sometimes Tane would wake up during the night and would feel that the insistent flashing of the cursor was reaching out to him. But mostly he just wondered if it was really doing anything at all, or if it was just stuck in some mindless loop because of some bug in Rebecca's program.

A third week went by. That week, Rebecca had another date with Fatboy, although she said she didn't feel very much like dating, with all that was happening. But she went anyway. That night, the flashing cursor seemed like a warning light.

The day of the auction, November 14, was the day that the program finally paused and displayed some data on the screen, but Tane wasn't there to see it. Neither was Rebecca. Painful as it was, they were both at the auction.

It was a bright, chirpy day and for that reason the auctioneer, who looked just like a dapper little English gentleman but who spoke with an Australian accent, held the auction outside in the small backyard. Tane had mown the lawn, and they had both spent an entire weekend weeding to make the place presentable. He thought it looked as good as it could look, as the potential buyers, the tire-kickers, and the nosy neighbors gathered around.

The auction turned out to be a disaster. It was over in less than ten minutes, and the house, Rebecca's family home, sold at a bargain-basement price to some flamboyantly dressed young entrepreneur.

Rebecca shuddered once or twice as the hammer fell, and Tane put his arm around her shoulders.

At that price, Rebecca and her mother wouldn't even be able to fully repay the bank. They'd have to keep making mortgage payments, plus pay the creditors, and they'd have no money for the move to Masterton. It was an all-around disaster.

Rebecca was crying silently as Tane led her inside. He offered to make her a cup of cocoa, but she shook her head and said she wanted to go to bed for a while.

He rang his mum and told her he'd be home a bit later than expected. She didn't mind and asked if there was anything she could do to help, but there wasn't really.

When dinnertime came, he found a few bits and pieces in the cupboards and the freezer and made some savory pancakes, but neither Rebecca nor her mother would eat them.

He ate them himself at the dining table, which was still covered in mounds of paper, and a bit later, he went to check that Rebecca was okay.

He pushed the door open noiselessly. The light from the hallway spilled inside. It was not a little girl's room, and it was certainly not a typical teenage girl's room. In place of the posters of boy bands, there were posters for Greenpeace and Amnesty International. The books on her bookshelf were by Stephen Hawking and Salman Rushdie, rather than Meg Cabot or Jacqueline Wilson.

She was lying on top of the bedcovers, still fully clothed but sound asleep. In sleep, the heaviness and the tiredness lifted from her face, and there was a stillness and a calm about her that wrenched Tane's heart.

He pulled a blanket over her and gently brushed his hand against her cheek by way of a goodbye.

It was still light, but only just, when he stowed his cycle in the garage and wound his way up through the many levels of his parents' house to his room, and there, waiting for him on the screen, was a long line of ones and zeros.

Rebecca's software had found a pattern.

"Thanks, Tane, thanks for everything." Rebecca smiled at him tiredly over the Sunday-morning cup of cocoa he'd made her. He'd quietly let himself back into the house at about eight, using Rebecca's key, which he had borrowed on his way home the night before. "You're a good friend. We'll keep in touch, after I move down to Masterton, won't we?"

"Of course we will," Tane said. "We'll probably be on the phone every night, and I can come and visit you on long weekends, stuff like that."

She smiled and nodded her agreement, although they both knew that it would probably never happen.

She said, "Yesterday was such a nightmare. I don't even want to think about what we're going to do now."

"When do you think you'll leave?" Tane asked.

"I dunno. I think the settlement date is in about three weeks, and we'll probably have to be out before then. I expect I'm going to have to organize it. Mum doesn't seem to want to have anything to do with it. I don't know how we're going to pay for it, though."

Tane had a thought and said, "Maybe my mum and dad can help out. A loan of some kind."

Rebecca looked down at her mug. "I'd say no and tell you that we're too proud and all that. But I guess we're not. We're just desperate." She laughed. "I just hope my BATSE analyzer finishes running before we leave."

"It already has."

"What?!!"

"I was going to tell you, but it didn't seem like it was important."

Rebecca put down her cocoa slowly, phrasing her words carefully. "Not important? Not important! It's probably nothing, just a random series of numbers that happens to look like a pattern, but if it is really a pattern, then we could be talking about the scientific discovery of the century!"

"I was going to tell you—"

"Bigger than the splitting of the atom. Bigger than the invention of the airplane. Bigger than . . . than . . . big. But don't get excited, because it is probably nothing."

It was a little hard not to be just a bit excited, Tane thought, considering that Rebecca was just about jumping out of her skin. "Do you want to come and have a look?" he asked.

"We'll take Mum's car. It'll be faster," was her answer.

Tane hesitated. "I don't have my license."

"Me neither," Rebecca said as she picked the car keys off the hook by the door.

```
0001100110010000100000011001100011
0000011001110011000001100111000000
1001100111100000000110011100101010
1100000000110001010101100000111101
0101100010000011111010101000000001
1111100110000111011110001100010100
0001001000001100001010101110001111
110001111010100101
```

Rebecca was still wearing the same clothes as the previous day, Tane noticed. But then the previous day had been a day from hell, so he supposed it didn't matter.

She had been poring over a printout of the numbers for nearly an hour, trying to make sense of it, but as far as Tane could see, it made no sense at all, not even to her.

"Look," she said, running her hand along a line of ones and zeroes. "It looks like a pattern all right, and parts of it repeat, which is not the sort of thing you'd expect from a random explosion of gamma rays."

Tane looked, and it appeared pretty random to him. Just a long series of ones and zeroes printed in fine black ink on a plain white piece of paper. "Really?" he asked.

"Look, see this section?" She drew some quick lines in pencil on the printout, marking out a series of six digits. *001100.* "Look how many times that sequence repeats throughout the data. Nine times. Too often to be a coincidence. Here's another sequence: 0101100."

She pored over it some more, making notes on another piece of paper and occasionally adding up some figures on a pocket calculator. "The next step is trying to decipher it. Like cracking a code."

Tane peered at it, squinting, turning his head slowly to each side, trying to see some kind of picture in the numbers, like one of those hidden picture paintings.

Something stirred a faint breath of recognition, as though he had seen patterns like this before, a long time ago. He breathed out slowly, which was his usual way of trying to relax into a memory that would not quite come. The memory tickled and teased agonizingly at the far corners of his brain, but the picture would not come into focus. The harder he tried, the more it kept darting just out of reach.

After a while, Rebecca shook her head. "Maybe it is just

random after all. Depending on how you group the digits, there could be any different number of recurring sequences, or none at all. They say that if you had enough monkeys and enough typewriters, one of them would eventually type *Hamlet*."

"What are you talking about?" Tane snorted. "Monkeys and typewriters? Hamlet?"

"Not literally," Rebecca tried to explain. "It just means that if you have enough random . . ." She saw the grin on his face and threw her pen at him.

"But wouldn't they be better off using word processors?" Tane asked.

"Who?"

"The monkeys."

"Whatever."

The excitement of the morning had worn off by lunchtime (cheese on toast, provided by Tane's mother). If there was any kind of a pattern there, it was proving to be elusive, and the dark circles under Rebecca's eyes had returned. Even her hair, normally spiky and sharp, was limp and lifeless.

"I thought I was on to something for a while there," Rebecca sighed. "I really thought I had it."

"What?"

"No. It's wrong," she said sadly. "Binary code. That's the language that computers talk in—I mean, way down in the depths of their operating systems. Information is stored in bits, which can be on or off—"

"Yeah, I get it," said Tane, even though he didn't. "Move along."

"Well, the BATSE data is actually in binary code. My

41

program just displays it in ones and zeroes to make it easier for us to read. So I had this bright idea of translating the binary code into ASCII characters."

"Um, ooohkaaay."

"God, it's like talking to a monkey some days," Rebecca stormed.

"Maybe, but I've written this really cool play about this guy named Hamlet—"

"ASCII characters," Rebecca cut him off with just a brief smile, "are eight-character binary codes for the letters of the alphabet. For example, 01000001 is *A*, 01000010 is *B*, and so on. So I translated the whole string of characters using ASCII."

"And?"

"Oh." She seemed distracted. "Nothing, just gibberish. So then I tried it in BASE 64, which is another kind of computer code, but no luck; then I realized there were two hundred fifty-eight characters, which is two too many for ASCII or BASE 64, which must be in groups of eight, so I took off the first two characters and tried that in BASE 64."

"And?"

She handed over a printout.

```
ZkIGYwZzBnAmeAZyrj8czAMVDDVz9UA/MO
8YycAkxQ==
```

" 'Zuhkiggy wazzabeen ameezy,' " Tane read out importantly. "You know this is a really significant moment, like when Alexander Graham Bell invented the telephone and said, 'Mr. Watson, come here.' Except our first message says, 'Zuhkiggy wazzabeen ameezy.' "

"Bell didn't invent the telephone," Rebecca said sourly.

"Maybe that's the language they speak in the future," Tane said. "Maybe 'Zuhkiggy wazzabeen ameezy' is future-speak for 'Hi, what's up?' or . . ." He trailed off, seeing that she was not laughing. "Sorry."

A tear appeared at the corner of Rebecca's eye and found its way slowly down her cheek.

"Let's go for a walk," said Tane, feeling stupid and useless.

From the back of the house, a narrow, little-used track wound through the trees and eventually joined up with one of the main hiking trails through the bush of the mountains. Not even forty-five minutes of steady walking along that brought them to the top of one of the dams that were scattered through the mountains to provide water for the city below.

This was a small, earthen dam that almost seemed a part of the hillside. They leaned on a solid wooden handrail, hewn from a half-round log, and looked down at the lush bush-covered hillside below.

The memory that had been tickling at Tane's mind was still there. He tried not to think about it. That was what his dad always said. Stop trying so hard. Let your subconscious sort it out.

"It's beautiful here," Rebecca said. "I love it. All you can hear is the water and the wind in the trees and the birds—" She stopped, interrupted by a loud bell-like sequence from just above their heads. "There, what's that one?"

"Korimako," Tane said. "Bellbird. And that's a saddle-back over there."

"How do you know all these?" Rebecca asked with a grin. "Are you a secret bird-watcher?"

Tane smiled and shrugged. "Nah, just Boy Scouts. Had to learn them all in Scouts. If you passed a test, you got a badge that . . . you . . . could . . ."

The delicate tendril of a memory tugged again at the back of his mind, tantalizingly close. He shut his eyes for a moment, and then, after what seemed like an age but was no more than a second or two, he said, "We've got to get back to the house."

"What is it?" Rebecca asked, but Tane was silent.

He flattened the sheet of paper out on the coffee table and smoothed it with his hand.

"You said it would be like cracking a code," he said, and pointed to the short pattern of numbers that Rebecca had marked: *001100*. "When I was a scout, I got a lot of badges. I got my New Zealand Birds badge, and I also got my Morse code badge. Now, if this was Morse code, then that would be a comma."

Rebecca froze and turned to him. Her eyes were wide. She didn't seem to be breathing. "Morse code?" she said in a dry voice.

"It's a method of signaling that ships—"

"I know what Morse code is," she rasped.

"Well"—he hesitated—"I can't remember much of it, but I can remember a few bits. If the ones were dots and the zeroes were dashes, that would be a comma."

"Okay. So what would this be, before the comma?"

"Ummmmm . . ."

"Google," said Rebecca determinedly.

A few moments later, they had a printout of all the Morse code characters.

A ·-	M --	Y -·--	6 -····
B -···	N -·	Z --··	7 --···
C -·-·	O ---	Ä ·-·-	8 ---··
D -··	P ·--·	Ö ---·	9 ----·
E ·	Q --·-	Ü ··--	. ·-·-·-
F ··-·	R ·-·	Ch ----	, --··--
G --·	S ···	0 -----	? ··--··
H ····	T -	1 ·	! ··--·
I ··	U ··-	2 ··---	: ---···
J ·---	V ···-	3 ···--	" ·-··-·
K -·-	W ·--	4 ····-	' ·----·
L ·-··	X -··-	5 ·····	= -···-

Half an hour later, they were no closer to solving the puzzle.

"It might be Morse code," Rebecca said. "But Morse code characters aren't all the same length, and that makes it really hard to decipher. Take this first bit, for example: 00011001100. That could be *O, I, M, I, M,* or it could just as easily be *M, N, P, W* or any of a hundred other combinations, none of which make sense!"

"Yeah," Tane said slowly, poring over the printout. "But if I was right about the 001100 being a comma, then we have 00011 comma 1000010000 comma 1100011000 comma, and so on."

"Well, 00011 is eight," Rebecca said, checking the chart, "and 10000 is one, 11000 is two, so that would give us eight, eleven, twenty-two, thirty-two, thirty-nine. . . ." She paused and looked at Tane. "Holy crap!" she said. "I think it *is* Morse code."

They looked at each other for a long time, desperately eager to carry on and translate the code but strangely afraid to. Slowly their eyes dropped back to the paper.

"That's it," Tane said after a moment. "See, 101010; that's a period. That must be the end of it."

"No, there's still a lot to work out. But let's start with this bit," Rebecca said.

They looked intently at the sheet.

$$8,11,22,32,39,40,3.$$

Tane said, "And . . ."

There was silence for a few moments.

"I don't know," Rebecca admitted. "They're just numbers. The fact that we picked them out of a gamma-ray burst using Morse code is pretty significant, but as for what they mean . . ."

"Are you sure this isn't just more monkeys typing *Hamlet*?" Tane asked after a while. "More random noise that just coincidentally happens to make Morse code characters? I mean, why use Morse at all? Why not use that ASCII stuff, or Moonbase 64 or whatever it was?"

"Base 64," corrected Rebecca. "Anyway, that's easy. Binary takes eight bits, eight ones or zeroes, to make a single letter like *A*. Morse code does it in less than half that. *E* and *T*, for example, take just one digit. *E* is dot, and *T* is dash. So they can fit many more letters into a single message. Maybe there's some kind of a limit, like on a text message."

"They need to change their phone company," Tane muttered.

"Eight, eleven, twenty-two . . . ," Rebecca read out loud.

"We're going to have to think creatively on this," Tane said. "Think outside the box. How many numbers are there?"

"Seven."

"The lowest number is three, and the highest is forty."

"Yes. The numbers start at eight and go upward, until they get to forty; then it suddenly drops back down to three."

Rebecca said, "Maybe it's a series, and we have to work out the next few numbers in the series."

Tane said nothing and closed his eyes.

Rebecca said, "It can't be letters of the alphabet, because there are only twenty-six of those. Maybe if I calculated the differences between each pair of numbers or . . ."

"No," said Tane suddenly, "you're thinking too logically. Try to think creatively."

"What do you mean? How can you think 'creatively'? We have to approach this logically."

Tane considered that for a moment, then said, "Okay, here's an example. It's a puzzle that my dad once gave me."

He took the pen and wrote a series of letters on a clean piece of paper: O, T, T, F, F, S, S, E.

"What's the next letter in that series?" he asked.

"Do we have time for this?" Rebecca shook her head.

"Try it."

"Okay, then." She took the pen from him and made a few notes on the paper. "*E* would be the obvious answer, because the other ones are doubled, but the *O* is not, so that can't be right. *O* is the fifteenth letter of the alphabet, *T* is the twentieth, *F* is the sixth—"

"See, you're already being too logical," Tane said. "It's much simpler than that."

"Simpler?" Rebecca looked confused. "How can it be? There's no numerical consistency. Ah, but working backward, *S* comes after *T*, and *E* comes after *F*, so maybe—"

"*N*," Tane said. "The answer is *N*."

"No, it's not. That's not logical—"

"One, two, three, four, five," Tane read out, pointing at the letters. "It is the first letter of each word. The next one is *N* for *nine*."

"That's stupid," Rebecca said. "Anyway, you're the creative one. You think creatively."

"Okay, then," Tane said. "Well, first of all, we need to consider that there are all kinds of numbers. Phone numbers. PIN numbers. Combination-lock numbers."

Rebecca agreed. "Dates are usually written as numbers."

"Room numbers, house numbers, decks of cards have numbers."

"Then there are serial numbers, like on money." Rebecca stopped, seeing the look on Tane's face.

"Money . . . ," he said very slowly.

Rebecca waited, watching him closely. Tane tried to keep his face steady, but it kept wanting to break out into a huge goofy grin.

"Well, share!" she said impatiently.

"What . . . if . . ."

"What?!"

"Six seemingly random numbers from one to forty . . ."

"Seven numbers, and from three to forty," corrected Rebecca.

"No, six, and from one to forty. The first six numbers fall between one and forty; it just happens that the first number is an eight. Then after those six numbers there's another number between one and eight."

Rebecca looked at him blankly.

"Don't you see?!" Tane shouted. He dived off the bed and ran out of the room, leaving Rebecca sitting there stunned and not quite sure why.

He was back in a few seconds clutching a newspaper, which he flipped quickly through, then thrust in front of her face. "Don't you get it?" he cried. "The six numbers are the Lotto numbers! The last number is the Powerball number!"

Rebecca, who had stood up when Tane had started rushing like a mad thing around the room, suddenly found herself sitting back down again without intending to.

"Holy crap!" was all she could say, looking at the winning numbers from the previous week's draw, crumpled in the paper in front of her nose: 3, 22, 27, 30, 39, 40, and 7 for the Powerball.

"Somebody sent us Lotto numbers!" Tane said. "From the future!" And then repeated himself two or three times.

"But who would . . ." Rebecca trailed off.

"I don't know!" Tane shouted.

"But why would—"

"I don't care!" he hooted.

"But for which draw?"

There was a long pause, and Rebecca slowly took the newspaper from Tane's hand and lowered it to the desk beside the computer, mesmerized by the short sequence of digits.

"I don't know," Tane said finally.

"If we are right about this, it'll be the scientific discovery of the century," Rebecca whispered.

"If we are right about this, we're going to be rich!" Tane cried.

It took at least an hour before Tane could settle himself down enough to even look at the piece of paper again, but the numbers were still there, and they still looked a lot like Lotto numbers.

Rebecca, when she had calmed down, turned back to the computer printout with all the ones and zeroes on it.

"What about the rest of it?" she murmured thoughtfully. "We've only worked out the first bit."

"I know," Tane agreed. "Let's get started."

```
1100000000110001010101100000111101
0101100010000011111010101000000001
1111100110000111011110001100010100
0001001000001100001010101110001111
11000111101010101
```

Rebecca nodded. "The periods are easy to spot. They are the 101010 sequences."

Tane said, "It looks like more numbers. That first 11000 is a two."

"I think you're right," Rebecca said, "Two, zero, two, period."

She quickly translated the next few characters and printed it out in neat block letters.

```
202.27.216.195,
```

"What does it mean?" Tane asked.

"I don't know." Rebecca frowned and tapped the pencil on the paper. "And this next bit."

```
0011101111000110001010000010010000
0110000101010111000111111000111101
0100101
```

"I don't think it's numbers. There's 00111011110, then a comma."

It took them about half an hour to come up with a combination that worked, but when it did, it was obviously correct.

"*G U E S T*—guest!" Rebecca said with relish.

Tane was still puzzling over the next section. "Does 'Compton1' mean anything to you? That's the only combination that seems like a word."

"Yes!" Rebecca exclaimed. "The Compton Gamma Ray Observatory, remember? That's where they pick up the BATSE data!"

"Of course." He rubbed at his temples. "My head hurts."

"Not much to go now," Rebecca said brightly. "I'll take the next bit, and you do the last sequence." She smiled sympathetically. "My bit is longer."

Tane looked at his segment. "0101." It made just a few combinations: *NN, KE, TR, TETE, TEN,* or simply just a *C.* He discounted the *TEN.* All the other numbers had been represented in digits, not spelled out. For reasons that he couldn't quite fathom, he decided that *TR* was the most likely.

He looked over at the section Rebecca was working on.

111000111111000111

She already had half a page worth of combinations scribbled out.

"I'm getting there," she said. "I think *I, A, M, S, I,* maybe a *J . . .*"

"I am Sij," Tane laughed, but the laugh suddenly died on his lips.

Rebecca noticed Tane's expression. "Why do you look so worried all of a sudden?"

"It's much simpler than that," Tane said strangely. "Every Boy Scout in the world knows that one. Dot, dot, dot, dash, dash, dash, dot, dot, dot. Then it repeats."

"Yes?" asked Rebecca, who had never been a Boy Scout.

"SOS!"

MR. DAWSON'S
TREE MUSEUM

The four science buildings at West Auckland High School formed a huge cross. Physics, Chemistry, Biology, and Geography, two-story gray concrete structures with a classroom on each level. The blocks were surrounded by the concrete of the playing courts and the asphalt of the teachers' parking lot.

In the center of the cross was an open courtyard where the corners of the four buildings touched, and in the 1990s, Mr. Dawson, a forward-thinking biology teacher, had claimed the area for his department. He had ripped up the cobblestone paving, thrown out the wooden bench seats, and wheelbarrowed in, with the help of a tenth-grade biology class, a load of fertile earth.

Then, with the blessing of the principal, he had planted the courtyard with New Zealand native plants. His aim was to re-create the wilderness of New Zealand as it had been two hundred years ago. Before Western civilization with its six-lane motorways and oxidization ponds and two-story gray concrete classrooms. He installed a small pump and piped in water from his biology classroom—carefully filtered to remove the chlorine and fluoride—and irrigated the plants with a small stony-bottomed brook that babbled happily across the courtyard and into a drain on the other side.

Mr. Dawson was only forty-two when he died of a massive stroke caused by a heart attack. There was neither rhyme nor reason for it. He wasn't overweight or unfit.

Some people just die young.

But Mr. Dawson's death, just a few months after completing his garden, ensured that the project, which had never been intended to last more than a couple of years, became a permanent fixture at West Auckland High School.

Students were not usually allowed in the Fred Dawson Memorial Garden, except when they were working on biology or environmental projects. The last thing the school wanted were chewing gum and chip packets destroying the carefully maintained environment.

Rebecca Richards was one of the few exceptions to this rule, but then, she was an exceptional student in many ways. The courtyard got a willing caregiver, and Rebecca got a quiet place to get away from the other fourteen-year-old girls discussing makeup and hair and fashion and bra sizes and the current romances of their favorite singers and TV stars.

Rebecca loved the peace and the seclusion of the garden. Tane, however, thought it was somehow sad in a small way that he did not quite understand.

Tane sat on a punga log, strategically placed as a seat, and stared quietly at the clear water of the brook, chewing slowly on a peanut butter sandwich. Rebecca, on the other hand, could not stay still for a second. She sat down; she jumped up. She found a weed and pulled it out; she fidgeted. She picked her nails; she scratched her head. She didn't touch her lunch at all. Tane had never seen her like this.

Oddly, Tane wasn't thinking about the Lotto numbers, and he wasn't thinking about the SOS. Both of them had talked and thought about little else over the past week, and Tane had found it almost impossible to concentrate on his studies, which was becoming a serious problem with final exams now so close. It was November 20, and the exams started on the 30th.

But just at that moment, he was thinking about chess. Not the game in general, but one chess set in particular. The chess set in question was extraordinarily beautiful. It was made of marble and all the pieces were famous sculptures. The king was Michelangelo's *David*, and the rook was Rodin's *Thinker*. Tane had been saving for most of the year to buy the chess set and had only one payment left to make. It wasn't for himself. It was for Rebecca. For Christmas. And he knew she'd love it, and he knew that she would know that he had saved for most of the year for it.

But strangely the Lotto numbers changed all that. If they really were Lotto numbers, then he and Rebecca were about to be rich beyond anything they could have imagined. And the fact that he had saved all year for the chess set would be meaningless. Rebecca would be able to buy twenty marble chess sets if she wanted.

He supposed it was a small price to pay. The sudden wealth would mean they could buy anything they wanted and, more importantly, that Rebecca and her mother could afford to buy a new house in Auckland and not move to Masterton.

But all that depended on whether they were right about the Lotto numbers. And then there was the question of which draw. Tane had had a moment of panic, worrying that the draw with their numbers might have already come and gone, but they had found an Internet site with all the Lotto results on it and had checked back six months. To their great relief, their numbers hadn't yet come up, so they resolved to buy a ticket every week until they did.

There was also the problem of the section of the cryptic message they had not yet solved. And the worrying SOS in the tail of it.

"The next Lotto draw is tomorrow night," Rebecca said. "What are we going to do about the problem?"

Tane looked up from the brook. Rebecca was pacing around the moss-covered dirt in small, darting movements, like a bird. "Sit down," he said, patting the log next to him.

She sat but kept twitching as if she wanted to keep pacing.

The problem. They had been discussing *the problem* almost since they had realized what the numbers meant. There was a Lotto draw every Saturday night. The *problem* was that to buy a Lotto ticket, or claim a prize, you had to be sixteen years or older. And Tane and Rebecca weren't.

It was a real problem. Tane's parents were out of the question. They didn't believe in gambling. Tane's mum believed that it was introduced by the pakeha, the European settlers, to keep the Maori people debt-ridden and down-trodden. There was no chance there.

Rebecca's mum was another possibility, but she hadn't left the house in over a year and wasn't likely to anytime soon.

Tane continued, "We have to do something. What if the

numbers come up tomorrow night and we miss it! The Powerball Jackpot is up to six million dollars. How many adults would you trust with that kind of money? They could just claim the prize and keep it for themselves. We would never be able to prove that we gave them the numbers."

Rebecca stopped fidgeting for a while and said, "Then it has to be Fats."

Tane turned away from her and said softly, so that his words were almost swallowed by the muttering of the small brook and swept away downstream, "Fatboy is the last person I would trust with six million dollars of my money."

"But at least he's family!"

"Only by blood. Not by choice."

Rebecca put her hand on his arm. "How can you say that? He's your big brother."

"I don't trust him," Tane said.

"I really don't understand why you're so down on him all of a sudden. Is it because he took me out a couple of times?"

The recorded sounds of a native parrot reverberated suddenly off the painted concrete walls around them. Tane looked at his friend. She was a different person than the one of just a few days ago. The light inside her was back, even brighter than before, despite the fact they had not yet proved, or won, anything. The light was excitement, he thought, but much more than that, it was hope. Her hope was a brilliant beacon in the darkness that had descended on her over recent weeks.

"Of course not. It has nothing to do with that."

"Well, I say we have no other choice. We'll sign him to a contract if that makes you feel any happier. Give him ten percent of the winnings—"

"Five."

"Okay, five percent. Now where is the message?"

Tane pulled a grimy, much folded, much looked at piece of paper from a back pocket, and they looked at it together, despite having both committed it to memory many times over.

```
8,11,22,32,39,40,3.202.27.216.195,
GUEST,COMPTON1.SOSSOS.TR
```

Rebecca said, "I'll ask Fatboy tonight, and if he agrees, we can write up some sort of a contract tomorrow."

Tane looked up in surprise. "Are you seeing him tonight?"

"Yeah, he's picking me up after school. We're going to the movies."

"I thought we were walking home together, to do some math study."

"Oh yeah." Rebecca was silent for a moment. "I forgot to tell you. Sorry."

"Final exams are only a few weeks away."

"I know. But I'm pretty comfortable with my math."

She was, and Tane knew it. She would probably top the country, even without studying. He said a little mean-spiritedly, "Well, if you're so clever, how come you haven't solved the rest of the message yet?"

```
202.27.216.195,GUEST,COMPTON1.
SOSSOS.TR
```

Rebecca ignored the barb. "How far in the future do you think the message has come from?"

"Who knows. Maybe thousands of years. What I'd like to know is who sent it."

"Me too."

The bell sounded distantly, beyond the concrete confines of the Fred Dawson Memorial Garden. The end of lunchtime.

That night, Friday night, while Rebecca was at the movies with Tane's big brother, Tane figured out the rest of the message.

Fatboy laughed. It was a friendly chuckle, but it sounded like an evil cackle to Tane, like the villain in a pantomime: "Moo-ha-ha-ha."

Fatboy said, "Five percent? Listen, little bro, I'm happy to go shares in a Lotto ticket with you; just don't tell Mum. But I'll chip in a third of the price, and we'll go thirds on any prize. You won't win the big one; the odds against that are enormous."

Rebecca and Tane shared a secret look. Saturday morning had dawned clear and calm in the forests surrounding Tane's house. It was the day of the big weekly draw, and that meant time was desperately short. Fatboy had picked up Rebecca from her place and brought her around on his Harley, because she'd told him that she and Tane wanted to discuss something important with him.

When he had found out that it concerned a Lotto ticket, he had roared with laughter. *Moo-ha-ha-ha!*

Tane said stubbornly, "All right, ten percent." He crossed out the figure on the contract that he had prepared, using his best legalese, and wrote in "ten percent."

He handed the paper to Fatboy, who promptly tore it

across the middle and laughed again. "Forget it. It's a silly bit of fun. You don't need a contract, and if I buy you the ticket, then we go thirds. Take it or leave it."

Tane growled under his breath, and Fatboy asked cheerily, "What, have you got it rigged or something?" and laughed again.

"Okay," Rebecca said, a little too loudly. "We go thirds. You buy the ticket, you claim the prize—"

"If we win," interjected Tane quickly.

"If we win. And you guarantee that you will give two-thirds of the money to me and Tane."

"Boy Scout's honor," said Fatboy, who, unlike Tane, had never been a Boy Scout.

Tane glared at Rebecca for a while before bringing out an envelope. The six Lotto numbers and the Powerball Jackpot number were clearly listed on the side. Inside were some crisp new five-dollar bills.

"Just these?"

"That's all," Tane responded. "For tonight's draw, and each week from now on."

"That's just one line. The more lines you buy, the better your chances."

"We don't want any other numbers, thanks all the same."

Fatboy persisted. "Look, you can't buy less than four lines, but if you're going to buy a ticket, you might as well give yourself a decent chance. Get a lucky dip with ten lines on it."

"No." Rebecca transfixed Fatboy with her gaze and spoke in a quiet, steady voice that eliminated all room for doubt. "No. Get four lines, then; you can choose the other numbers. But whatever you do, make sure you get the numbers on the side of the envelope."

Fatboy stopped laughing and looked at them both a little strangely for a moment, then shook his head as if dismissing a fanciful idea. "Cool, kids." He took the envelope with a sweep of his hand and stood up. "See you, Becks. See you, little bro."

"If we win the six million, you promise you'll share it?" Tane asked one last time.

"If we win the six million, I'll eat my motorcycle helmet!" Fatboy was out the door, his final laugh echoing back in through the open window. *Moo-ha-ha-ha.* Then the throaty roar of his bike and he was gone.

"He'll be honest," Rebecca said in a conciliatory way to Tane, who felt anything but conciliatory.

He nodded. "He'd better. But you're right. What else could we do? Imagine if the numbers come up and we haven't got a ticket!" He looked at her for a moment and she looked at him. Then, at exactly the same time, they both burst out laughing. It had nothing to do with Fatboy, Tane thought. It was just the sheer excitement of it all, and maybe a bit of relief at having finally solved *the problem.*

Now the new problem was how to fill in the time until the live televised Lotto draw at eight o'clock that evening. Tane looked at his watch. Only nine hours and forty-seven minutes to go.

He said, "Our share would be four million dollars. What could we buy with that?"

"A new house," Rebecca murmured, almost to herself. "But don't forget the SOS. There's more to this whole thing than getting rich. Whoever sent those numbers did so for a reason."

Tane stood up with a mischievous glint in his eye. "You'd better come see this."

Tane's computer was on in his bedroom. Rebecca sat on the bed while Tane took the chair and opened an Internet browser. She watched with a fascinated frown as he typed some numbers into the address bar.

```
202.27.216.195.
```

"Those are the numbers from the message . . . ," she realized.

Tane nodded. "It's an IP address. We learned about those last year."

"An Internet address. Of course!" Rebecca actually smacked herself on the forehead like they do in cartoons. "I should have recognized the pattern. What Web site does it take us to?"

"Have a look."

She stood behind him as the page slowly loaded onto the screen. The first thing that came up was the bright blue NASA logo. The next was a series of letters that they both recognized: BATSE. Below that were Username and Password boxes. Tane carefully typed "guest" into the Username, and "Compton1" into the Password.

He said, "It took me a couple of goes to get it right, because it was case sensitive."

"You clever bunny," Rebecca breathed. "Is this what I think it is?"

Tane nodded. "All the BATSE data." He pointed at a list. "That's the one we got from Professor Barnes. And that one arrived yesterday. These are all the ones in between. Want to analyze them?"

"Wanna try and stop me!" She almost kicked him out of the chair.

A moment later, her program was whirring away.

"It'll be quicker this time," she said. "I reprogrammed it to look for the Morse code patterns. It's quite clever but also quite complex. Do you want to know . . ."

"I—"

She didn't give him time to answer. "I went back and examined the raw data, and I found out something interesting. You see, the bursts are radiation waves, like an AM radio signal using amplitude modification to convey the ones and zeroes—"

"I'll take your word for it." Tane grinned.

"No, it's simple!" Rebecca said. "Imagine waves on a beach. There are big waves; those are ones. And there are little waves; those are zeroes."

"Okay." Tane nodded. "That much I understand."

"But sometimes there are gaps between the waves. And those are the gaps between the Morse code characters!"

"That is clever! And it'll make it much easier," Tane said. They had spent ages trying to work out all the possible combinations of the first message.

"Yeah, and faster . . ." She paused, noticing Tane's sly smile. "What are you smiling at?"

"I think I know who sent the message."

"You do?! Who?"

"Well, my guess is that was the final part of the message. Kind of like a signing off."

"TR?"

"Who do you know with the initials TR?"

Rebecca looked blank, and Tane's grin grew bigger.

"Isn't it obvious? TR. Tane and Rebecca. It's us. We sent the message to ourselves!"

Rebecca blinked rapidly a few times but said nothing as the enormity of that sank in.

Eventually she said, "Makes you wonder about the SOS, then, doesn't it."

Tane looked at his watch again. Nine hours and forty-three minutes to go.

SATURDAY NIGHT

Tane's watch said twenty minutes to go, and he was sure the hands were standing still. But as he watched, the second hand inexorably flicked over. From where he was sitting, on the soft leather sofa in the middle lounge of his parents' house, the lights of the city blazed up into the clear night sky. The flashing lights of an airplane made a staccato string of pearls through the sky above the city. He barely noticed it. The second hand ticked over again.

Rebecca's program had already decoded a second message from the future and was busy working on the third. The second message was just as cryptic as the first.

```
PROFVICGRNCHMRAPRJCTSTOPIT.
BUYSUBEONTLS.DNTGOMST.DNTTLNE1.
```

Rebecca was clicking her fingers in front of Tane's face to get his attention.

"Concentrate," Rebecca said. "This is important."

Tane didn't think it was all that important, but it was taking Rebecca's mind off the last twenty minutes, so he tried to concentrate, for her sake.

It was hard. His hands were shaking and he wanted to vomit. If the numbers were right, then Rebecca would be able to pay all their bills, and they wouldn't have to move to Masterton. Everything would be all right.

"It's called the grandfather paradox, and it goes like this. What if you went back in time and killed your own grandfather?"

"Why?"

"Why what?"

"Why would I go back in time and kill Grandad? He's nice. I've got nothing against Grandad."

"Tane! Focus! That doesn't matter. We're just saying *if*. Okay. *If* you went back in time and killed your grandfather when he was just a boy, then you would have never been born. Therefore, you could not have gone back in time to kill your grandfather. And so you would have been born, and so you could go back and kill him, but then you wouldn't have been born . . . and around and around it goes."

"Grandad takes me fishing," Tane said, but quickly added, when he saw that he was about to get thumped, "But I get it, I get it!"

"Some people say that time is like a Möbius strip. An endless loop with no start, no end, and a single surface, called the present."

Tane just shook his head. This science stuff was elementary to Rebecca, but it was way beyond him. His watch said nineteen minutes to go. *What if the numbers were wrong! What if they weren't Lotto numbers at all?*

"What's a Möbius strip?" he asked.

"Oh, come on! Do you ever stay awake in math?" Rebecca cried, and jumped up. She disappeared into Tane's room for a second and reemerged with paper, scissors, tape, and a pen. Tane watched intently as she cut a long strip from the paper and held the ends together in a loop.

"A Möbius strip is a piece of paper with only one side and one edge."

Tane tried to imagine that. "No way. If a piece of paper has a top, then it has to have a bottom. How can a piece of paper have only one side?"

"Watch."

Rebecca took one end of the strip of paper and twisted it over, just once. She taped it to the other end. "There you go. A piece of paper with only one side."

Tane took it and examined it. "Nope. Look, a top and a bottom. Or I suppose you'd say an inside and an outside." He knew he wasn't going to win this argument, but it was always fun to try.

Rebecca offered him the pen. "Draw a line longways, around the strip. Don't lift your pen off the surface. Stay on one side of the paper only."

Tane shook his head but took the pen and started drawing.

What if there was no Lotto win? No great scientific discovery? And Rebecca would still go to Masterton.

After a few seconds of drawing, he found himself right back where he started, joining up with the start of his line.

"So?"

"So you drew on only one side of the paper, right?"

"Yeah?" He looked at the Möbius strip. He had drawn around both the inside and the outside of the loop.

"See, it has only one side."

Tane frowned and forgot about his watch for the first time that day.

"But what has this got to do with us?"

"It's like we're on that loop. And when someone in the future sends a message to the past—"

"When *we* send a message to ourselves . . ."

"Whoever. But it's like they have made a hole in the paper and passed the message through to where we are in the past. But instead of paper, it's quantum foam, and the message is the gamma-ray burst."

"And what has my grandfather got to do with all this?"

"Well, they sent the Lotto numbers, right? But when we win—"

"If."

"Okay. Just suppose for a moment that it is us sending the messages."

"It is!" Tane insisted. "Think about it. Who else would know that we had thought of analyzing the BATSE data just at that precise time. Only us!"

"All right, us. If we win the Lotto but then forget to send the numbers to ourselves, then we won't win the Lotto, and around and around it goes!"

"Wow." Tane could think of nothing else to say, really.

Rebecca held up a notebook. "So I've got this notebook, and I have recorded the exact dates and times of the gamma-ray messages. Along with what the messages said, of course. Sometime in the future we have to send the messages, and any others that arrive, exactly as we received them. Otherwise, *kaboom*, the grandfather paradox."

"Leave my grandad out of this," Tane muttered. "And

where are we even going to get the gamma-ray time-messaging-machine thingy from anyway?"

"That part I'm not sure of. In the meantime, let's see that new message again."

Rebecca opened the notebook and they pored over it together. Rebecca lightly drew some lines in pencil to separate what she thought were the words.

```
PROF VIC GRN CHMRA PRJCT STOP IT. BUY
SUB EON TLS. DNT GO MST. DNT TL NE1
```

She said, "I think it's like text-messaging. That kind of truncated English."

Tane picked up the rest of the paper that Rebecca had made the Möbius strip from. "So what have we got?"

"I think the first part is easy. *PROF VIC GRN* has to be Professor Vic Green. I don't know who he is, but we can Google him or check with the universities later."

"What about *CHMRA PRJCT*?"

"Something project. Chim, cham, chem, chom, chum. Where's your dictionary?"

It was five to eight by the time they found the word.

"*Chimera!* That's the only word that fits." Rebecca pronounced it slowly. "Ky–mere–rah."

"What does it mean?"

Rebecca looked, and frowned. "In Greek mythology, it's a monster with a lion's head, a goat's body, and a serpent's tail."

Tane blanched, remembering the SOS. "I don't like the sound of that!"

"Wait, in biology, it means an organism formed by

grafting tissues or splicing genes from two or more different organisms."

"Chimera Project. Stop it. We are supposed to stop the Chimera Project. That's what this whole thing is about." Tane frowned. "I'm starting to wish they'd sent the message to someone else."

"We sent the message, according to you. Who else were we going to send it to?"

Tane's watch said seven fifty-seven. "Better turn the TV on," he said, and did so.

Rebecca was still examining the message. "We have to buy a 'SUB EON TLS,' whatever that is, and don't go to the 'MST.' Mast, mest, mist, most, must. Don't go in the . . ."

"Masterton," said Tane brightly. "Don't go to Masterton!"

"Okay," Rebecca said, "and the last bit is easy. 'Don't tell anyone.' "

The live, televised Lotto draw came on the TV, and Tane turned the sound up. He could hardly breathe. If the numbers were the same . . . *What if they weren't?* Then again, from the cryptic clues in the last message, maybe they'd be better off if they weren't!

Rebecca and Tane sat on the couch to watch the short program, the original crumpled piece of paper on the coffee table in front of them. The numbers stared back at them: 8, 11, 22, 32, 39, 40, 3.

"What time is your mum coming home tonight?" Rebecca asked idly during the theme tune and preamble.

"Not till after eleven. Why?"

His dad was away in the bush, and his mum was out at some community council meeting.

"No reason," Rebecca said quietly.

Tane dragged his attention away from the screen and

looked at her. He asked thoughtfully, "How's your mum? Will she be okay on her own tonight?"

"She's fine. Stop worrying."

Tane stopped worrying, but only because the Lotto hostess, elegant and sophisticated in a long blue gown, came on and started talking. Her blond hair was pulled back in a tight bun, and her smile was wide and toothy.

After an interminable introduction, the overly effusive hostess started the barrel rolling, and the Lotto balls began to tumble.

He barely felt Rebecca's hand slip into his. She was scarcely breathing.

The first number out was thirty-two.

"We've got that! We've got that!" Tane yelled.

Rebecca still wasn't breathing.

The second number was eleven.

"We've got that too! It is this week's draw! It is this week's draw!"

The next number rolled down the slope from the barrel and Tane froze.

"Thirty-six? Thirty-six?" He screamed, "It can't be thirty-six!"

The ball stopped rolling. The Lotto hostess announced, "Thirty-nine."

Rebecca collapsed against Tane.

He said, "Thirty-nine. It looked funny when it was rolling. It was a thirty-nine."

Rebecca didn't reply. She hadn't breathed since the start of the show. She finally took a breath after the next number, though. Eight. By that stage it was just a formality.

Forty. Twenty-two.

He didn't even bother watching the bonus numbers and

found to his great surprise that he was hugging Rebecca, and she was hugging him.

The Powerball Jackpot had been sitting at $6,325,450 by the time the Lotto booths had closed at seven o'clock that evening.

It was almost anticlimactic seeing the three ball come wobbling up the little tube.

"We proved it. Messages through time. It's the scientific discovery of the century!" Rebecca breathed out slowly, and added almost as an afterthought, "And we're rich!"

"No." Tane shook his head. "Not yet. At the moment, we've got nothing. Fatboy is the rich one. Let's see if he does the right thing."

Rebecca nodded. "He will. But now that we know it really works, we've got the important stuff to discuss."

Tane knew what she meant. That was one thing his mind kept coming back to again and again. This wasn't a get-rich-quick scheme.

It was a cry for help.

EVENSONG

Sunday was a good day. A day of celebration. Rebecca stayed over in the guest room, and Tane's mum made French toast for breakfast.

They didn't mention the Lotto win to her, even though to keep it inside when it kept trying to burst out was like trying to hold in an enormous belch after drinking a whole can of Coca-Cola. Tane wasn't quite sure why they kept it a secret. "Don't tell anyone," the message had said. But did that include his own mum?

Tane had tossed and turned during the night, dreaming of Greek monsters with teeth of fire, but even so, he was up at six, before the sun, and Rebecca was already awake when he got up. It felt a bit like the day after Christmas when all the excitement is over and done with, but the real fun of playing with all your presents is about to begin.

They just talked until his mum got up and made the

French toast. They talked about the money mainly. What to do with it. What to spend it on.

There were some dark thoughts lurking, but those didn't get a mention in the early light of Sunday.

By nine o'clock, they had solved most of the second message. Professor Vic Green turned out to be a woman, Professor Victoria Green, a highly respected geneticist. According to the Auckland University Web site, she was currently heading a private research laboratory on Motukiekie Island in the Bay of Islands.

But *SUB EON TLS* turned out to be the biggest surprise: *SUBEO NTLS*.

"It's a submarine!" Tane's eyes were wide. "We're supposed to buy a submarine! Cool!"

"I wonder why?" Rebecca said curiously.

Subeo was a British company. They had achieved international fame a few years earlier when they had produced what they called the world's first underwater sports car: the Subeo Gemini, a two-man submarine, designed mainly for recreational purposes.

The Subeo Aquarius had followed, a three-man version that also proved quite popular for commercial operators. But the latest model, not yet released, according to their Web site, was the Subeo Nautilus. If the Gemini was a sports car and the Aquarius a sedan, then the Nautilus was an underwater motor home. It was large enough for six people, an entire family, and could stay underwater for months on end. It was the first of the Subeo products to incorporate a diesel engine as a generator, to charge the banks of sealed-cell batteries that were the power source for the submarine.

Tane ran through three sheets of specifications that he downloaded as a PDF file before he came to the price.

"Holy cow!" he said.

"Where? Let me see." Rebecca grabbed the piece of paper off him.

"One and a half million pounds! What's that in New Zealand dollars?" She found a currency converter on the Internet. "That's over four million dollars!"

"We'll only just have enough, after Fatboy takes his share," Tane said grimly, the thoughts of riches vanishing before his eyes. "Are you sure we have to buy this thing?"

Rebecca nodded. "I wish I wasn't. There is a reason they, we, went to so much trouble to send this message back through time. I don't know what it is, but I know that we have to buy a Subeo Nautilus, and if they're in England, then we'd better get started."

Tane looked carefully at her. If they spent all their money on a submarine, then how would they afford to buy a new house for Rebecca? He opened his mouth to say so, but decided against it. Instead he just sighed and composed a quick inquiry e-mail to Subeo. He hesitated before clicking the SEND button but eventually sent the message on its way through cyberspace.

"Where the heck is Fatboy?" he wondered aloud.

That evening, after Rebecca had gone home and there was still no sign of his brother, Tane went for a walk out amongst the treetops. His dad had built the ropewalk himself, off the end of the deck, but it was sure and safe, if a little wobbly in places. There was a heavy rope for a base, like that of an anchor rope from a sailing ship. On each side, at about shoulder height and just in arm's reach, two more slender ropes gave you something to hold on to.

Tane didn't bother to open the safety gate; he just

swung his legs over it and walked the first few steps without even holding on to the handrails, balancing like a tightrope walker.

He came out here often. Some days because he wanted to, and other days the evensong of the native birds seemed to call to him.

The breeze had come up with the closing of the day, but the sun had yet to disappear behind the mountainside, so it was pleasantly warm. The leaves on the trees that surrounded him ruffled softly, but the branches and the rope were still. All around him, birds sang joyfully in an enveloping chorus.

His dad came out here a lot also. He said it beat the hell out of watching television in the evening, and Tane supposed he was right.

The last time he had seen his dad was a couple of weeks ago, just before he had gone bush on another painting project. Fatboy had come around that day to show off his *moko,* which he had somehow managed to persuade their mum to keep a secret.

Fatboy had walked in and taken off his helmet, and after an initial look of surprise, their father's face had cracked slowly into a smile, and his eyes had sparkled with pride. His dad had embraced Fatboy and pressed their foreheads and noses together in a *hongi,* the traditional Maori greeting. Then he had hugged his eldest son, and Fatboy, the cool, leather-clad, rock-star-in-the-making that he was, had hugged him back without embarrassment or backslapping.

Tane thought back on that now and shook his head. He and his brother couldn't be more different. He was getting messages from the future, but Fatboy was still stuck in the past.

Where the heck was Fatboy anyway? He had not called, and when they tried his mobile phone, it went straight to voice mail. Had he even watched the Lotto draw? Did he know? Maybe he did, *and that was why he hadn't called.*

A tui landed on the rail just in front of Tane's left hand. The distinctive white feather under the bird's chin looked like a miniature clerical collar. The parson bird, the early European settlers had called it, because it looked like a churchman. Tane didn't move. The tui looked at him suspiciously for a moment, then fluffed up its feathers and began to sing. The call of the tui was legendary, and they seemed to sing a different song every time you heard them. This bird, this day, had a slow, sad, rhythmical pattern that sounded like a lullaby.

After a while, the bird stopped and looked back at Tane, turning its head from side to side in small darting movements.

Tane raised a hand slowly toward the tui, inviting it to perch on his finger. The tui took a step backward on the rope. *I'm not scared,* it seemed to be saying, *but I'm not stupid.* Then it was gone in a whirling dash around and through the branches of a nearby macrocarpa.

Tane stayed put for a while, looking out across the valley toward the concrete spires of the city.

It would be a shame when this was all gone. He knew it was coming. The subdevelopers with their tractors and bulldozers would be here one day. Already, across the ridge in the next valley, he could see the brown scar where a construction crew had felled the trees and cleared the bush, preparing the foundations for a new lodge and conference center.

One day, this ropewalk would be something he would

tell his grandkids about, and they'd laugh, he thought, unsure whether to believe him.

He walked on to where he knew there was a new nest of young fantails. The mother was busy feeding them worms and didn't notice him.

Where the heck was Fatboy?

excitement beneath the words. Fatboy, too, was trying hard to maintain the ice-cool rock-star persona, but the excitement was seeping out into his inflection like a little kid with a new toy.

"No way. Exams start next Monday," Tane said steadily.

"Lunchtime, then. I'll meet you both at McDonald's."

Fatboy rang off, and Tane realized that he had forgotten to ask why he'd had his mobile phone turned off.

He speed-dialed Rebecca's number.

Lunchtime was at twelve-thirty, but by twelve thirty-seven, Fatboy still hadn't showed. Tane could barely restrain his excitement, and a Quarter Pounder and fries didn't help.

Rebecca, by contrast, was oddly silent and ate nothing.

"What's troubling you?" Tane eventually asked. "Is it the SOS?"

"No, no. Yes, I'm excited. It's just . . ." A small tear squeezed itself out of her left eye, and she wiped it away quickly. "I know you should never say 'What if.' What if this had happened, what if that had happened. But I just can't help thinking, what if we had thought of the whole thing a year earlier? Fourteen months earlier."

Tane reached across the small Formica-topped table and put his hand on her arm. He knew where she was heading.

Rebecca said, her voice choked, "They could have warned us. We could have told Dad to stay at home that day. Everything would be different." Rebecca struggled to contain the sobs. "Mum . . ." She couldn't continue.

"You're right," Tane said. "You should never say 'what if.' "

He wanted to say more, something to ease Rebecca's pain, but he couldn't find quite the right words, and then it was too late because Fatboy pulled up, right outside their

TRUST

Fatboy rang when Tane was getting ready for school, bleary-eyed and headachy. He'd been unable to sleep the night before.

His mum answered the phone, and from the tone of her voice, he knew instantly who it was.

His schoolbag dropped, spilling his pencil case and English study notes across the kitchen floor. He barely noticed.

"Harley wants to speak to you," his mum said, holding up the phone.

Tane had to restrain himself to avoid snatching the phone away from her. "Where are you?"

Fatboy's voice sounded cheerily in his ear. "We're millionaires, little bro. All three of us. We need to get together."

"We have school today." Tane tried to sound cool, as if he had never even remotely considered the idea that Fatboy might have absconded with the money.

"Can't you take the day off?" Tane could hear the

window in a brand-new, metallic green, soft-top Jeep Wrangler. There was a nervous-looking man sitting beside him in the passenger seat.

Rebecca grabbed Tane's napkin and patted at her eyes. By the time Fatboy and the stranger sat down, her smile was forced but believable. Just.

Fatboy slid across the bench seat with a flourish and put his arm around Rebecca's shoulders. He grabbed Tane's Coke. "*Kia Ora,* kids."

"Hey!" Tane protested.

"Buy yourself another," Fatboy laughed. "Hell, buy yourself the whole factory if you want to."

The stranger sat timidly on the end of the bench seat. He was tall and balding in a flat line across the top of his head. He had a black mustache. He said a little unsteadily, "Actually, the Coca-Cola Amatil factory would be worth considerably more than the six million you have available to invest."

"Don't you just love lawyers!" Fatboy and his *moko* grinned at them. "They're so literal."

"Nice wheels," Rebecca said cautiously.

"Yeah. Goes like stink too," Fatboy agreed. "I almost got it up on two wheels coming around Seymour Road."

Tane thought that might go some ways to explaining the rather nervous-looking lawyer.

"And we need a lawyer, do we?" he asked pointedly.

Fatboy reached inside his jacket and pulled out a thick, folded orange-colored booklet. He tossed it in front of Tane, who picked it up and examined it. *Realize Your Dreams. Winner's Information from the NZ Lotteries Commission.*

"Page twelve," said Fatboy. "Seek professional advice. Tane, Rebecca, this is Anson Strange; Anson, my brother Tane and my um . . . Rebecca."

They both shook the man's hand.

Fatboy continued, "I didn't have a spare helmet for the Harley with me. But it was no problem. I just ran next door to the Chrysler yard and picked up the Wrangler."

"I hope you got a discount," Tane muttered. "Why couldn't we get hold of you?"

Fatboy looked aggrieved. "I was on my way to Wellington to claim our winnings. You can't just run into the nearest Lotto shop and ask them to cash out a six-million-dollar ticket!"

"We tried your mobile phone."

"Can't use them on a plane."

Rebecca asked, "Are you sure we need a lawyer? I thought you said that was all unnecessary."

Fatboy answered, "Things are different now. With six million dollars to play with, we've got to do things properly. Otherwise we might go and do something stupid like spend it all on a flight to the moon or something."

"Or a submarine," said Tane under his breath.

Rebecca said, "Does anyone else know about our win? Like your mum and dad?"

"Or the press?" Tane added.

Fatboy shook his head. "Nobody. I requested that our details remain anonymous." He turned to the lawyer. "Anson, would you give us a few minutes?"

Anson rose dutifully and went to stand in a queue behind the counter.

"What are you guys into?" Fatboy asked as soon as Anson was out of earshot.

"What do you mean?" Rebecca asked innocently.

"You knew those numbers were going to come up. I'm not entirely stupid. Something's going on."

"Nothing's going on," said Tane quickly.

"Can you do it again? Pick the numbers?" Fatboy stared directly at Tane.

"No."

"Maybe."

Tane and Rebecca said it simultaneously. Tane was louder.

Tane could just about see the dollars ticking over behind Fatboy's eyes.

"I want in," Fatboy said. "I want a part of it."

You want a part of everything, Tane thought, and said sullenly, "You don't even know what *it* is."

"That's true." Fatboy grinned. "But I want in anyway. How's that? Is it illegal?"

Tane didn't think it would worry Fatboy if it was. "No."

"There are some big up-front expenses," Rebecca said cautiously.

"Bigger than six million dollars?"

Rebecca nodded slowly. "Maybe."

Fatboy whistled. "But you could do it again, right? The Lotto thing?"

"Maybe," Rebecca repeated, but it was clear that Fatboy interpreted that as a definite yes.

"So if I understand what you're saying . . . We all pool our money together now, and we all get an equal third of anything later."

"You don't know what you're getting into," Tane insisted. "Stay out of it."

The more Tane insisted, the more interested Fatboy seemed to get.

Fatboy said slowly, "Okay, I'm in. My two million for a one-third share."

"We need to talk about this," Tane said.

"I'll give you a minute," Fatboy said, and went to chat with his nervous-looking lawyer.

"No way." Tane was adamant, although he kept his voice low.

"We don't know what we're getting into," Rebecca reasoned. "He might be a good person to have around."

"I'd rather sell my soul to the—"

"Look, he came through all right with the Lotto ticket, didn't he?"

"I still don't trust him. And anyway, he thinks this is all some kind of moneymaking scheme."

"Well, trust him or not, and whatever he thinks, we need his share of the money."

"No, I figure we'll just scrape through without him."

Rebecca dropped her eyes and there was a sudden catch in her voice. "Sure. And where are Mum and I going to live? On the submarine?"

Tane's next sentence froze on his tongue.

"Come on, Tane."

"I think we'll regret it."

Rebecca reached over and kissed him on the forehead.

Tane realized that he already regretted it.

They told Fatboy everything. Tane hadn't intended to tell him any more than they had to, but once you showed a tiny corner of the picture, it just kind of led to more questions and they led to more questions, and before long, Fatboy knew as much as they did. He didn't quite believe them at first, but the Lotto ticket was a quite convincing argument.

Tane thought Fatboy would change his mind when he

found out that it wasn't just about picking the Lotto and was quite surprised when he didn't.

After that, Fatboy waved over their patiently waiting lawyer, who recommended a trust to cope with the financial arrangements.

After school, Fatboy picked them both up in the new Jeep, and they went to the bank to sign some documents and pick up cash-cards for their new bank account, which had almost as many zeroes in it as the messages from the future. Then Fatboy took them around to Tane's house to check their e-mail.

There had been no response from Subeo, but Fatboy, ever practical, suggested a phone call to the UK. He felt they could probably afford the cost of the call.

It turned out that the Subeo sales representative was in Sydney on a visit to the Australian Navy, and Fatboy didn't have to tell him too many lies to persuade him to add Auckland to his itinerary.

It was Rebecca who finally asked the question that Tane had been dreading. "What are we going to do about Professor Green?" she asked.

That brought reality crashing back into the excitement of the money and the trust and the submarine purchase. There was a reason for all this, they suddenly remembered. Some time in the future, they were going to be in big trouble.

Tane said, "If we believe the instructions in the message and understand them correctly, then we are supposed to somehow stop the Chimera Project."

"But what *is* the Chimera Project?" Rebecca wondered.

"Look it up on Google?" Fatboy suggested.

"I did," Rebecca said. "Nothing. So I looked up Professor Green and the research facility. There's a lot of stuff about their research into rhinoviruses—"

"Rhino viruses?" Fatboy looked up incredulously.

Rebecca smiled. "Nothing to do with rhinos. It's the virus that causes the common cold."

"Oh." Fatboy looked quite disappointed.

Rebecca continued, "But researching the common cold isn't going to cause a worldwide disaster, so that can't be the reason for the SOS. But then again, Prof Green is a geneticist, and playing with genes can be playing with fire. Maybe there's something else going on at the lab that they don't want the rest of the world to know about."

"The Chimera Project," breathed Tane.

"And we're supposed to stop it," Fatboy said.

"I think we should go and see the professor," Rebecca said, "ask her about the project, and perhaps ask her to stop it."

"And if she says no?" Tane asked.

"We'll worry about that when the time comes."

"Why don't we just tell the police?" Fatboy asked. "Or the government? Or someone official. I mean, what are the three of us supposed to do?"

Tane looked at Rebecca, who shook her head. "Not yet. I doubt they'd believe us, but more importantly, the message told us not to tell anyone. Until we know the reason why, we should follow the instructions."

Tane looked at her closely. That made sense, but he couldn't help wondering if there was a bit more to it than that. Was she afraid that someone else would whisk this discovery away from them and claim credit for their ideas and hard work?

• • •

The next day, school or no school, exams or no exams, SOS or no SOS, Tane and Rebecca took their new cash-cards and went shopping. It wasn't every day that you became a millionaire, after all. They didn't go wild, though. Nothing extravagant.

Rebecca bought a new pair of jeans that she'd been admiring for a while, then a couple of pairs of shoes to go with them. Tane bought a new leather jacket that he thought looked really cool.

Then Rebecca bought a few CDs—music she couldn't afford to buy before, just twenty or so of her favorite groups—and Tane bought a new joystick for his computer and a couple of new computer games. There were a few other odds and ends, too.

At lunchtime, Tane said he was going to take Rebecca to the best restaurant in the whole of Auckland, and according to the driver of the limousine they hired, the best restaurant in town was Number Five, which had just reopened up in City Road, near the Sheraton Hotel.

It was very nice. So nice, in fact, that it wouldn't let them in. Not in the clothes they were wearing. But half an hour in Smith & Caughey's fixed that, and Tane toasted Rebecca across a very fine cut of eye-fillet steak wearing the first suit he had ever owned and the second he had ever worn. The first being at Rebecca's father's funeral.

By the end of the day, the score was fifty-seven CDs, eleven DVDs, one top-end laptop computer for Rebecca, twenty-two articles of clothing, one computer joystick, four computer games, seven pairs of shoes, two books, four items of jewelry (of which Tane's new necklace was by far the most expensive), a bicycle, two pairs of sunglasses, a life-sized stuffed toy baboon that sat in a spare seat in the limo and laughed at them the rest of the day, three mobile phones, and a two-storied cliff-top house for Rebecca and her mother to live in that happened to have a boatshed, looking out over the water at West Harbor.

Nothing extravagant.

THE MAN FROM SUBEO

The man from Subeo was Arthur Fong, which sounded Chinese, although he wasn't. He said he'd be there on Thursday evening, November 26, at seven-thirty on the dot and rang the doorbell as the clock in the hallway just ticked over.

Tane, Rebecca, and Fatboy had gathered at Rebecca's new house for the meeting. Fatboy had picked up Tane after school, and they had had a quick dinner of fish and chips while waiting for Arthur Fong to arrive.

It was Tane who answered the door. He'd jumped up like a shot and practically sprinted for the door while the others were still registering the sound of the bell. Then, not wanting to appear too eager, he had sedately strolled down the polished wooden floors of the hallway to the front door.

The door was solid kauri inlaid with panels of stained glass. It was a nice door. It was a nice home. It wasn't new; in fact, it must have been fifty years old, but it was elegant, and a lot of money had been spent restoring it. None of which had really mattered to Tane, Rebecca, and Fatboy when they had found the place. What had sold them were two things. Firstly, it was vacant and available for immediate possession. Secondly, the back lawn led straight down to the edge of a high cliff above a secluded inlet of the upper harbor. At the bottom of the cliff, down a series of wooden staircases, there was a large, brown, slightly ramshackle boatshed.

From an upstairs room, the sound of a television washed faintly through the floorboards. Rebecca insisted that her mum was only grieving, that her mind was all right, but she had not questioned her daughter when she told her that they had bought a new house. Had not asked where the money had come from. Had just moved in, quietly accepted the room that Rebecca pointed out to her, and turned on the television.

As sad as it was, it was also convenient. It was good that she didn't ask too many questions.

Arthur Fong was tall. Thin of face but wide of bottom, he was rather like a pyramid in shape and when he realized that his appointment was with three teenagers, suddenly found several pressing reasons to leave.

"Sit down," Fatboy said, and added, "please," for good measure.

Mr. Fong sat down. People had a habit of doing things when Fatboy told them to.

"Listen," Mr. Fong said, "I admire your initiative. If this is for a school project, then I'd be happy to send over some brochures, even some of our technical drawings, which we don't normally release. But I am on a very tight schedule."

Tane said, "Mr. Fong—" But Fong held up his hand to

interrupt him. "I have spent time—and money—flying over here because I thought I was going to be meeting with a company who was genuinely interested in purchasing one of our products." He rubbed vigorously at his face with both hands, a gesture of tiredness and frustration.

"Can I get you a cup of tea?" Rebecca said demurely, and Tane glanced at her. That was not really like her.

That seemed to soften his attitude slightly, although he declined.

"Not had a good week?" Rebecca asked.

Mr. Fong smiled tightly. "You could say that. I've had flights delayed, lost luggage, canceled orders, and now a wasted trip to New Zealand, so excuse me if I seem a little brusque. You do realize, don't you, that the price of the Nautilus is over a million pounds. It is not a toy!"

"Canceled orders?" Rebecca asked casually.

Fong said nothing.

"In Australia?" she coaxed.

Fong sighed. "Yes. Six months of negotiations all down the drain. And now this." He made moves to get up again.

"Why did they cancel?" Rebecca asked quickly but still with a casual tone. "Is there something wrong with the submarine?"

"Of course not," Fong said indignantly.

"Because if there are problems with it, then—"

"The sub passed every test they gave it with flying colors. The cancellation was all to do with bureaucracy and politics in upper management. The sub is fine. It's brilliant, in fact."

"So where is the sub now?" Rebecca coaxed.

Fong looked at her and smiled, realizing where she was heading.

"It's still in Sydney," he said. "But please be serious. It costs a million pounds. I don't know what that would be in New Zealand dollars—"

"Four million, one hundred twelve thousand, two hundred and twenty-nine dollars," Rebecca said from memory. "And ten cents. At today's rate."

Fong rose to his feet.

"It was nice to meet you. But right now, I am going to leave. I don't like my time being wasted."

"Your time is not being wasted," Fatboy said. "We represent a trust that has substantial funding. The Nautilus you have in Sydney. We'll buy it."

"A trust," Fong said skeptically.

"I said we'll buy it."

Mr. Fong looked at Fatboy with a kind of exasperation, as if he were speaking to an idiot who wouldn't see sense. "Sure. It's yours," he said. "Just write me out a check for, hell, round it off to four million New Zealand dollars. It's yours."

The doorbell sounded and Rebecca went to answer it.

Fatboy stretched out a hand and said, "Mr. Fong, you have a deal."

Fong ignored the hand.

Fatboy continued, "There are two conditions. You ask no questions, and you don't inform the press. This deal is just between you and us."

Mr. Fong looked at him cynically for a moment, but then laughed and shook Fatboy's hand. "Absolutely. Anything you say. No questions asked. And the check?"

Fatboy shook his head. "We don't have a checking account yet, but—"

"What a surprise." Fong didn't sound surprised at all. "Then I'm afraid the deal is off."

Rebecca's voice came from the doorway. "Mr. Fong, I'd like you to meet our lawyer, Anson Strange."

"Just in bloody time," Tane said out loud, without intending to.

MOTUKIEKIE

The engine of the small plane roared and spray flew past the window. Tane peered out at the water slipping away faster and faster underneath the hull of the small seaplane. The harbor was smooth, but even so, small waves drummed faster and faster at the hull of the craft.

"I thought it would be bigger than this!" Tane shouted over the noise of the engine, gripping the back of the seat in front of him.

Rebecca seemed unconcerned by the fact that they were about to take off from the surface of the sea and head thousands of feet up into the sky in a piece of motorized tin that was probably built by the Wright Brothers. Fatboy was in the copilot seat, joking with the pilot.

The pilot, a blond-haired man who seemed far too young to be in charge of an airplane, heard and called back, without taking his eyes off the controls, "It's a Grumman Super Widgeon. It's quite large compared to most seaplanes you see nowadays."

"I'd hate to see an ordinary Widgeon," Tane shouted.

He'd been on planes before, plenty of times. But they had video games in the backs of the seats and sixteen music channels and a cabin crew who brought you cold drinks and cookies.

And they took off and landed on land.

This was the fastest way to get to Motukiekie, though. Professor Green had recommended the company herself. Tane was a little surprised that she had agreed to see them, but it seemed that having a famous scientist for a father opened quite a few doors for Rebecca, even if (or perhaps because) he was no longer around.

It was a Friday, but there was no school, as it was the last Friday before exams, and it was officially a study day. Which is exactly what Tane's parents thought he was doing. Studying. At Rebecca's house. Not flying to the Bay of Islands in a prehistoric seaplane.

The rippled surface of the ocean outside turned to a mosaic of blue tiles, painted in flowing brushstrokes, then to a continuous blur, and then it disappeared, and all Tane could see was the sky as the plane banked around in a tight circle, back over the city.

They climbed as they turned, but they were still so low as they passed back over the wharves and the harborside apartments and office blocks that Tane could see people eating lunch.

They kept climbing and by the time they passed the enormous Skytower, the largest building in the Southern Hemisphere, it was well below the large floats hanging outside Tane's window. From this angle, it looked surprisingly small.

The city slipped away beneath them, and the harbor bridge

beckoned, a gray coat hanger joining the central city to the North Shore.

"You should fly under it!" Fatboy grinned at the young pilot.

Tane gripped the back of the seat.

"That's illegal." The pilot smiled back. "I'd lose my license. It's been done, though."

"Really!" Rebecca exclaimed.

"Captain Fred Ladd, back in the sixties or seventies. He was a bit of a legend apparently."

"Did he lose his license?" Tane wanted to know.

"Yeah, but they gave it back to him. He was a bit of a legend, after all."

It took little more than an hour to reach the Bay of Islands, even in this old museum piece. The pilot seemed to know the area well.

"That's Cape Brett," he said. "My great-grandfather used to be the lighthouse keeper there. Of course, it's all automated nowadays. Down to your right, that's the Hole in the Rock."

It was a tiny island with a hole punched right through one end. As they passed over it, a launch packed with tourists cruised right through the gap, seemingly oblivious to the danger from the rock walls that surrounded them.

"If you like big-game fishing, we can organize a tour for you," the pilot said. "There's great marlin fishing up here, but if you prefer kingfish, tuna, shark—"

"Sportfishing is murder," Rebecca said quietly, but loud enough to be heard.

The pilot took no offense. "Then I guess you'd be more interested in the bird sanctuary on Roberton Island."

"Another time," Fatboy said. "We're on a tight schedule, this trip."

"Well, that's where we're headed, right there." The pilot pointed. "That's Motukiekie Island."

There were islands everywhere, but the one he was pointing at was easily recognizable thanks to the small complex of buildings surrounded by a wire fence, not far from a small cove at the end of the island. It seemed a stark contrast to the lush verdure of the surrounding islands.

The seaplane began to descend, and they flew low over a small hill at the opposite end of the island.

Fatboy drew in his breath suddenly. "Look at that. A Pa."

Tane heard the undertone and looked, but he saw only a lumpy hillside with curious circular ridges. Fatboy was right, he realized; it was indeed the remains of an ancient Maori fort, a Pa. But it still seemed like just a lumpy hillside to him.

Then, as the plane passed alongside the hill, preparing to land, it all changed. For a moment, the hillside seemed to come alive in his mind. He saw women in flax skirts weaving baskets, children playing. Strong-shouldered men preparing a feast in a dug-out earth pit. Suddenly, an attack by warriors of a neighboring tribe, screaming and charging up the hill at the wooden battlements with their *wahaika* and *taiaha*— their weapons—held high.

Just for a moment.

Then the floats of the plane hit the water, and a cloud of spray obscured the hillside, and when it cleared, the Pa was gone and he was looking at nothing more than a lumpy hillside.

Professor Green met them at the jetty herself, which seemed a little unusual, Tane thought. Surely the head of the organization didn't meet all her visitors personally at the wharf?

"Call me Vicky," she said brightly, her emerald-green eyes matching her name. Her hair was red and constantly trying to escape from the loose bun she had it pulled back into. Tane figured that loose hair was probably not a good idea in a science laboratory, but Vicky's hair seemed to have a mind of its own.

"We don't normally allow visits, for security reasons," she said, leading them up a concrete path through dense native bush. "But I thought I could make an exception." She looked sadly at Rebecca. "I knew your father. By reputation anyway. And I did meet him once at a conference in Dunedin."

Rebecca nodded silently.

Vicky continued, "And is your mum still conducting research into climate change? I seem to remember that her work was quite radical. Groundbreaking. But I never saw anything published in the scientific journals."

"She's taking a sabbatical this year," Rebecca said.

Tane thought of the blue flickering windows of Rebecca's mother's room and said nothing.

They reached a high wire fence, topped with vicious-looking barbed wire. There was a gate set into the fence and beside it an electronic keypad.

Tane glanced over as the professor tapped in a four-digit pattern. He caught the last number. Three. Like the Powerball number. Like the three of them.

The path continued inside the fence, and they made their way through some brightly colored flowerbeds to another door, another keypad, and through some polished corridors to her office.

Vicky fussed around them, getting them each a glass of cool water, despite the fact that they hadn't asked for one.

There was a painting on the wall of her office that Tane recognized immediately and knew that Fatboy would, too. It was one of their father's works, entitled *Tuatara Dawn*. It was worth a lot of money, Tane remembered.

"So how can I help?" Vicky's emerald-green eyes flashed brightly once again.

Rebecca began, "Well—"

"What kind of security reasons?" Tane interrupted, looking up at the CCT security camera mounted in the corner of Vicky's office. Another had stared at them in the main entrance area.

"I'm sorry?"

"Earlier you said you don't usually allow visitors, for security reasons. What kind of security reasons? Do you work with dangerous viruses here?"

Vicky laughed, a soft, bell-like trill. "Good heavens, no. Nothing like that. All our work is with rhinoviruses, nothing dangerous. The security, and the reason we operate all the way out here on an island, is to get away from protestors, who have no idea what we are doing but object to it anyway. Because we're a genetics lab, they assume we are creating genetically modified tomatoes or cloning sheep or something like that. Do you know what rhinoviruses are?"

Fatboy answered smugly, "Of course. It's the common cold."

Tane caught a brief smile from Rebecca.

"Come and have a look," said Vicky.

She talked as they walked along a short corridor with large glass windows looking in on a laboratory where technicians and scientists in white lab coats and plastic hair caps were doing unguessable scientific things with microscopes and test tubes.

"This is our level-one lab. That's what we call a biocontainment level. The lab is sealed while people are working in there, but there's no real danger to anyone."

"And if there was an accident?" Fatboy asked.

"Well, you might catch a cold, I suppose." Vicky laughed again, pleasantly.

Tane had been expecting to meet some evil scientist with devious plans, thick glasses, and maybe a Persian cat on her lap. Vicky Green didn't fit the bill at all.

Vicky continued, "We made provisions for a level-two lab when we built the complex, but we haven't used it yet."

Tane noticed that her eyes involuntarily flicked toward a solid-looking door at the end of the corridor as she spoke.

She continued, "That would be for any dangerous pathogens, like influenza or hepatitis C. Labs go all the way up to level four, you know, but that's only for people who are working with the really deadly viruses like Ebola. The United States has one at the CDC, their Centers for Disease Control, and I think the Russians have a couple."

They stood and watched the lab staff at work for a while.

"What area of rhinovirus research are you conducting?" Rebecca asked.

"Well, our main area is conserved antigens. Are you familiar with that field?"

"Slightly," said Rebecca.

"I'm not," Tane said quickly.

"Okay, do you know how your body's immune system works?"

"Antibodies?" Fatboy queried.

"Well, that's a part of it. *Antibodies* are your body's watchdogs against viruses and bacteria. *Macrophages* are your body's soldiers. When the antibodies recognize something dangerous—a *pathogen*—they latch on to it, smother it, and send out a call for the macrophages to come along and swallow it up. But viruses like the rhinovirus keep changing. Mutating. Your body learns to recognize one rhinovirus but next winter along comes a new one with a different shape, and your antibodies don't recognize it."

She stopped and looked around them, to make sure they were following her, which they were. "We are looking for conserved antigens, which means looking for common characteristics."

She drew a felt pen out of her pocket and, seemingly absentmindedly, drew a diagram on the glass window looking into the lab. Tane suspected she did things like that a lot.

Her diagram looked a bit like a flower, a central circle, with smaller circles surrounding it, joined to the center by stalks.

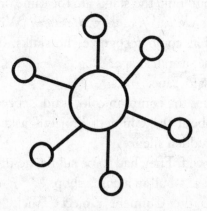

"Suppose this is a rhinovirus. Our antibodies recognize these shapes here"—she pointed to the smaller circles—"but then along comes a new virus." She rubbed out the small circles with her thumb and drew in small triangles. "With a different shape, which they don't recognize."

"Then it wouldn't be able to smother it," Rebecca said.

"Right, but look, the stalks are the same on both viruses. That is what we call a *conserved antigen*. What if you had antibodies that could recognize the stalks, instead of just looking at the overall shape?"

"Wow," said Tane.

"You'd cure the common cold," said Rebecca.

"What about the Chimera Project?" asked Fatboy, and there was a sudden silence.

Tane winced. They had to be subtle, he thought. Fatboy was as subtle as a bull in a china shop.

"What is the Chimera Project?" Vicky asked after a while.

"We were rather hoping you could tell us," Rebecca said.

Vicky thought for a minute, then shook her head. "Never heard of it. It could have something to do with genetics, though. A chimera is what we create if we splice together genes from two different organisms. The University of California created a 'geep' a few years ago, part goat, part sheep, but there was a lot of hoo-ha about that, and you don't hear about that sort of thing very much anymore."

Tane looked carefully at her. Was she telling the truth? If there was no Chimera Project, then maybe they could just get back to Auckland, cancel the order for the submarine, and get on with spending the six million dollars. That sounded like a good plan. However, he couldn't get three small letters out of his mind: *S, O,* and *S.*

Rebecca said, "What if you were to genetically splice together two, or more, different cold viruses? To help find your conserved antigen. What if you did that?"

Vicky laughed, a little too quickly this time. "A chimera rhinovirus. I'm afraid that's just science fiction, young lady."

The trip back was silent. Even the pilot sensed the mood and cut his usual cheery chatter. It wasn't until they were almost about to land that Rebecca said what they were all thinking.

"Professor Green was lying through her back teeth."

WATER WORKS

```
WTRWKSBTMP1000:2.80,24,341,55,500.
80,24,342,54,499,1.80,24
```

Rebecca's software, trawling through weeks of gamma-ray bursts, had found the next pattern, but this one made no sense at all.

All three of them stared at the characters dotted across the computer screen, trying to see order in the chaos. The early Saturday sun cast long streaks of light across the carpets of the lounge of the West Harbor house but did nothing to illuminate the puzzle.

"So you've checked earlier messages too?" Fatboy asked.

"Weeks of them," Rebecca replied. "The messages start on the day we visited Dr. Barnes."

"As if they knew you would visit him that day."

"Exactly. That can't be just a coincidence."

"I still don't understand where we're going to get this time transmitter from." Fatboy frowned.

"Me neither," Rebecca said with a smile. "I'd invent one, if I had the slightest idea of where or how to start."

"SOS means an emergency," said Tane, whose mind was somewhere else entirely. "It means 'help, save us,' but from what?"

"Water Works," said Rebecca, looking at the printout. "Like on Monopoly. You know, the Electric Company and the Water Works."

The other two looked at her and she shrugged. "Still doesn't make much sense, though, does it."

"Maybe it's a plague," Tane said. "Maybe Dr. Green is going to accidentally create some horrible disease and wipe out half of mankind!"

Fatboy asked, "What if we just went and saw her again? Maybe she'd listen to us if we told her about the message."

"Maybe she'd deny everything again and have us arrested," Tane said.

"What are you up to?" It was Rebecca's mother, drifting through the room. They hadn't heard her come in.

"Runescape," Tane lied quickly.

"What's that?" she asked vaguely.

"It's an online game where you get to be a kind of a character, called an . . ." He trailed off as she drifted out of the room, not listening to his answer. Tane stared at the computer screen, careful not to look at Rebecca.

"I think we have to involve the authorities," Fatboy said. "If it is the end of the world that we are talking about, then that's too big a problem for the three of us to deal with."

"You're right," Rebecca agreed. "But first we have to

prove it. So far it's all just guesswork, and as Tane says, maybe we have misunderstood the message."

"And what if we tell the authorities, and they don't believe us, and they alert Vicky, and we lose our chance to do something about it?" Tane said. "Then the end of the world will be our fault!"

"Maybe that's why the message said, 'Don't tell anyone,' " Fatboy considered.

Rebecca said, "We need to know more about the project. I mean, what's it about? What are they really trying to do? I think we need to go back to the island."

Fatboy shook his head. "She's not going to admit anything."

"I know," Rebecca agreed. "That's why we have to go when she's not around. When nobody's around."

"Ooooh kaaay . . ." Tane drew out the words.

Rebecca continued, "We get in there at night when nobody is working, and go through her files. Find out what she's up to, then figure out what to do about it."

"That sounds pretty reasonable," Tane said, "but what about her security? The barbed-wire fences and alarms."

"Worry about that next," Rebecca said. "Are we agreed on the basic idea?"

"Sounds pretty good to me," Fatboy said. "And I might have an idea about the security."

Tane just nodded. "It's okay with me."

Fatboy said, "Okay. We definitely do it at night, when nobody's around. Wear masks so the security cameras can't identify us later." Fatboy idly doodled while he talked. Tane looked at the paper. It was a rough map of Motukiekie.

Rebecca was busy on her new computer and soon had a satellite image up on the screen, courtesy of Google Earth.

The lab was clearly visible, a large cleared area amidst the dense bush of the island. Northwest of the lab, along a narrow path, was another complex of buildings, consisting of one large block and a number of smaller ones on a hill nearby.

"What are those buildings?" Tane wondered. "More labs?"

Rebecca shook her head. "Accommodation. The scientists need somewhere to live, don't they?"

Fatboy studied the picture and added a few notes to his map.

"Okay, but how do we get to Motukiekie Island without being seen? I don't want to get arrested." Rebecca was suddenly quiet and Tane knew what she meant. She'd already been arrested once. Who would look after her mum if she was in prison, or reform school, or wherever it was they sent teenage criminals?

"Underwater," he said with dawning awareness.

"The submarine!" Fatboy snapped his fingers.

"The Subeo Nautilus," breathed Rebecca. "So that's why we had to buy the submarine."

"This just might work," Fatboy said, "but there is still the problem of their security system. I think I caught the first few numbers when Professor Green pressed them on the keypad."

"Me too!" Rebecca said cautiously.

Fatboy closed his eyes, remembering, and said, "Five, one, something, maybe four . . . I couldn't see the last numbers because of the way she was holding her hands."

"That's right." Rebecca nodded. "Five, one, and four. I saw them too, but they're no good. We might as well have nothing without the last number."

"Three," Tane said, "like the Powerball number."

"Are you sure?" Fatboy asked.

Tane nodded. "I'm not totally useless."

Fatboy ignored him. "Okay, then. When? Any ideas when we should do this?"

Rebecca said quickly, "Soon. As soon as possible. Before it's too late."

Tane asked, "But how do we know when 'too late' is?"

"That's easy," Rebecca said, staring Tane straight in the eye. "The day after Professor Green releases the virus, or whatever it is that she is going to do . . . that's a day too late."

Fatboy said solemnly, "The sooner the better, then."

"Okay. Moving on. We still have more message to decode," Rebecca said slowly. "Bottom P. Bat Map. Butt Mop."

"Butt Mop?!" Tane burst out laughing, a little too loudly. Then Rebecca got the giggles, which set Tane off again, and the combination was too much even for Fatboy, who laughed so hard his hat fell off.

Exam week came and went, and Tane was convinced that he failed every darn thing. He couldn't concentrate, he couldn't focus, he couldn't even remember. Things that he had known all year suddenly seemed like distant memories. Subjects he was strong in were all of a sudden his weak points.

It was unfair, he thought. How many of the other kids sitting the exams were trying to solve cryptograms from the future and planning to break into a genetics laboratory? Well, just one other that he knew of, and she was going to breeze through her exams and probably still top the country despite everything that was going on.

SEA OF GREEN

Imagine the biggest, best, most exciting toy you ever unwrapped on Christmas morning. Then times that feeling by ten. It still doesn't even come close.

Technically, this wasn't a Christmas present, but with only a couple of weeks to go until the twenty-fifth, it certainly felt like one. The drudge and slog of exam week was over, and the freedom of the holidays was here. Tane hadn't felt he had done very well, but that seemed of little importance now.

He had felt like celebrating on the weekend and had been going to suggest something to Rebecca, but she was going out with Fatboy, so he had sat home by himself and watched TV.

Tane stood at the entrance to the boatshed and stared at their brand-new, bright yellow, six-person submarine. Rebecca stood beside him and Fatboy beside her.

The single one-hundred-fifty-watt bulb hanging on a

piece of wire from the ceiling reflected off the rounded sides of the Subeo Nautilus, giving the whitewashed walls of the boatshed a warm yellow glow, which complemented the streaky orange hues of the sunset across the harbor behind.

Arthur Fong and Wee Doddie, the mad Scottish engineer who had arrived with him, were still on board going through some final delivery checks, although that seemed a little bit late in the day considering that the sub had sailed, if that was what you called it, under its own steam from the delivery ship anchored out in the gulf, all the way up through the harbor, under the harbor bridge, and out through the upper harbor to Beachhaven. It had traveled underwater, as a bright yellow submarine sailing through the harbor might have attracted the kind of attention that Mr. Fong had promised not to attract.

"What are we going to call her?" Rebecca asked.

Tane looked at her and noticed that Fatboy's arm was casually draped around her shoulders.

"Tane, you're the creative one. You think of a name," Fatboy said.

He already had. "Möbius Dick." He thought it was a clever play on the name of the infamous whale.

"You gotta be kidding," Fatboy laughed.

Tane bit back his annoyance. "How about just Möbius, then?" he suggested.

"I like Möbius," Rebecca offered.

Fatboy shrugged. "I could go with Möbius."

Wee Doddie, who insisted that was his real name, climbed out of the top hatch grinning cheerfully. He was in his fifties or sixties, tough and wiry, completely bald, utterly mad, and had a gold ring through each eyebrow. His forearm was tattooed with a picture of two dolphins above the word *Dreadnought*, which Tane thought might be the name of a submarine he had once served on.

He was their training instructor, according to Arthur, although Tane wondered if that was such a good idea. Not because of his knowledge or experience, which were un-doubtedly excellent, but because of his thick accent.

He was from "Gluzgi," which eventually turned out to be Glasgow, and when he spoke, it was just a jumble of syllables that their brains instinctively tried to turn into English words. Only none of it made any sense.

"Rate kids way rid utter gore. Giddy arses blown will tea coffee a waste-bin."

Tane looked at Fatboy who looked at Rebecca.

Rebecca struggled to suppress a smile. "I think he wants us on board."

"You sure?" Tane asked doubtfully.

"My uncle Iain talks like that," Rebecca whispered. "What he said was, 'Right, kids, we're ready to go; get your asses below and we'll take her for a wee spin.'"

Doddie jabbed a thumb toward the open hatch and said emphatically, "Wedgie wheaten fur? An invite o'da queen? Giddy arses blown will tea coffee a waste-bin."

"Come on, then," Fatboy said.

Doddie shook his head and folded his arms as they climbed the short ladder onto the top hatch. "Do they nay spike English reindeer."

"I think I understood that one," Tane whispered to the others as they climbed inside.

Doddie's voice came clearly in through the open hatch. "Aye, an than yer arse fell orf."

It was dark by the time they took the *Möbius* for her first dive, which suited all of them just fine, as the last thing they wanted to do was draw attention to themselves.

Arthur and Wee seemed to accept, if not to understand, the need for discretion.

It turned out the bright yellow color had nothing to do with the old Beatles song and everything to do with safety. It made the craft more visible underwater, and most commercial submarines were painted yellow for that reason.

Everything inside was space-conscious. Not an inch of room seemed to be wasted, and every surface seemed to have at least two or three uses. The main control room of the sub was separated from the central cabin by a thick pressure door, operated by a wheel lock. In the event of a rupture or leak in the rear of the sub, they could seal the control room and steer the boat to the surface.

The central cabin had three round portholes on each side, made of an impossibly thick glass that still somehow gave a good view of the surrounding ocean. There were floodlights built onto the hull of the sub outside the portholes on each side. In the central cabin were three bunks on either side.

At the back of the main cabin was a small galley and at the rear of the sub, through another watertight door, was the battery room with its rows of sealed-cell batteries, tiny diesel-powered generator, and storage cupboards in every conceivable nook and cranny. There was a marine toilet in one corner of the battery room, which had been modified in some way for use in the pressurized hull of a submarine, but Tane could not understand most of what Doddie had to say on that subject.

Everything was computerized and automated. They didn't have to blow ballast tanks or adjust diving planes or any of the stuff Tane had seen in the old submarine movies, which was a relief. There was no *Ah-OO-gah* diving horn either, though, which was a shame.

The Subeo Nautilus was controlled with a two-handled joystick, like that of a small airplane. Forward to go down, backward to go up, turn to go left or right. The top hatch was actually a pressure chamber, like an air lock, which meant that it could be opened underwater. The hatches were syn-chronized so that they couldn't both be open at the same time while the boat was submerged. Of course, it paid to be wearing scuba gear when you did this, unless you were par-ticularly good at holding your breath.

The sub could go forward, or backward, although the steering was "krarp" in reverse according to Wee Doddie.

A detachable buoy on the rear of the hull provided a number of important links with the outside world. Once re-leased, it floated to the surface. It had an air intake, to pro-vide air for the diesel generator as well as for the passengers; a radio antenna; and a solar panel that could recharge the sub's batteries while it was underwater.

But the bit that Tane liked best about the buoy was the gimbal-mounted video camera, linked to an LCD screen, which could be controlled with a small joystick on the console.

"A periscope!" Tane exclaimed.

Arthur Fong showed them how to change the Sofnolime scrubber cartridges in the carbon-dioxide filter. If they were staying for a long period below the surface, without sucking in fresh air through the buoy, then they would have to change the cartridges regularly or the carbon dioxide would build up in the craft's atmosphere and kill them.

They all paid particular attention to that part.

Wee Doddie showed each of them how to run the sub and made each of them do it over and over until he was "suss fee" that they could "date purply": *satisfied* that they could *do it properly*, Rebecca translated.

They stayed well clear of the harbor bridge for fear that someone on the bridge or in one of the high-rise towers in the central city might notice the bright underwater lights of the *Möbius*, and they kept pretty much to the center of the harbor to keep away from any anchor chains of boats moored near the shores.

It was black underwater at night, darker than Tane had expected. The lights penetrated a certain distance into the water, turning the black into a dirty, murky green, and there were surprisingly few fish. Tane had expected to see schools of them, but there were only a few, here and there, caught in the lights of the submarine.

He was about to ask Doddie about it when a dead fish floated into the lights of the *Möbius*, belly-up, bloated, its head stuck inside one of the plastic rings of a beer six-pack holder. Tane held his breath and watched it drift slowly, diagonally, across the bow and into the darkness beyond the lights. Rebecca and Fatboy didn't see it. They were busy playing with the periscope camera.

It was only one fish, but it took some of the fun out of the test dive for Tane.

Arthur left the next morning for Sydney, so they spent two full days, or rather nights, training with Wee Doddie and one day out amongst the islands of the Hauraki Gulf, well away from the eyes of any spectators on the myriad of yachts that painted the surface of the gulf in long loving brushstrokes.

When Arthur returned on Thursday, there was a small ceremony that included the handing over of the keys to the boat (Doddie had been insistent that it was a "boot" not a "shape") and the signing of all sorts of papers that basically said that if they drowned themselves, then it was their own silly fault and not the silly fault of Subeo UK Ltd., its shareholders, directors, or subsidiaries.

"Are we old enough to sign these?" Tane whispered to Fatboy, hesitating over the dotted line.

Fatboy shushed him. "If it makes Fong feel better . . ."

Rebecca impulsively hugged Wee Doddie when the taxi arrived to take him and Arthur to the airport.

She said, "Spooner greet cup laddies. Text February thing!"

It's been a great couple of days. Thanks for everything!

Tane and Fatboy looked at each other with raised eyebrows, but Wee Doddie gave her a big mad smile and tousled her hair affectionately.

"Suez can spike English off troll," he said.

THE MÖBIUS TRIP

The next day, they left before dawn to be clear of the crowded harbor before daylight. This time of the year, the harbor and the inner gulf were awash with boats of all kinds enjoying the summer sun. Sailing boats, for yachting was a fire in the blood of many New Zealand people; motor boats, because some people just like to go fast; and a multitude of smaller craft, from Windsurfers to Jet Skis to kayaks.

There were families and fishermen and foreign freighters. Tane hoped they wouldn't run into any scuba divers, and luckily they didn't.

The plan was simple. Too simple, Tane thought, but they just didn't have any more information to make more detailed plans with. It would take them two days to cruise up to the Bay of Islands in the *Möbius*. That second night, they would sneak onto the island, break into the lab using the passcode, and look around for . . . for what?

He was glad that Rebecca was going to be there. He'd

have no idea what to look for and wouldn't even know it if he found it. But no doubt she would make sense of what was in the filing cabinets, or the petri dishes, or whatever it was that they found.

And how to stop the Chimera Project. That bothered him the most. But he guessed that would depend on what they found.

They stocked the compact refrigerator of the *Möbius* with five days' supply of perishables and packed the small larder with bread and tins.

There was no bath or shower on board, for space reasons, but Tane cycled down to the local boat shop and picked up a few bars of sailor soap, the kind that lathers in salt water.

"We can take a bath every day," he said. "Just open the hatch."

"Yes, Mother," Fatboy said with a grin.

Because there were only three of them, there was plenty of room on the three spare bunks for extra clothes, towels, and assorted gear that you would usually take on a camping trip. The three black wet suits, masks, fins, and assorted other gear took up one of the bunks.

Tane brought a pack of cards, and Fatboy even squeezed his guitar on board. Rebecca brought her computer, which by now had a wireless connection that allowed her to access the Internet from anywhere. Even, they discovered, using the aerial on the buoy, from underneath the surface of the ocean.

Exams were over, and whatever the results might be, there was nothing Tane could do about that until the next year. They were now on vacation, and when the weather shone out clear, blue, and calm on the first morning, it seemed that all was right with the world.

Tane's mum and dad had been given a story about a camping trip, which they had no reason to disbelieve, and Rebecca's mum came down to the kitchen the night before they left while they were packing up the last few odds and ends.

Tane could never quite understand, although he would never say this to Rebecca, how normal her mother looked. How *sane*.

She wore jeans and a casual T-shirt, just like any other mum, around the house. Her hair was always brushed in a neat bob, and she always wore makeup. Not over the top, just a little, like his mum wore to go to the shopping mall.

She came down just like any other mother and wished them well on their boat trip.

"Thanks, Mum," Rebecca said. "I've made you a casserole. Enough for two or three days. It's in the fridge, and there's leftover pizza in the freezer if you get hungry."

"Oh, you didn't need to fuss around like that," her mum said. "I'm quite capable of looking after myself."

Tane caught a small glance from Rebecca and knew that being capable of looking after yourself and actually doing it were two different things.

Rebecca gave her mum a kiss and said, "See you in a couple of days, Mum. Love you."

"Love you too," her mum said absently. "Take care, now." Then she disappeared back into her room and they heard the theme tune start from *Survivor: New York*.

The *Möbius* made better speed underwater, but the air quickly got dry and tinny, so when they were well clear of any other boats, and far enough away from land not to be seen, they surfaced and opened the twin hatches to let the fresh cool sea air wash through the boat.

It was a sunny day, and there was a small flat area in between the two glass domes of the cockpit where you could just about lie down comfortably. Rebecca changed into her bikini and did some sunbathing, while Fatboy steered and Tane lounged half in and half out of the hatch, playing a happy bluesy tune on his harmonica.

The *Möbius* might have been cool, and she was very discreet, but she wasn't fast, and it seemed to take an eternity even to get out to the tip of the Whangaparaoa Peninsula, at the northern end of the Hauraki Gulf.

"Don't spend too long out there; you'll burn," Tane said. He had put sunblock on his face and arms half an hour ago and had put on a hat. Rebecca was still soaking up the sunshine, swaying gently with the movement of the boat in the water and squealing occasionally when a rough wave splashed spray over the front fins.

"Yes, Mother," Rebecca laughed, and it would have been funny, except that Fatboy had said the same thing the day before.

"Seriously. They reckon the ozone hole is extra large this year. You'll burn fast."

She craned her neck up past the right-hand dome and squinted at him. "I know, you're right," she said. "But it's luvverly! Nice to know you care, though."

Tane shrugged. The sun was nice and warm on his skin; that was true. And the occasional splash of seawater provided a pleasant, refreshing spray.

He felt, rather than saw, Rebecca looking at him out of the corner of her eye and knew she had something on her mind. He shut his eyes and let the sun warm his eyelids while he waited for her to come out with it.

Rebecca said after a while, "Why do you care? Why are we such good friends? Why do you like me? Some of the kids at school won't even talk to me."

Tane thought about it for a while and played a few more bars before answering. "I guess they haven't known you as long as I have."

"What's that got to do with anything?" she asked, then said, "Chuck us the sunblock."

Tane carefully slid the plastic bottle down the rounded yellow side of the *Möbius* into her outstretched hand. He said, "Think of it like this. Other people see you and they only see you as you are right at that moment. And they make up their minds about you based on that one tiny instant in time."

"Yeah?"

"But I've known you all my life. I look at you and I see the little girl who wet her pants in the sandbox at kindy and blamed Mary Mackey. I see you at your tenth birthday and at your dad's funeral. I look at you and I see all the different yous, and . . . ." He paused. "I wonder about the ones still to come."

Rebecca laughed, a slightly embarrassed sound. "Jeez, you talk a load of crap. I'm not sure if you're being nice or being rude!"

"So why do you like me?" Tane asked.

Rebecca said immediately, "What on earth makes you think I like you?"

She kept a straight face long enough to make Tane think she was serious, before dissolving into another fit of laughter.

Tane thought that, despite what she said, she was secretly

quite pleased with his answer. It felt good. Like the old days, before Fatboy stuck his nose in.

"Of course, some days," he said, "you can be a real pain in the ass."

"What do you mean . . ." She looked around and saw his smile and threw the bottle of sunblock at him. It bounced off the hatch and disappeared into the ocean.

"Oops," she said.

They stopped for a while in the evening, and Rebecca, who was the most experienced cook, made a quick fry-up on the gimbal-mounted electric stove. Electric, not gas, Arthur had pointed out, because it was easier to replace electricity than oxygen.

They ate on board and continued for another hour after dinner into a sheltered cove on the lee side of Little Barrier Island. There was no point in continuing farther, as the light was fading, and running with the lights on used up the batteries twice as fast.

"It's deserted," Tane said, scanning the cove with binoculars. "Let's park the sub up on the beach for a while and go for a swim."

"Hauturu." Fatboy shook his head, giving the island its Maori name. "We're not allowed to land there. It's a wildlife sanctuary."

"We're not allowed to break into science labs either," Tane pointed out, "but that's not stopping us. And what do the wild lives need sanctuary from anyway?"

Rebecca smiled but said softly, "Us."

They did go for a swim eventually, after Fatboy jury-rigged an anchor by tying a nylon rope to the bow and diving down to secure it around a heavy rock in shallow water near the northern tip of the small cove. It seemed strange that the *Möbius* did not have an anchor of her own, but maybe, as Rebecca surmised, nobody ever thought she would need one.

Once the boat was secure against the gradual draw of the tide, and with the sun a dusky memory on the horizon, they fooled around for a while, dive-bombing each other off the end of the boat, dunking each other, and generally acting like a bunch of lunatics until the light faded a little too far, and the water darkened a little too much, and they climbed back on board for the night.

They sealed the hatches, released the buoy, and with a whisper of bubbles, slowly sank to the bottom of the cove, landing gently in soft sand between a small underwater ridge and a few scattered boulders.

And there, in the tranquility of Little Barrier Island, they slept, serenaded only by the gentle sounds of the sea and the hum of the air hose from the buoy.

BUTT MOP

Rebecca downloaded the next batch of BATSE data the next afternoon while Tane had his turn steering the sub. A few boats had been cruising the area, and the fine weather of the previous day had disappeared, replaced by squally showers, so they had taken the precaution of submerging and continuing the trip in the relative calm of the ocean depths.

"More of the same," Rebecca said, peering at the characters on the screen of her laptop. "Just more of the same."

Since the "Water Works" and the as-yet-indecipherable "Butt Mop," there had been nothing but numbers. Always a series of numbers, separated by commas, then a full stop, then another series. Not Lotto numbers; they didn't fit the pattern. Something else. Something with a *lot* of numbers!

Every day it seemed there were more transmissions captured by the satellite and uploaded to the BATSE Web site. They had set both Tane's computer and Rebecca's shiny new laptop running Rebecca's program, day and night, and were working through the backlog of transmissions that had been coming in ever since they had visited Dr. Barnes at the university.

Rebecca had tried every combination and calculation she could think of to make some sense out of the numbers, but the answer still eluded her. She was convinced, and had said so many times, that the solution would be something not logical. Something lateral. Something that Tane's creative imagination would be needed to solve.

"Come on, Tane," she said. "We need you to think outside the box."

Tane stared out at the monotonous sameness of the ocean. It was hard to think creatively when you had a splitting headache, and he had one now. He hadn't slept much the previous night but had lain awake worried about breaking into the lab. That was against the law. It was a criminal act. He had never broken the law before (unless you counted that packet of gum he had "borrowed" from the corner store when he was seven). He had rolled over and over in his tiny bunk, and now his head throbbed with the pulse of the engines. *Think outside the box.*

He wasn't the only one feeling the stress of the mission. He could see it on the faces of the others, especially Rebecca. She could not afford to go to jail. Could any of them? No. But especially not Rebecca. Yet it had to be done. What were the consequences if they did it? What would be the consequences if they didn't?

In the clear open water here, there was nothing much to look at. Just the occasional school of fish or curious shark. Ahead at Poor Knights Islands there was a world-famous diving spot, renowned for its clear waters, colorful marine life, and the wreck of the *Rainbow Warrior*. But that was a bit off course for them, so he had to be content with the blue-green infinity of the open water.

Think outside the box. It was a well-worn phrase from an old puzzle that he had once seen. Nine dots that formed a three-by-three grid. Join all the dots using just four lines. It seemed impossible to most logical people, but creative thinkers quickly realized that it was easy, if you allowed your four lines to extend beyond the confines of the grid. Outside the box.

He sketched the puzzle on a notepad, then completed the lines to make the answer.

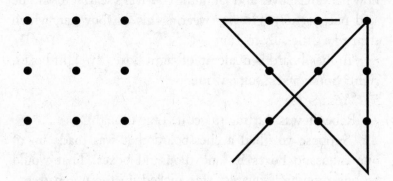

Something struck him about that phrase. *Think outside the box.* He stopped trying to solve it and let his mind drift idly, like the ocean around them. The dead fish in the beer rings came to mind, but he shook that away quickly. Quick flashes of many things, superimposed on each other—Fatboy's hand on Rebecca's shoulder, the nervous lawyer absentmindedly pulling at his mustache, the fantail family naively fearless in their flimsy nest, the chessboard he had bought Rebecca for Christmas. And as it usually did, the answer just floated into his mind and was there for quite a while before he realized it.

The chessboard. *Think outside the box.* Black and white chess pieces, black and white boxes on the chessboard. Boxes. *Think outside the box.* The chessboard itself was a box, made up of smaller black and white boxes. Think *inside* the box!

"The chessboard," he finally said out loud.

Rebecca was in the main cabin, sitting on one of the bunks, working on her computer. She looked through the pressure door at him. "What chessboard?"

"Any chessboard," Tane said quickly.

Fatboy had been lying on one of the other bunks, but now he walked over and sat in the codriver's seat. "Go on," he said purposefully. He was wearing his cowboy hat, which seemed a little silly to Tane.

"A chessboard is made up of eight boxes by eight boxes, right? Some black, some white."

"Yes."

Rebecca was starting to get it, Tane thought.

"Suppose you had a chessboard that was made up of one thousand boxes by one thousand boxes. That would be one thousand squared." He picked up the notepad and wrote it: 1000^2. "In the first row, instead of alternating black and white, suppose the first, say, eighty were white, and the next—what was it . . ." He checked the printout.

```
BTMP1000:2.80,24,341,55,500.80,24,
342,54,499,1.80,24
```

" . . . twenty-four were black. And so on and so on for all the rows. What would you have?"

"A bloody great, stupid-looking chessboard," said Fatboy, who was cool and popular but wasn't really all that bright.

"A photograph," said Rebecca, who was.

"Or a fax," said Tane who, just at that moment, thought he was the brightest of them all. "A fax is just a lot of rows of black and white dots, arranged in a particular pattern to form a picture."

"Brilliant!" Rebecca cried. She put down her computer and rushed into the control room. She threw her arms around Fatboy's neck and gave him a huge hug from behind.

Hey, thought Tane, *it was me who solved it!*

"What should we do?" asked Fatboy. "Get a big piece of paper and start to draw it up?"

Rebecca shook her head. "It'd be easier to do on the computer. I'll do it in Photoshop. I'll just create an image one thousand dots by one thousand dots and save it as a . . ." She stopped, and then strangely, and rather tiredly, began to laugh again.

"What?" asked Tane, a little defensively, thinking she was laughing at him.

"Save it as a *bitmap*."

It took Rebecca nearly two hours to take the data they already had and convert it into dots on the bitmap. All the weeks of data they had received and it made up less than a third of the image. It was clear enough from that what the image was going to be, though.

"It's a diagram," Rebecca announced from the main cabin, studying the image on the screen of her laptop. "A schematic."

"Of what?" Fatboy asked.

"Of what the hell do you think?" Tane answered a little testily, his head still throbbing.

Rebecca said, "Easy, Tane. Of the gamma-ray time-message-sender device, Fats. I have a feeling that we are going to need this, sooner than we thought."

"How soon?" Fatboy asked, but nobody answered.

Rebecca came back into the control room and, there being no spare seat, sat on Fatboy's knee. Tane stared out of the viewing window of the sub. He said, "I think I have a name for it."

Rebecca looked up. "Yes?"

"Well, it's like a telephone that sends text messages through time, right?"

"Well, sort of."

The name had floated into Tane's mind in between throbs of pain. *Tele* was ancient Greek for "distance," and *phone* was ancient Greek for "speech." So a "telephone" was a machine that let you speak across a distance. The ancient Greek word for "time" was *chronos*.

"It's a Chronophone."

Rebecca said, "I like it."

"Wouldn't it be a Chronograph?" Fatboy asked. "I mean, it's more like a telegraph, sending Morse code, than a telephone."

"Maybe, but a Chronograph is a kind of watch, so I think Chronophone is best," Tane insisted.

"Actually, Fatboy is right," Rebecca said.

"Okay, whatever." Tane shrugged and turned away.

There was an awkward pause. Fatboy coughed.

After a moment, Rebecca said brightly, "Chronophone will do fine. But what a paradox."

Tane groaned, "Oh, here we go. I suppose you want me to kill Grandad again."

"You killed Grandad?!" Fatboy asked.

"No, Fatboy, don't worry about it. What paradox?"

"Think about it." Rebecca's eyes were wide. "We're in the middle of sending ourselves plans for the Chrono . . . phone, right, from the future."

"This much we know already."

"But where did we get the plans from?"

"Which 'we' are you talking about?" Tane asked.

"Okay," Rebecca said. "Call the future Tane and Rebecca 'them.' Now, where did they get the plans from? From us, right?"

"From us?" Fatboy queried. "How did we send the plans to the future?"

Rebecca sighed with exasperation. "We didn't send them. We just hung on to them. Think about it. Tane and I are the future Tane and Rebecca, just not yet. So future Tane and Rebecca get the plans from us, but where did we get them from? *From them!*"

"So who had the plans in the first place?" Fatboy asked.

"Exactly!" Rebecca thundered, leaving Fatboy no more the wiser.

"And this has something to do with Grandad?" Fatboy asked, and couldn't understand why Tane and Rebecca got the giggles.

"The plans must have come from somewhere," Fatboy insisted.

"Maybe this is one of those kinds of questions that our brains just can't comprehend," Rebecca said, wiping laughter tears from her eye. "Like the infinite size of space. Or what existed before the universe."

"Or why in automatic cars you pull the gear lever backward to go forward, and forward to go backward," Tane contributed, and even Fatboy started laughing, in a confused kind of way.

Eventually Fatboy said, "Okay. So I don't really get all this paradox stuff, and I don't understand where the plans for the Chronophone came from, but did you guys ever think about what a weird coincidence this whole thing is?"

Rebecca, still sitting on his knee, twisted her head around to look at him. "Yeah, I know."

She idly lifted off his cowboy hat and put it on.

Tane asked, "What do you mean?

Fatboy hesitated. "Well . . ."

Rebecca said, "He means that us, well, you really, Tane, thinking up the idea of receiving messages from the future, just at the right time to stop Dr. Green and her Chimera Project, is a very unlikely coincidence. Right, Fats?"

Fatboy nodded. "Did anything else unusual happen, when you thought up the idea?"

Tane asked, "Like what?"

"Like, did you see anything, hear anything . . ."

Tane shut his eyes, remembering. "There was a shooting star."

Rebecca looked up sharply. "What?"

"The moment that I thought of the idea of messages from the future, I saw a shooting star. That's it. Nothing else."

Fatboy shook his head. "Maybe it wasn't an ordinary shooting star. Maybe the shooting star was actually a thought from the future hurtling through the atmosphere in some cosmic ray from the depths of the universe just before embedding itself in your brain."

Tane said, "That's nuts."

Rebecca was already adding it to the notebook where she kept the message dates and times. She spoke as she wrote.

"Please remember to send a shooting star above West Auck-land on the twenty-seventh of October at exactly nine-fifty-three p.m. That was the right time, wasn't it?"

"Close enough."

Fatboy grinned. "So maybe the whole thing wasn't Tane's idea at all."

"Bite me," Tane laughed. "I thought of it by myself."

Fatboy said, "Sure, with a little help from the future and their intergalactic brainwashing machine!"

He put his arms around Rebecca's waist and she leaned back into him.

Tane gritted his teeth. "I thought of the basic idea," he said.

His annoyance must have shown because Rebecca said, "He was only joking, Tane."

Tane snapped back, "Well, I'm sick of it."

He regretted saying it immediately. The confines of a submarine were no place for bickering and fighting, but the words were in the open now and there was nothing he could do about that.

"Easy, Tane," Fatboy said calmly.

Once started, it was difficult to stop, and his head was pounding.

"Easy! You blackmail us out of two million dollars, worm your way into our project, and start barking orders around like you're running the show. And you tell me to take it easy."

"Hey, Tane," Rebecca said gently.

"No, stuff it!" Tane shouted. "And stuff you! None of this, the submarine, the money, none of this would be here if not for me, and you just weasel your way into everything and take it all!" Even Tane knew that it wasn't the money that he was talking about.

"Chill out," Fatboy said, his jaw set.

"I'm sick of it," Tane cried, his voice suddenly hoarse. "I'm sick of it and I'm sick of you."

"Enough!" Rebecca said suddenly and firmly. "That's enough, Tane." She stood and took Fatboy firmly by the hand and led him back into the sleeping cabin. She pulled the watertight door shut between the two compartments, pausing only to say, "We'll keep out of your way until you've calmed down."

The clang of the metal door and the whir of the wheel-lock turning were like a knife in Tane's chest. For some reason, he had thought she would agree with him. That she would tell Fatboy to back off and remember that he was just a one-third partner and there only by the grace of Tane and Rebecca. Friends since forever.

But it hadn't turned out like that at all.

"Crap!" he yelled suddenly at the top of his voice into the void of the water all around. "Crap!"

Then, after a quick consultation with the map, he changed course, just slightly.

It was a childish display of emotion. An ill-considered, impulsive thing to do.

And it probably saved their lives.

THE RAINBOW WARRIOR

"Holy mother . . . ," Fatboy said, his body still halfway through the doorway from the bunk compartment. "Where the heck are we?"

Tane stirred uncomfortably. He had slept in the driver's seat, and his back and neck now ached. He stretched, trying to work out the knots.

"Sorry about yesterday," he said.

"We all have days like that." Fatboy flashed a quick smile. "Don't worry about it."

Tane smiled. Fatboy picked his guitar out of a narrow locker, sat on one of the fold-down seats, and began to play. *Music to soothe the savage beast*, thought Tane.

Rebecca emerged silently from the compartment behind Fatboy and said nothing.

Fatboy asked, "Was it something to do with Rebecca? Do you not like that we—"

Tane interrupted, to avoid more pain, "I was just tired and grumpy, I'm okay now."

He avoided Rebecca's eyes.

"Where the heck are we?" she said at last, startling Fatboy, who dropped a chord but picked up the tune and continued.

Through the large twin glass domes of the *Möbius*, the rusted bow of a ship reached plaintively out toward them. The water was clear and still, and the early light of the morning washed the bow in cobalt hues. The seabed around the ship merged with the blue of the sea behind, in a soft vignette. The railings of the bow were intact but encrusted with green and brown marine life. In death, the ship was the foundation of life.

"The *Rainbow Warrior*," Tane said.

"Wow," Fatboy said, "it's amazing."

Beyond the prong of the bow, the rest of the ship lay on its side on the sandy bottom of the ocean, an artificial reef. The back of the ship was broken, and she lay twisted in her final resting place.

Tane wasn't quite sure why he'd diverted the sub. It just seemed like the right thing to do. For Rebecca.

"We are a long way off course," Rebecca said curtly.

"No," Tane said, "only a couple of hours. I . . . just . . . felt like a diversion."

"It'll cost us a day."

"But it's only a couple of hours out of our way," Tane protested.

"It means we won't make Motukiekie today. We'll have to stop over for an extra night, and do"—she hesitated—"the thing, tomorrow night instead. It's cost us a day."

"It's just one day," Tane mumbled. "I'm sorry."

"Tane, something bad is going to happen. We don't know what and we don't know when. One day extra might mean one day too late. We already talked about this."

Crap! Tane thought. *Crap!*

Rebecca's eyes were frosty, but she shut them for a while, and when they finally opened, they were clear.

"What a tragedy," she murmured, watching a school of colorful fish flit through the encrusted handrail on the point of the bow.

"The guy who died?" Fatboy asked.

Fernando Pereira, a Dutch photographer, had drowned when French secret agents bombed the *Rainbow Warrior* in Auckland harbor.

"That too," she said softly.

They spent the third night at sea on the wave-washed bottom of a bay just south of Cape Brett, which they had flown over a few weeks earlier in the Grumman Super Widgeon with its underage-looking pilot.

The island was closer now, and in Tane's mind it loomed large and frightening. Breaking and entering was against the law. And what if there was some virus loose on the island? The uncertainty and fear grew as a storm blew up overnight, and even on the seafloor, the ferocity of the crashing waves above thudded against the little yellow boat, seesawing them from side to side and shunting them small amounts across the sand of the bay.

By ten-thirty, when they were just bunking down for the night, the nerves and the uncertainty became overwhelming. *I can't do this,* Tane realized. *I can't go onto an island in the middle of the night and break into a science laboratory that might be infected with a superplague.*

He would be letting them down. He knew that. But what choice was there? *I can't go through with this*, he thought again as another violent wave rocked the sub from side to side. He took a deep breath and held it for a moment before opening his mouth to speak. They'd think him a coward, but he had to let the others know.

"I'm really not sure if I can go through with this," Fatboy said while Tane's mouth was still open like a fish. He shut it with a snap.

"What do you mean?" Rebecca asked, emotion rising in her voice.

"I've done a few dodgy things in my life," Fatboy said, "but I've never broken the law. Well, not a big law. Not the kind of law they put you in jail for. Maybe we should just wait and try to talk to Vicky again."

Rebecca said in a small but determined voice, "That won't help. And if we don't do this, who else will?"

"I'm just not sure if I can go through with it," Fatboy said again quietly.

"It's gotta be done," Tane said firmly, as if he had never considered any alternative. "And we've got to do it."

There was a long pause.

"I know," Fatboy said at last, reluctantly.

The next day they rounded the tip of Cape Brett, passing Motukokako Island and its famous Hole in the Rock, then into the Bay of Islands itself.

"Waewaetoroa Passage," Fatboy said, looking at the chart. "That's Waewaetoroa Island on the right and Urupukapuka Island on the left. We could go all the way around, but it would be quicker to go through the passage between the islands."

"Any reason why not?" Rebecca asked.

"Not really." Fatboy frowned. "There are a lot of big rocks and shoals, and it gets quite shallow at the other end, but boats navigate through there all the time."

"On the surface of the water," Tane noted.

"Yeah, but I think we'll be okay."

Fatboy drove the sub, as he had proved the most adept at handling its idiosyncrasies, and in the confined space and currents of the passage, that might prove to be vital.

The mouth of the passage slipped past them before they realized it. Just two gradual upward slopes on the seabed that slowly resolved into the underwater sides of the two islands.

Beneath the surface of the water, the Waewaetoroa passage was far from a straight and clear path between the islands.

Rocks jutted out at odd angles from the sides of the islands, which were at times shoals and other times sheer vertical cliffs. Huge boulders on the seabed rose up to meet them, well beneath the keels of the pleasure boats that frequented the passage but big enough to stop larger ships from traveling this way. And certainly big enough to keep Fatboy on his toes.

He had to slam the boat into reverse at one point as they rounded a curve on the side of one of the islands and were confronted by an unexpected underwater ridge, almost a reef, teeming with fish of many kinds and colors.

Rebecca sat in the codriver's seat and pored over the chart holder, marking rocks and sketching in ridges and rises with a pencil.

Huge fronds of seaweed reached out toward them from the sides of the islands and from many of the scattered boulders. At times the weed blocked visibility, and at other times it threatened to wrap itself around the main propeller and draw them into a watery grave.

It was a scary, underwater obstacle course.

"I'm glad we're taking this slowly," Fatboy said at one point.

"And in daylight," Tane added.

Finally the massive shapes to each side began to fall away, and deeper water beckoned. They continued on for a while as Tane raised the buoy and opened the iris on the video camera.

A fuzzy green shape bounced around on the screen as the light chop above rocked the buoy about.

"That's Motukiekie," Tane breathed.

Motukiekie Island. Their second visit, but a vastly different trip from the first one in every possible sense.

Motukiekie. Professor Green. The Chimera Project. It was suddenly very real. Far too real. The dangers that lay ahead of them were exposed on the video screen in front of them, a fuzzy green shape on a blue ocean.

Rebecca heard it first. "What's that?" she said.

It started off as a kind of far-off rumble, but quickly became a throbbing, whooshing sound that reverberated through the hull of the sub.

"I don't know," murmured Tane, twisting the joystick to spin the small camera around on the flat gray buoy above.

The answer was suddenly there on the screen before them.

"Dive, dive, dive!" Tane yelled. Fatboy had already rammed

the controls forward and hit the manual override for the trim tanks, flooding them all at once to make the *Möbius* sink like a stone.

"What is that?" screamed Rebecca.

Tane grabbed at the switch for the winch that lowered the buoy, but his fingers slipped and it took him two goes to get the motor winding and the buoy lowering.

The bow of a Navy frigate looks large from any angle, but bearing down on you in the water, it looks like the end of the world.

"I hope it's deep enough," Fatboy muttered as the hull hit the sand and the ocean floor with a thud that jarred the vehicle.

The rumble of the engines in the ship grew louder as it closed in on them, and they could hear each individual rotation of the huge propellers.

The sound passed right overhead, shaking the hull and its terrified occupants, but then the ship, and the stark terror, passed them by.

"What the hell is a frigate doing here?" Tane wanted to know, raising the buoy again once he was convinced there were no more surprises like the first one.

The ship had slowed once it had passed them and was rapidly disappearing around the end of the island.

"What is it?" Rebecca asked. "One of ours?"

Tane nodded. The New Zealand flag was clearly visible on the short pole at the stern of the ship. "Must be the *Te Mana* or the *Te Kaha*."

"Probably on exercises," Fatboy said.

"Will that stop us?" Rebecca asked.

Tane and Fatboy looked at each other.

"I don't see why," Tane said after some thought. "They won't be interested in Motukiekie. Just cruising past, I think."

Even so, they stayed on the ocean floor for more than an hour, to make sure the frigate would not return, before resuming their journey to the island.

When the last rays of the sun were a long-ago memory, they took the wet suits off the top bunk.

"Who's coming with me?" Rebecca asked, pulling the wet-suit trousers up over her bikini.

"I am," Tane said.

Fatboy said, "I can go if you like, Tane. I'd be happy to do it."

"No," Tane said firmly, "I started this, and I'm going to help finish it."

He put on his weighted belt, heavy enough to compensate for the buoyancy of the wet suit.

Fatboy helped Rebecca with hers, then handed them the oxygen bottles. Not full scuba gear, just small pressurized metal bottles, about the size of a small Coke bottle. There were no straps; they simply gripped the mouthpieces tightly with their teeth. Waterproof flashlights dangled from their wrists on flexible cords.

It was three a.m. when Tane and Rebecca slipped out through the open top hatch of the *Möbius* and slowly swam toward the island.

LAUNDRY PILES

They came ashore on the beach at the base of the wharf. Moonlight silvered the waves in the channel, but here in the shadow of the island, it was dark. A large boat was moored back along the wharf, but there were no lights and it looked deserted, so they decided to ignore it and carry on. If anyone was on board, they were well asleep at this time of the morning.

They hid the fins, weight belts, and oxygen bottles behind a pillar beneath the end of the wharf but left on their masks to hide their faces from the security cameras.

Rebecca started off down the wharf but stopped after just a few yards and touched her hand silently to Tane's arm to stop him also.

She squatted and cupped her hand around the end of her flashlight so it couldn't be seen from a distance. Before turning it on, she instinctively also put her back to the island, to shield the light from any watching eyes. In the dim light, Tane could see something on the ground.

Tane squatted with her and examined the find. It was a cloth of some kind. Made of a soft pink material. He picked up one end of it. It immediately resolved into a distinct shape. It was a woman's nightie. A smaller, separate shape slipped out of the end as he raised it, and Rebecca caught it with the light. It was a sensible, white pair of ladies' panties.

"Seems a strange place to leave your laundry." Rebecca's voice, low and soft in his ear.

Tane nodded his head, unsure of what to say. It was a disturbing thing to find.

It took them a while to find the entrance to the path, even though they had been here once before. Tane risked a quick flash of his flashlight.

"Over there," he whispered, and followed Rebecca as she trod lightly and carefully up the concrete pathway.

He looked back at the water just once, before it was obscured by the trees surrounding the track. It was dark and deep and peaceful. It had been that way for millions of years and would still be the same in another million. Just looking at the expanse of water gave him a steadiness and a resolve to complete this mission, no matter what.

He caught up to Rebecca and whispered in her ear, "Kids will read about this in history books one day."

He felt her smile rather than saw it in the darkness.

After only a few paces, Rebecca stopped again. Another pile of clothing, this one a small mound. She separated it with her flashlight. A white lab coat. Inside of that a bright red T-shirt and a pair of jeans. Inside the jeans, which were still done up, a pair of blue boxer shorts. Underneath the clothes was a pair of Nike's, complete with socks. A watch fell out of the sleeve of the lab coat when she moved it.

"This might explain the nightie," Tane said with a grin.

"Maybe a couple of scientists out skinny-dipping for a bit of a lark."

Rebecca nodded, as if she agreed, but said, "In other circumstances maybe. But not here. Not now. And why are the jeans still fastened?"

The pathway leveled out as they approached the top of the rise and emerged from the native bush into the cleared area that housed the laboratory complex. Here they were no longer in the shadow of the island, and the flat area in front of them was bathed in moonlight.

They found no more piles of "laundry" as they silently approached the building complex.

They had both memorized the security code for the gate, but the moonlight brushed it with silver, and Tane could see that there was no need. It was not locked. It was not even shut.

He looked at Rebecca, and the moonlight shining into her diving mask showed a furrowed brow. Why was the gate unlocked?

They moved through the gate and crept forward along the short concrete path that led to the lab.

Back at home, and on the *Möbius,* the plan had seemed simple. Open the gate with the keycode. Open the door to the lab the same way. Snoop around inside and just like in the movies, surely they would instantly find all the incriminating evidence they would need to shut down the project and save the world from extinction.

But no one could have planned or prepared for the reality. The door to the lab was open, swinging idly in the light breeze that blew in from the east, here on the more exposed top of the island.

Not that long ago, a red-haired professor with a big

bright smile had opened this door for them and welcomed them into the lab. But nobody was here to welcome them this time. The light from inside spilled outward from the doorway, clearly illuminating the smashed doorjamb and ruined hinges.

"Something's really wrong here," Tane whispered. "That door's been smashed open. Someone's broken in before us!"

Rebecca grabbed his arm and pulled him down into a crouch beside her. Enough light spilled out from the broken doorway for him to see her eyes, stark, wide, and terrified inside the scuba mask.

"No," she said. "It's worse than that. Much worse. We've got to get off this island now!"

"What is it?" Tane asked, wondering what had her so spooked.

"Look at the door, Tane," she said. "Look at the hinges. Someone—or some*thing*—has smashed that door open from the *inside!*"

All the breath in his body suddenly froze. *What the heck . . .*

He rose slowly and took a step backward. Rebecca's hand slipped into his. Another step, then another. Walking backward, unable to take their eyes off the smashed door and the carelessly spilling light.

They were just back past the gate when the bright spotlights crashed on all around them, twenty or more, brilliant white lights that hurt his eyes, which were still adjusted to the darkness. He spun around and instantly recoiled, shielding his face with his arm, desperately frightened, unsure whether to turn and run or to stand still.

Rebecca screamed and clutched at him. In that single instant, he felt like a possum on a highway at night, transfixed by the headlights of an onrushing car, knowing that this was certain death but paralyzed beyond saving himself.

A voice—deep, authoritative, American—shouted at them from behind the screen of lights, "Drop your weapons. I say again, drop your weapons and lie on the ground, facedown, toward my voice. Drop your weapons, or we will open fire."

Weapons?! Tane tried to scream, "It's just a flashlight!" but his throat wasn't functioning.

"We are unarmed!" Rebecca shouted. "We are unarmed."

Tane found his voice and joined in. "We are unarmed," he called, lying facedown as he did so. "We're just kids!"

He saw only dark dirt as strong boots thundered around him and strong arms twisted his arms up behind his back before some tight plastic wire was pulled harshly around his wrists, and he was hauled to his feet.

His mask was wrenched down and left hanging around his neck. One of the bright lights was shone in his face. He winced from the pain of the glare. Even with his eyes tightly shut, it was bright enough to hurt. It felt like a dream, like he was in some strange bright fantasyland where nothing made any sense and nothing was expected to.

"Where are the others?" the same voice shouted. "Where are the rest of you?"

If he could have, he would have helped them willingly. "On the submarine," he would have said. But his throat had closed up again and he couldn't speak.

Beside him he heard Rebecca's voice. "There are no others! We are just kids!"

The man's voice again, talking, not shouting this time. "Crawford, this is Crowe. Any more warm spots showing on the scope?"

As he spoke, the soft chop of a helicopter—a very quiet helicopter—slid smoothly through the dark sky overhead.

Then the man was back a few inches from Tane's face. It was strange how muffled his voice was, in the midst of all the fear, darkness, bright lights, and confusion. As if the man were talking from behind a glass window. Or a mask of some kind.

"Where are the others? Where are the hostages?"

What others? What hostages?

When there was no answer from either of them, the man's voice softened a little. "Get them back to the boats. We'll interrogate them properly on board the ship. Crawford, remain in position. I want to know if a mouse farts on this rock. Red and Blue Teams exfil now."

Strong hands gripped their arms, at least two fully grown men to each child, wrenching their arms up behind their backs so high that it brought tears to Tane's eyes. He heard Rebecca cry out in pain, and a fierce anger flared inside him. How dare they do that to a girl. To Rebecca. But there was nothing he could do.

The frigate was the *Te Mana*. Her name was stenciled in huge letters on her side, near the stern. She looked very different from the side than she had from beneath the bows. They boarded her via thick rope netting hung down the side of the ship, a quick clip of some cutters behind them freeing their hands for the climb.

Compared to the darkness of the island, the deck of the frigate was a city of light. Men and women in naval uniforms kept their distance from the black-clad soldiers who had arrested them.

"Take them below?" one of the soldiers wanted to know.

"Not till we're a hundred percent that they're clean." The soldiers all looked the same, but the voice was the first one they had heard on the island, obviously the leader of the team. "What does the RPAD say?"

A large man was scanning them with a handheld device connected to something on his back. All of the men were armed with an unusual, rounded-looking rifle, with some sort of sprayer attached to the front of it. They wore black, armored space suits, with oxygen masks covering their faces and a small flat TV screen pulled back over their heads, some kind of night-vision system, Tane thought.

"Nothing," the man said. "No pathogens."

There was a hiss and a click and the man with a red "1" on his shoulders pulled his mask away from his face. He was thin, with a face that looked to have been chiseled out of granite. Even when he spoke, there was no expression, no movement on his face except for his mouth.

"Where are the rest of your people? And where are the hostages?"

Tane looked at Rebecca. None of it made any sense. No sense at all. What people? What hostages? How had the soldiers known they were coming? Rebecca's jaw was clenching and unclenching, and veins stood out in her neck. *As long as we don't get caught.* That was what they had said from the very beginning. *As long as we don't get caught. I can't afford to go to jail.*

The man continued, "Where are you holding the scientists? Have they been harmed in any way? And what about the fog? How did you create that?" He glared at Tane for a moment, then switched his gaze to Rebecca. "Cooperate with us now, or things are going to get real ugly, real fast."

Fog? What fog? It wasn't making a whole lot of sense,

Tane thought. Perhaps if they told them the whole truth, they would understand. They wouldn't believe them at first, but they could show them the Lotto numbers and the other messages, and they would have to believe them, wouldn't they? And they hadn't actually committed any crime yet. They were about to, but they hadn't had the chance to go through with it.

"We got a message from the future," he said quietly.

"What?!" the leader asked.

Tane looked him in the eye and continued a little more strongly, "We found a way to detect—"

"Oh my GOD!" Rebecca screamed, staring wild-eyed at the island and holding up her hands to shield herself.

Tane jumped out of his skin and stared past the soldiers to the black shape of the island behind. He strained his eyes, desperately seeking the cause of the alarm but could not see what Rebecca was seeing.

He wasn't the only one. There was not a man on the deck of the ship who did not instinctively turn to face the island. Those with weapons already had them raised, seeking targets, in an awesome display of instant reactions.

It all happened at once—the scream, the men turning to face the island, the slap on his arm—that he hardly noticed that Rebecca was running. Running away from the soldiers, away from the island, straight toward the side of the ship.

The leader shouted, "Hey!" But Rebecca was already three or four yards away from them and moving fast. A split second later, Tane was moving, too. One of the soldiers made a grab for him, but Tane ducked out of his reach and sprinted after Rebecca. The tall man with the scanner was there, but he had to drop the device to grab at Tane and that slowed him down, just enough. There were running boot-steps behind him but Tane didn't look back.

Rebecca reached the railing at the edge of the ship and leaped up lightly, one-footed, onto it before diving down into the darkness.

Tane didn't risk anything so fancy. He just grabbed the railing with two hands and hurdled it. Then he was falling, and falling, and falling.

The deck of the frigate was a long way from the surface of the ocean, and in the dark, it seemed to take forever to reach the water.

In that fraction of an instant before he splashed deep beneath the waves, he saw what Rebecca must have already seen, or perhaps had just guessed would be there. The dim, underwater glow of the *Möbius,* and the raised flat platform of the periscope buoy, just visible in the moonlight.

WAEWAETOROA
PASSAGE

The shock of landing felt like a car crash; then dark water enveloped him.

His nose filled with salty water. It seemed to take an age to kick back to the surface, but then he shot up above the waves like a cork, the wet suit giving him buoyancy. He gasped in a huge lungful of air and coughed and spluttered the water out of his sinuses.

Then there was a loud splash nearby. Someone had followed him over the side of the ship!

He jackknifed in the water and began to swim down. It was hard. Harder than he had realized. The wet suit kept trying to drag him back up to the surface.

He opened his eyes despite the sting of the salt and saw the bright lights of the *Möbius,* barely a few meters away, the submarine itself just a dark smudge in the water behind the glare of the lights. A couple more strokes and he was nearly at the sub. The top hatch was open, he saw, and Rebecca was already inside, silhouetted against the hatch lights.

She was waving frantically at him, and he suddenly realized that she had been down there, holding her breath, waiting for him to come so she could close the hatch.

Suddenly a strong hand closed around his ankle pulling him backward in the water. He kicked frantically but the grip was viselike. Desperately, he kicked out with his free foot and felt it connect solidly with something soft, like a person's face. The steel ring on his ankle loosened, and he kicked away down toward safety.

The hatch neared, and then Rebecca's hand reached up and pulled him closer.

He dived down into the hatch. Rebecca was already spinning the wheel to close it, but she seemed tired, listless. He swiveled around inside the narrow compartment and grabbed the wheel off her, twirling it around. The hatch snicked shut and locked, and in the same instant, Tane's hand found the flush lever.

Compressed air roared and the water level dropped, an inch, two inches, then enough for him to get his mouth and nose above water. He sucked in the tinny air and thought it tasted wonderful. Rebecca, where was Rebecca? She was just floating in the chamber and had not raised her head.

The water level continued to drop, and Tane grabbed Rebecca by the hair, wrenching her head above the water. She didn't breathe in.

"Oh crap!" Tane muttered. There was nowhere to lie her down in the narrow chamber, so he pressed her body against the rounded wall with his, the black neoprene suits clinging to each other. He pressed into her stomach with his fists and a torrent of seawater poured out of her mouth. She still wasn't breathing.

They had done this stuff over and over in first-aid classes at school, but that all seemed like a million years ago. *Finger in the mouth, check for obstructions.* He remembered that much at least. There were none. *Seal the nostrils.* Her mask, still hanging around her neck, was getting in the way, so he tore that off over her head. He gripped her nose tightly between two fingers. The rest of the training was a blank, so he just sealed his mouth on hers and blew. He counted to three— *was that in the training?*—and blew again. The water was around his waist by then. He breathed into her lungs again, and by the time the chamber was empty, she was breathing on her own.

The only thought in Tane's mind was, *It works. That stuff they taught us. It really does work.*

He spun the wheel for the side hatch and dragged Rebecca's semiconscious body out onto the floor of the main cabin. He could hear the engines of the *Möbius* running at full speed.

Fatboy looked back through the open door from the control room. "What's wrong?" he shouted.

"She's okay," Tane yelled back.

Rebecca coughed and spluttered and her eyes began to open. He was wedged against the side of the sub. Her head was in his lap.

"Tane," she said weakly.

"Are you okay?" he asked.

She just nodded and closed her eyes again. A moment later, she said, with her eyes still shut, "I couldn't hold my breath any longer."

"You did great; you did great," Tane reassured her. She had been holding her breath *for him.*

She tried to get up, and Tane put an arm underneath her shoulders to assist. He helped her lie down on one of the bunks and fastened the Velcro safety strap around her waist. He unstrapped the torch from her wrist and loosened the wet-suit jacket to help her breathe.

"I need some help up here!" Fatboy yelled from the cockpit, and Tane scurried forward.

Water rushed past the steering dome as he strapped himself into the codriver's seat.

Fatboy said, "Grab Rebecca's chart, the one she marked the rocks on. We're going back through the Waewaetoroa Passage."

"At night?" Tane asked incredulously. "At this speed?"

"Got no choice," Fatboy said, and as if to prove him right, there was suddenly a loud pinging sound against the metal of the hull.

"What the hell was that?"

"Sonar," Fatboy said. "I knew that was coming. They're chasing us. Now they know exactly where we are. They're much faster than we are, but they're big and heavy and it'll take them a while to get moving."

"We can't go through the passage at night." Tane was horrified.

"They can't go through it at all. They draw too much water. They'll have to go all the way around Okahu Island, by Whale Rock. And they won't be able to ping us through the passage—too much rock for the sound to bounce off. I'm thinking that we run the passage and try to make it to the Hole in the Rock before they round the island. We can hide from the sonar behind Motukokako Island, and they won't know which way we've gone."

The pinging sounded again and again, vibrating against the little hull.

"Get that chart ready," Fatboy said. "Here we go."

The rocky mouth of the passage loomed, and then they were between the two rock walls. It was much faster this time, and not just because Fatboy was driving the boat hard. The current must flow in this direction, Tane realized. The last time they had been fighting against it. This time it was dragging them along.

"What happened up there?" Fatboy asked, not taking his eyes off the rushing rock walls ahead of them. "I was watching the ship on the periscope when it came back into the bay, and I saw them take you on board."

"I don't know," Tane replied. "Ridge coming up on your right. Better come up a bit and steer a bit left."

The ridge, a gnash of jagged, hull-piercing teeth, growled away rapidly to their right, a school of dark fish scattering in all directions as they burst through the middle of them.

Had they known that they were coming? If not, why were the soldiers there? Had something bad happened on the island? There was no time to talk or even think about that now.

The pinging reverberated off the walls of the underwater canyon, bouncing around and around in echoes of echoes of echoes, creating its own wall of sound and shielding them from the ship. In here they were invisible to the sonar, just as Fatboy had said.

"Big rock, center of the passage," Tane said calmly, and Fatboy pulled the steering back, swerving up over the seaweed-covered behemoth as it loomed in their lights. Both of them scanned the water ahead intently. Their lights did not reach far enough ahead to give them enough warning of obstacles, and if not for Rebecca's map, they would have smashed into the rock of the seabed many times already.

"Ridge to your right, no, your left, your left!" Tane called as Fatboy almost steered them into a pancaked rock formation.

"Get it right, Tane." Fatboy gritted his teeth.

A large shark, apparently dozing near the exit of the passageway, twirled its tail and spun out of their way as they shot out the end of the canyon, and the seabed began to drop away beneath them.

"Now the race is on," Fatboy murmured. "If we can't make Motukokako in time, they'll pick us up on the sonar and haul us in like a fish on a line."

The pinger behind them fell silent. They were shielded from the *Te Mana* by the islands of Waewaetoroa and Okahu.

They said nothing, lost in their own thoughts. Tane checked on Rebecca once, but she was resting and just smiled up at him.

Only when they had passed Motutara Rock did Fatboy relax a little. "I think we've got a good enough head start," he said.

Almost immediately, the pinging started again, but this was long off and distant: just a faint echo against the hull.

Tane looked at his brother in concern, but Fatboy shook his head. "I think we're okay. The sound has to reach us and then travel all the way back to the ship like an echo. That pinging is too weak. I reckon we're out of sonar range for them at the moment."

The pinging, faint as it was, grew steadily louder as they

continued on toward Motukokako and its famous Hole in the Rock.

"They're chasing us," Tane said worriedly.

"No. They don't know where we are. They're just guessing. If we can make Motukokako, we can lose them." He patted the control console. "Come on, little submarine, you can do it."

Tane didn't smile. He felt sick.

Motukokako rose suddenly out of the seabed before them. A huge rock wall in the lights of the *Möbius*. The pinging was getting louder now.

"Here we go," he said, slowing the submarine down and crawling along the face of an underwater cliff. The currents were strong and volatile, throwing the small craft from side to side, but Fatboy kept the *Möbius* as steady as he could.

Another cliff rose on the starboard side, and Tane realized that they were in the "hole," the short passageway that cut right through the rock of the island.

When the rock walls disappeared, Fatboy steered to the port side and held the craft steady in one spot, using the motor to adjust for the currents that threatened to drive them back into the cliff. The pinging grew in intensity, but Fatboy shook his head at Tane's querying look.

"We are behind the island. They can't 'see' us here. But better get that periscope up and let me know when they come around the point."

Tane raised the buoy and tried to look around. It was difficult in the swelling waves, even with the gimbals that kept the camera steady.

The moonlight illuminated the edge of the island and sea beyond, but the water kept spinning the buoy around, and he had to constantly maneuver it.

The pinging surrounded them by the time Tane caught the first glimpse of the bow of the frigate, a dark silhouette against the moonlight.

"There she is!"

Fatboy was already turning the submarine, and rock surrounded them again for a moment as they ducked back through the hole in the rock.

Tane aimed his camera at the edge of the island just in time to see the stern of the frigate disappear behind it.

"What now?" he asked.

"Wait," Fatboy replied.

Less than thirty minutes later, the ship returned, but they were through the hole to the other side of the island long before it would have been able to ping them.

"It's like playing hide-and-seek," Fatboy laughed.

It sort of was, but Tane still felt sick.

They stayed in the shadow of Motukokako for another hour as the pinging receded into the distance. Only then did they start the journey back to Auckland.

Tane spent most of the trip sitting on the floor by Rebecca's bed, watching her. She woke up at one point, looked at him, and said, "Nothing makes any sense." But most of the way she slept. She vomited once or twice and he cleaned that up and reassured her gently that she was okay.

She had held her breath for him.

BOOK 2

THE LONG WHITE CLOUD

BAMBI

Gazza Henderson poured the remains of his dinner onto the last embers of his fire with a hiss and a small puff of steam.

The dregs of his coffee went the same way, but there was barely enough heat left in the fire to raise a sizzle.

Technically, the campfire was illegal here deep in the bush at this time of year, but rules like that were for hikers and tourists. He had been hunting in the forests of Northland for more than twenty years and felt as at home in the bush as he did in his own living room. He certainly knew how to put out a campfire properly.

He heaped earth on top of the fire's remains and stamped on that carefully, making sure there was no chance of residual warmth flaring up again later and causing a forest fire. He had no wish to do that. It would be like burning down his own house.

Bambi's cold dead eyes stared up at him from beside his pack. Bambi wasn't a fawn, like in the movie. It wasn't even a doe. He was a buck, a hoary old stag, but Gazza always called the deer he shot "Bambi." It was a kind of twisted joke that had started when he used to go hunting with his mate Trevor in their teens.

This Bambi was a beauty. His antlers were worth at least two hundred on the Douglas points scoring system. Plus he had the Kaipara split in the antlers, which traced his ancestry directly back to the original fallow deer released in New Zealand in 1864.

The Kaipara split wasn't worth any extra points, but it was certainly worth a few pints in the clubrooms when he got back. Besides, he was sure that Bambi would take out the New Zealand record this year.

"Won't you, old boy," he said out loud. Bambi just stared at him coldly.

The sun was setting through the tall straight trunks of the kauri of the forest, and a light haze was rising as the day cooled. It softened the shadows of the trees, already elongated by the low angle of the sun, and gave the forest a quite otherworldly feeling.

Gazza debated with the dead stag for a while whether to de-head him and leave the body in the bush. He was a trophy hunter, a sportsman, he told all his mates, not a butcher, and the whole stag was a lot of weight to lug all the way back to Russell.

As he watched, the haze thickened into a light mist, swelling up around the tree ferns and rata vines. It seemed a bit unusual for this time of day. Mists were common in the early mornings, and many times he had awoken to find himself in a whitened-out world. But not usually in the evening when the land was still warm.

In fact, he couldn't ever remember a mist through the forest at sunset like this.

The tall kauri made ghostly spires as the delicate tendrils of the fog—for it really was turning into a fog—wrapped their way around trunks and through the fanned-out leaves of the pungas. Already those trees, more than twenty or thirty meters away, were dissolving into the mist, leaving a wall of white behind the trees closer to him.

There was a vague movement in the mist, more of a stirring than anything else.

"Anybody there?" he called out. He didn't expect there to be, but the alternatives were a deer or a Captain Cooker, one of the ferocious wild boars with razor-sharp tusks that populated the Northland forests.

He reached for his rifle but left the safety on. Hunting was a dangerous enough sport in the full light of day. But in the twilight, in a fog, it could be a death sentence. The last thing he wanted to do was shoot some innocent tramper, or another hunter, thinking it was a deer or a Cooker.

But at the same time, he didn't want to leave himself defenseless in case a wild boar did suddenly materialize out of the mist and charge toward his little campsite.

There were more movements then, more stirrings in the mist, around and in between the trees.

"Anybody there?" he called out again curiously, but not nervously.

The mist was thickening all the time, and he could see barely a few meters now. He had a strong sense that someone or *something* was out there. He slid a round into the chamber of his rifle and flicked off the safety.

"I am a hunter," he called out. This time there was a slight nervous catch in his voice. "I have a rifle. Please identify yourself."

There was no reply, and all around him now, he had the sensation that the woods, the mist, were alive. Indefinable shapes swirled around him in the fog, ghosts amongst the trees.

A short while later, two rifle shots echoed through the tall kauri of the forest.

When Gazza hadn't returned by Thursday, December 17, his wife, Lorna Henderson, reported him overdue. Gazza was never back late from a hunting trip.

New Zealand's Most Wanted

"I can't believe," said Tane with a serious expression, "that they fell for that corny old look-out-behind-you routine."

"Actually it was 'Oh my God,'" said Rebecca with a grin. She had woken up after that first miserable night feeling one hundred percent fine and full of vim and vigor, if with a slight raspy cough to remind her of her brush with death.

Tane wasn't sure if she knew just how close she had come to dying, or what he had had to do to save her life, and he didn't enlighten her. It was something that was probably best forgotten.

"Seriously, though," he said with a smile, "whoever those guys were, they were tough, they were hard, they were professional combat soldiers. And yet they fell for the oldest trick in the book."

"Who were they?" Fatboy asked, without any trace of humor. "And is there any way they can identify us?"

They were seated around the wooden dining room table of the West Harbor house. The journey back had been a slow one, creeping from bay to bay, point to point, watching, always watching for the sharp bow of a naval frigate. It had taken them four days, but the *Möbius* was now safely tucked away in the boatshed, away from prying eyes.

"No, I don't think so," Rebecca said.

"What about fingerprints?" Fatboy asked.

"I've never been fingerprinted by the police," Tane said. "So even if they got my fingerprints on the island, they wouldn't help."

"I have," Rebecca said carefully. "After the Save the Whales march. And that was going through my mind the whole time after they captured us. On the rubber boat, we had our hands tied behind our backs, and when we got on board the ship, I was careful not to touch anything. Not even the guardrail."

Tane remembered how she had skipped lightly over it.

"What about the netting?" he asked. "When we climbed up the side of the ship."

Fatboy shook his head. "They won't be able to lift fingerprints off wet rope," he said. "I am almost certain of it."

"Which just leaves the air bottles and weight belts," Rebecca said. "Should we go back to the island and get them?"

"Too risky," Fatboy said. "They'll be watching the island from now on. Better just pray they don't find them."

"What I think we need to work out most urgently," Tane said, "is what they were doing there. There was minimal security when we visited the island a few weeks earlier, and then when we turn up, suddenly the entire fifth cavalry is waiting."

Rebecca nodded. "I think something bad has happened on that island."

"Something to do with those piles of clothes you found?" Fatboy asked.

"Maybe," she replied, "and the broken door."

"The soldiers might have broken that door down," Tane said hopefully.

"From the inside?" Rebecca reminded him.

"Well, at least it's off our shoulders now," Fatboy said. "Now that the army and the navy are involved, it's not our problem anymore."

"Thank God for that," Tane agreed.

"Maybe," said Rebecca without conviction.

Tane looked closely at her. "Maybe?"

"It's not up to us anymore," Fatboy said emphatically. "We tried. We failed. Let the authorities sort it out."

"They won't," Rebecca said. "Or they can't. Or they just don't."

"You've got to be kidding," Fatboy said. "They've got soldiers and scientists and . . . and . . . other stuff. Of course they can sort it out."

Rebecca looked down at the tabletop, which was covered with copies of the almost-complete diagram, neatly printed out on crisp new sheets from their new inkjet printer.

"Tane, Fats, if the authorities are going to sort it out, then why have we been getting SOS messages from the future? They are going to fail. Just like we failed. The only people who can sort this out is us—that is, if we can figure out these messages and do the right things. In time."

Tane caught the sting in the tail of that and glanced away.

Rebecca asked, "What about the Chronophone?"

With two computers working almost nonstop, they were quickly chewing through the backlog of BATSE data. There was now less than a third of the image to go. The plans lay tantalizingly close to completion in front of them.

"We can't build it yet," Fatboy said. "Not until we have the missing bit. But we could start buying some of the components."

"Where from?" Tane asked. "The local Chronophone shop?"

Rebecca laughed, and Fatboy said, "They're all just standard components, looking at the diagram. Resistors, transistors, diodes. We can pick them up at any RadioShack. But I'll get a mate of mine to look over it in any case. Goony. He's the electronics technician at the recording studio. What he doesn't know about circuit boards is not worth knowing."

"Will he help us build it?" Rebecca wondered out loud.

"Probably," Fatboy replied.

"Can we trust him?" Tane asked.

"I don't think we have any choice," Fatboy responded. "But anyway, he doesn't have to know what it does to assemble the components."

"Hi, Rebecca. Hello, boys," a new voice said, and they all looked up with somewhat guilty expressions. They hadn't heard Rebecca's mum come in.

"Hi, Mrs. Richards," Tane said. "How are you feeling?"

He saw Rebecca's cross look out of the corner of his eye.

"I'm fine, thank you, Tane. How is your mum? I haven't seen her in such a long time."

"Oh, she's fine, thanks," Tane replied.

"What's happening on your program?" Rebecca asked conversationally, casually turning the Chronophone plans upside down on the tabletop as her mother poured herself a glass of orange juice from the fridge.

"Oh, I don't know." Her mum looked quite annoyed. "It's getting hard to follow. They keep interrupting it with those blasted news reports."

"News reports?" It was Tane who asked.

"Oh, all those cordons up past Whangarei. Mad cow disease, something like that."

The three of them sat openmouthed as Rebecca's mum disappeared back upstairs.

"There's a TV in the lounge," Rebecca said unnecessarily.

The newsreader was as smooth and polished as a greenstone tiki. They watched with increasing shock as the details of a quarantine zone were announced. A police spokesperson was interviewed and urged residents to stay calm but to avoid any unnecessary travel. Mad cow disease had been discovered on a Northland farm, a cattle disease potentially damaging to New Zealand's dairy exports.

The main highway had been cordoned off at Kawakawa to the south of Russell and at Kerikeri to the north. All ancillary roads had also been blocked. There was no movement in or out of the quarantine zone without special permission of the police and military who were policing it.

In the same bulletin, but declared as an unrelated story, the police were searching for two teenagers and an unknown number of accomplices in connection with the disappearance of a prominent scientist from a research station in the Bay of Islands.

A photo of Professor Green was displayed, along with a potted summary of her career, followed by a police sketch of Rebecca and Tane. It wasn't a good likeness.

"What the hell is going on?" Fatboy wanted to know when the bulletin had finished.

"Disappearance!" Rebecca's mouth just about hit the floor. "So that's what the soldiers meant by 'Where are the hostages?' They think we kidnapped Vicky!"

"And the rest of her team!" Fatboy realized.

Tane said, "But we didn't. So who did? And what's this about mad cow disease?"

"It's not mad cow," Rebecca said. "That's just a story, to avoid panic."

"So what is it?" Tane asked.

Rebecca said chillingly, "Isn't it obvious? Something bad *did* happen on the island. The Chimera Project."

Tane got up and turned the sound off on the TV. The sudden silence in the room seemed to take all the warmth out of the day, despite the unfettered sunshine outside.

Rebecca said, "I think we were too late. That whatever it was that we were supposed to stop has already happened."

3

'TIS THE SEASON

HE SEES YOU WHEN YOU'RE SLEEPING,
HE KNOWS WHEN YOU'RE AWAKE.
HE KNOWS IF YOU'VE BEEN BAD OR GOOD,
SO BE GOOD FOR GOODNESS SAKE!

—J. FRED COOTS AND HAVEN GILLESPIE,
"SANTA CLAUS IS COMING TO TOWN"

The week leading up to Christmas was full of the noise and fun and shopping that is like no other time of the year.

Carolers sang joyously on street corners, whole streets of houses were festooned with thousands of tiny lightbulbs, and children sat fearfully on Santa's knee in the shopping malls and asked for outrageous gifts like ponies and spaceships and magic rings that could make them fly.

Shops promised pre-Christmas sales, large corporations sponsored nighttime light shows and drew Santa's sleigh on the clouds in colored laser light.

Drivers and shoppers alike grew increasingly irritable as stressed-out motorists and frazzled parents gesticulated at each other over places in motorway queues, or parking spaces, or the last stock of a special-priced toy.

In other words, the year progressed just like those that preceded it, and apart from the occasional slightly disturbing news report from the north, life was pretty good.

To Tane, Rebecca, and Fatboy, it all seemed like sheer insanity.

The man in the Santa suit glanced casually over at Tane again. Too casually. For the third time.

"Let's get out of here," he said to Rebecca, who was comparing the component numbers on some electrical parts with the list that Fatboy had given them.

Fatboy was still circling the block. He had given up looking for a space after half an hour of trying. Kmart had a sale on and there wasn't a free parking space this side of Western Springs.

"But we haven't got the capacitors yet." She frowned, running her finger along a row of small, labeled plastic bins.

"Santa Claus has been watching us for the last five minutes."

Rebecca looked around at the man, who quickly looked away. "Might be a store detective. The way you're acting, I'd be watching you too."

"A store detective in a Santa suit?" Tane took a deep breath and tried to calm down. It didn't help. A police car went past outside with its siren crying, and he accidentally knocked over an entire stand of *Dummies* books. He picked them up quickly, before the sales assistant could come and help.

Santa was watching them again, Tane realized, half hidden on the other side of a circular stand of electronics magazines. He was curiously thin-faced for a Santa, who was usually a chubby, jovial fellow. This Santa had a scar above one eye, not quite masked by the stuck-on bushy eyebrows. He looked like a spy in a Santa costume. Or a hired killer. Or a soldier.

"He's still got his eye on us," Tane whispered, covering his mouth with his hand in case Santa could read lips.

"You'd better watch out," Rebecca said quietly.

"What? Why?" Tane hissed urgently.

"You'd better not cry . . ."

"Cry?" Tane stared at his friend in confusion.

"Got it," said Rebecca, picking up a couple of small metal objects out of a plastic tray. "Let's get out of here."

"Cry?" Tane asked again.

Rebecca laughed gaily and sang in Tane's ear, "He's making a list and checking it twice; he's gonna find out who's naughty and nice . . ."

Tane groaned and punched Rebecca lightly on the arm.

For all her frivolity, though, he noticed that her hands were shaking as she handed over the money at the counter.

Fatboy swept into the curb in the Wrangler as they emerged from the electronics shop. They swung on board, Rebecca in the front, Tane in the back, and Fatboy pulled out again in a seamless maneuver.

He handed a newspaper to Rebecca as he steered carefully around a family of four lugging two long plastic kayaks across the parking area.

"Made the front page!"

Rebecca looked at it and wordlessly handed it back to Tane.

HUNT CONTINUES FOR TEENAGERS, the headline blared over the police drawings of him and Rebecca. Rebecca's was a reasonable resemblance, he thought, but his picture looked like an axe-murderer.

Rebecca had dyed her hair jet black since the escape from the soldiers and had started wearing a cap. It was summer, so they all wore sunglasses. All in all, Tane didn't think they were in any danger of being recognized by a passing stranger. But what if one of their school friends recognized the pictures?

"What do we do?" he asked.

"Nothing," Fatboy replied immediately. "It doesn't change a thing. They'll never recognize Rebecca from a picture like that, although yours is a pretty good likeness."

"Bite me," Tane said.

The Wrangler was an open-top jeep, which would have seemed like a lot of fun on such a lovely, sunstruck day. But it made Tane feel elevated and conspicuous. There was nothing to hide behind.

They sat silently in a queue to get out of the car park. Tane pretended to rest his face on his hand to shield himself from an elderly couple in an old Volvo in the next lane.

"The worst thing is feeling like a criminal all the time," he said, almost to himself, "when we haven't done anything wrong."

"I know what you mean," Rebecca said in a small voice, and Tane thought, not for the first time, that she was a lot more fragile than she was making out. She had that tired, heavy look about her again. Perhaps she felt that she, of all of them, had the most to lose.

The car radio was tuned to a news talk station.

"Any news on the plague?" Tane asked.

"Nothing," Fatboy replied. "Quarantine zone is still in place, apparently, but there's been no other reports."

"Let's hope it stays that way," Tane said.

SILENT NIGHT

A strange fog rolled through the streets of New Zealand's northernmost city—Whangarei—on the night before Christmas, blanketing the city. Streets that were usually full of festivity and Christmas Eve revelers became unusually, deathly silent.

By morning, not a creature was stirring in the city of nearly fifty thousand people, except for the birds in the trees and the small animals of the undergrowth; the pets, now howling and yowling for their owners; a few farm animals; and, of course, the occasional mouse.

WHITE CHRISTMAS

SLEEP IN HEAVENLY PEACE
SLEEP IN HEAVENLY PEACE.
—JOSEF MOHR, "SILENT NIGHT"

Crawford landed the Sikorsky MH-60S Knighthawk helicopter in the middle of the main road, touching down with a gentle sigh.

Crowe was out before the engine had even been switched off, ducking his head against the wash from the rotors.

He stopped next to his second in command, Big "Mandy" Manderson, and stared to the north. His shoulder itched and he absently reached up to scratch it, realizing the futility only as his finger connected with the solid Kevlar of his armored combat biosuit. The suit was black. It was a positive-pressure suit, so even if it was damaged, the higher air pressure inside would keep pathogens from getting in. Scientists in biohazard labs wore positive-pressure suits but the air pressure was about the only similarity. Crowe's suit, and those of his team, were made of bulletproof Kevlar with ceramic chest and stomach plates. They were not only protection from germs, but also protection against human germs with guns. For all that, it was lightweight and about as comfortable as a black combat biosuit could be.

"Still think it's terrorists?" Mandy asked in his slow Southern drawl.

Crowe didn't answer.

It was dark. The sun was still hiding a couple of hours away behind the forests and the ocean to the east, but even so, all over New Zealand, excited children would be waking up—with that natural, internal alarm clock that kids have on Christmas morning—and eagerly unwrapping presents.

Except in Whangarei.

Crowe stood in the middle of the road and looked at the fog. He had never seen a fog quite like it before. The edge of it was so well defined that it looked as if you could walk up to it and touch it. It was as if a puffy cumulus cloud had dropped from the sky and settled on the road in front of him.

A road sign just in front of the fog was perfectly clear, but everything behind it was blanketed in white. WHANGAREI 2 KM the sign announced.

The calls to emergency services had started at eleven the previous night. The local police station had gone off the air, so police officers from surrounding areas had rushed to the scene. They had reported seeing the fog; then their radios had fallen silent.

"What did you find out?" Mandy asked.

Specialist First Class Evans, the unit's newest and youngest recruit, appeared at his side, holding a bunch of large-scale photographs. "The satellite images you asked for," he said, handing them over to Crowe.

Crowe flicked through them quickly. They were in series, with a date/time stamp at the top of each photograph in black computer lettering. The photos themselves were grainy black-and-white weather satellite images showing the top of the North Island of New Zealand.

"There it is," Crowe said, pointing to a small fuzzy spot on one of the photos. "That's the fog over Motukiekie."

He flicked forward a couple of photos. "Here it is moving south, across the water."

He looked up at Manderson. "It comes inland here, to the east of Russell, but misses Russell, Paihia, Kawakawa, and travels through the Russell forest, then down the coastline through this area here. What is this area?"

"Mainly forests and farmland," Mandy said, consulting a map.

"Okay, it rolls over the top of this small town here, Hikurangi, and ends up in Whangarei."

Crawford joined them, the rotors of the Knighthawk slowly winding down behind them.

Crowe pursed his lips and nodded, then looked up. "Any luck finding those kids?"

Mandy shook his head. "No leads as yet. The local guys are currently reviewing the security camera footage from the lab. Going back a couple of weeks. See if the cameras noticed anything suspicious in the days leading up to the . . . accident."

"What about the days when the scientists disappeared? What do the cameras show on those days?"

"Nothing. Not a thing. The image is completely fogged for a couple of days. Some kind of jamming equipment perhaps."

Crowe looked at the high bank of fog a short way up the highway and said nothing.

Manderson straightened up to his full height and stood

next to Crowe, facing the mist. He said, "Something's been worrying me, Stony."

Crowe said nothing but looked at the big man.

Manderson continued, "How did those kids get from their submarine onto the island without us noticing?"

"They swam." Crowe frowned.

Manderson shook his head. "Crawford was overhead in the helicopter the whole time. He would have seen them on the heat-scope."

Crawford said, "I saw nothing until they appeared at the end of the wharf."

"Underwater!" Crowe realized.

"But they had no air tanks when we picked them up," Manderson noted.

Crowe said, "Get some men back to the island. Search around the wharf."

Evans said suddenly, "Skipper, the mist!"

Crowe swung around back to the wall of fog in front of them. It was glowing.

"What the hell . . . ?" Manderson drawled.

Crowe wasted no time. "All teams, seal masks and get up here now. Set your fields of fire and kill zones. Be ready for anything."

Jackboots sounded all around them as the members of Red and Blue Teams fanned out across the road, dropping to one knee or even lying on the roadway, their special-issue XM8 automatic weapons trained on the glowing mist.

The glow slowly split in two and gradually resolved itself into two distinct lights, brightly luminescent in the mist.

"It's a car!" Crawford said.

"No," Crowe said, "the lights are too large, too far apart. It's a truck."

It was crawling toward them. Just rolling slowly forward through the mist. The lights brightened, yard by yard.

The dark bulk of the truck gradually materialized through the ethereal white clouds. It was big, an eighteen-wheeler.

The long snout of the truck now poked its way out of the wall of the edge of the fog. The name SLIPSTREAM WARRIOR was painted in bold lettering across the front of the hood.

"Hold your fire," Crowe called. "We may have a survivor."

At a painfully slow crawl, the big truck rolled forward out of the fog, past the WHANGAREI sign, and gathered momentum down a short slope before a small bridge across a stream. It was no more than fifty or sixty yards in front of them now.

"They're not in a hurry, are they," Evans murmured.

"Stay alert," Crowe ordered.

As it turned out, there was no need. For alertness. The truck failed to take the small bridge on a mild bend in the highway. It never turned. It never tried to turn. It just rolled forward in a dead straight line and hit the railing of the bridge on an angle.

The concrete wall of the bridge disintegrated under the impact of the massive truck, and the juggernaut toppled slowly off the side of the bridge and crashed down, nose-first, into the small stream below.

The back wheels of the cab and the large trailer remained on the highway. The wheels of the truck continued to grind for a few seconds; then it stalled with a huge shudder that ran through the body of the truck like that of a dying animal and was still.

"Crawford, Manderson," Crowe said tersely, "check it out."

The two men ran in a crouch over to the dead body of

the beast, sliding down the embankment beside the bridge and peering in through the shattered windshield of the truck.

"It's empty." Crawford's voice sounded in his earpiece. "No driver."

"Stranger and stranger," Crowe said.

"Around here, if you ask me, 'strange' is pretty normal," Manderson said.

Crawford spoke again, his voice suddenly low and serious. "Crowe, you'd better come and look at this."

"Evans, don't take your eyes off that fog," Crowe said, running across to the edge of the broken bridge. Crawford and Manderson were crouched over something on the bank of the stream. Crawford turned and looked up at him, and then he could see past the man, to the object they were crouching over. It was a body.

Crowe slithered down the embankment and splashed through the stream to where the other two crouched. His heart wrenched. It was the body of a small boy, half in the water, faceup in the mud. The body was covered in mud, and it was incredible that even the eagle-eyed Crawford had spotted it.

The boy couldn't have been more than four. It was all Crowe could do to say, "Get the body back to the lab."

Manderson said, "Let me do it," and Crowe remembered that Mandy had a five-year-old son of his own. More than any of the others, he would be feeling the anguish of the little boy's death.

Manderson stowed his weapon and carefully, respectfully, worked his hands into the mud underneath the neck and knees of the tiny body. He lifted and the body came free of the mud with a sucking sound.

The boy opened his eyes, took one look at Manderson's black suit and face mask, and screamed his little lungs out.

A police doctor went back in the ambulance with the boy. They still called him "the boy" because he had been unable to tell them his name.

He had done nothing but scream until the ambulance had arrived. The U.S. Army Bioterrorism Response Force soldiers in their black combat biosuits must have looked a fearsome sight to a half-drowned, terrified four-year-old.

So far, he was the only known survivor of the calamity that had embraced the city, but as an eyewitness he was useless. Only two coherent words had come from the terrified little boy the entire time, and they made little or no sense at all.

"Jerryfish," the boy had screamed over and over. "Jerryfish! Jerryfish!" and "Snowmen!"

The "jerryfish" was the most confusing. It seemed he was saying "jellyfish," but there was no rationale in that. Jellyfish were saltwater creatures and the boy had been found in a freshwater stream.

But the word "snowmen" had Crowe worried. A white biosuit could be mistaken for a snowman, particularly by a young boy. If he had seen terrorists in biosuits, that could well explain the "snowmen."

"It's starting to drift," Manderson noted.

Already the WHANGAREI road sign had disappeared into the maw of the mist.

"I noticed," Crowe replied. "It's coming south. Get the men ready to evac."

"A bit strange, don't you think?"

"Strange, why?"

Manderson looked at him oddly. "The breeze is nor'east, Stony."

Crowe peered up at the leaves on the branches of some nearby trees. It was true, he realized with a profound horror. The fog was coming south.

But the wind was blowing the other way.

ON CHRISTMAS DAY

It was half past nine in the morning. On Christmas Day.

The Christmas tree sat in the corner of the middle lounge, the largest of the three. It was a tall tree, perfectly shaped in the traditional Christmas tree cone, with deep green needles—or were they leaves?—and a dark wooden trunk scored with the intricate and random patterns of bark. It was a luxurious tree—vibrant, exciting, larger than life—that embodied the spirit of Christmas in its very form.

And it was made in China, according to the not-quite-covered-up sticker on its base. Aluminum, fiberglass, and plastic, if you cared to read the small print.

"Be there in a moment," Tane's mum called cheerily from the kitchen, busy with some final putting-away.

They had all helped clear away the remnants and dishes of the champagne breakfast, which was a Christmas morning tradition in the Williams household and happened before the presents were opened. They all helped; that was part of the tradition also. Even Rebecca.

It was the first time that Rebecca had spent Christmas morning at Tane's house. Her mum's cousin had come and picked her up, but Rebecca had asked to go to Tane's and nobody had minded.

Tane thought it was strange to be having a day of celebration with all that was going on—quarantine zones, kidnappings, nationwide police hunts, and so on—but it seemed even stranger *not* to celebrate Christmas, and certainly it would have raised some tricky questions with his mum and dad if they had decided not to show up.

His mum wandered in at last from the dining room and found an empty armchair.

"Right, then," she said. "Who's the youngest?"

That was another Williams family tradition. The youngest person would play Santa Claus and hand out the presents to the others, starting from the oldest person. As there were no grandparents or young cousins this time, that made his dad the oldest and Tane the youngest. Rebecca shared his birthday, but she had been born in the morning and Tane had been born in the evening.

Tane didn't answer. He was too busy watching the spider. It was a big one. Not huge like an Avondale spider or a tarantula, but big enough to be scary. It was brown with an elongated body and thick, sectional legs. It had woven an intricate web in the corner of one of the large picture windows of the middle lounge, a tightly woven web, almost honeycomb in appearance, with many layers of strands on top of other layers.

The spider was quivering, shaking. He had never seen a

spider do that before. A thin band of white crossed over the dark brown body. It struggled to move, and he suddenly realized what was happening. The spider had become trapped in its own web.

"Tane's the youngest," Rebecca said brightly, showing no sign of the worry that must surely be festering inside.

Tane hunted in the pile of brightly wrapped parcels until he found something with his dad's name on it.

"Merry Christmas," he said jovially, making a bit of a performance of the handover. His dad grinned and snatched it off him, scanning the tag to see who it was from and ripping off the paper with gusto. It was a book, the latest John Grisham thriller, from his uncle in Wellington.

His dad laughed now, for no real reason. Just the joy of the day.

If only he knew!

Tane was already rummaging for a present for his mum. His mind was elsewhere, though, and he skipped over one a couple of times before noticing it.

He found a present for Fatboy from Rebecca, and then one for Rebecca, from Fatboy.

Fatboy's present to Rebecca was a silver necklace. Tane didn't look at it too closely, but it looked expensive. Still, with over a million dollars still earning them interest in their trust account, what was money anyway? It was the thought that counted, and he hoped that Rebecca would realize the effort that had gone into the present Tane had chosen for her—the chess set.

She still hadn't opened it, saving it till last probably, because it was the biggest. Or maybe, he hoped, because it was from him.

He opened Rebecca's present slowly. It was delicately,

femininely wrapped in layers of colored tissue, bound by ribbons. That wasn't like her at all. Maybe they had wrapped it in the shop for her, he thought. Inside the wrapping was a white cardboard box. He pulled the top off carefully and stared down at what was inside.

It was a brand-new harmonica. Engraved on the silver top of the instrument were the words FRIENDS FOREVER.

He gave Rebecca a hug, with a warm feeling that went from his toes up to the hair of his scalp.

His parents' presents for him and his brother were the same, he realized as he opened his. Fatboy had opened his a few moments earlier. It was a genuine hand-carved *patu pounamu*, a greenstone club, almost a foot long with a leather cord through one end, carved with traditional symbols of their Tuhoe tribe.

"Goes with the *moko*, don't you think?" Fatboy said proudly.

Tane put his carefully to one side, conscious of the close scrutiny of his parents. It was a kind of cool present, but he had been hoping for a new Xbox console. He forced a smile.

"Thanks, Mum, Dad, it's great!"

Rebecca came over and sat next to him as she unwrapped the chess set. Tane crossed his fingers behind his back.

It was a hit.

Rebecca actually squealed with delight as the paper fell away. She slid the wooden case out of its plastic covering and pulled each piece individually out of its velvet casing, noticing the fine detail of the replications.

She even held up the king, Michelangelo's *David*, to show the rest of the room. "Look at the detail!" she exclaimed. "You can see every muscle on his tummy. And what a tiny willy."

They all roared with laughter.

"Thanks, Tane," Rebecca said, and hugged him warmly.

Tane never got to see what Rebecca had bought Fatboy, which was the only jarring note on the day. Fatboy unwrapped it, looked inside without revealing the contents, smiled at Rebecca, and wrapped it back up. He gave Rebecca a hug after that, but Tane looked the other way.

It was a lovely day, and the worries that faced them receded for a few hours at least. They ate, they drank more champagne than they were allowed by sneaking into the kitchen and topping off their glasses just a little at a time, and they listened to "Snoopy's Christmas" over and over on the stereo until his dad got sick of it and put on "The Little Drummer Boy" instead. They just spent time enjoying their presents and each other's company. Fatboy got his guitar out after lunch (leftovers from the breakfast) and Tane joined him on his new harmonica. The big windows were open to the forest, and the sounds and smells of the native bush drifted gently inside. The sun was fiery, but sheltered by the trees of the forest, the house was cool and peaceful.

It was a lovely day.

In the midafternoon, they went back to the West Harbor house to do some more work on the Chronophone. Rebecca's mother was still out at her cousin's, so they had the house totally to themselves. They had already purchased most of the parts for the machine, and Fatboy had arranged for his mate Goony to come over and start building it the moment the rest of the plans came through.

Rebecca went to sit on a large sofa in the corner of the living room and wrapped her arms around her legs, rocking back and forth slowly. Tane watched her silently. They had managed to put it all out of their minds for a few hours on Christmas morning, but now the reality was breathing down their necks.

At six o'clock, Tane turned the television on to watch the news. The queen was on, broadcasting her Christmas message, and he flicked over to TV3.

There was only one story. The news had apparently been running all day. Breathless reporters behind police road-blocks and helicopter shots from a distance told a story of the most catastrophic disaster in the history of New Zealand. Fifty thousand people, cut off, missing or worse. A strange fog. The evacuation of the small town of Maungaturoto, south of Whangarei, the next in the path of the fog as it drifted down toward Auckland, New Zealand's largest city.

Auckland residents were urged to remain calm and to not try leaving the city. Civil defense managers assured reporters that special teams of experts had already been brought in from overseas to deal with the problem.

Rebecca had been drinking some water, but her glass shattered suddenly on the floor. Her face was white.

"Rebecca?"

She turned and ran outside onto the patio. Tane ran after her. He sensed Fatboy following.

"Oh no. Oh no, oh no, oh no."

Rebecca gripped the edge of the patio table with both hands as if she would fall down without it. She was breathing strangely, Tane noticed, hyperventilating. She kept lurching forward.

"Oh my God, no," Rebecca said.

"What is it, Rebecca? Do you think we were exposed to a virus when we were on the island?" Fatboy asked urgently.

"No. Worse than that. Much worse than that."

Worse than that! The world seemed to be spinning around Tane's head. "What's wrong, Rebecca?"

She shut her eyes for a second and breathed out a long, slow breath. "I've just put it all together. The island. The fog. The cryptic messages. I know why we had to buy the submarine."

"To visit the island. We already knew that, didn't we?" Tane asked with a growing apprehension.

She shook her head. "What if there were two reasons? A plan B in case our trip to the island failed."

"Which it did," Fatboy noted.

"What if we were right? What if this . . . virus . . . or whatever it is, is so dreadful, so devastating, that plan B is to give ourselves a refuge, a kind of a fallout shelter under the sea."

"A sanctuary," Fatboy said softly.

Rebecca asked, "What if we're supposed to hide underwater in our little yellow submarine to keep ourselves safe from a plague that is about to wipe out the rest of New Zealand?"

"Or the rest of the world," Tane said.

It was ten past six in the evening. On Christmas Day.

SANCTUARY

On Boxing Day, while other kids all over the country went swimming or cycling on new Christmas bikes or were just playing with their Game Boys and other presents, Tane, Rebecca, and Fatboy planned for the apocalypse.

"How long do you think we will be underwater?" Tane asked.

"However long it takes," was Rebecca's answer. "Months, maybe years."

The Chronophone plans had finally finished with a last long list of numbers, followed by the single word *END*. They had printed out the schematic and pored over it.

"Why even bother?" Fatboy had asked at one point. "It's too late. It's no use to us now."

Rebecca had looked at him incredulously. "Are you insane? If we don't build the Chronophone, then we can't send the messages back through time. If we don't do that, then we won't know anything and we'll just be out there like everyone else, playing with our Christmas presents and lying on the beach, and not even knowing that we are about to be wiped off the face of the planet."

Fatboy had looked at Tane in alarm, but Tane had said, "She's right. No Chronophone, no Lotto, no nothing. We'd better get it built."

That had been three days ago. That day, Tane had opened the front door to possibly the thinnest person he had ever seen in his life. Goony seemed to be made of just cling-film wrapped around a skeleton. He introduced himself shyly with a big droopy grin and lugged inside a huge plastic toolbox that looked heavier than he was. He was supposed to be a genius at electronics and, according to Fatboy, had once built a guitar amplifier out of an old kitchen mixer just to prove he could do it.

The Chronophone plans had given him no trouble at all.

"It's a transmitter," he had said after a cursory look at the diagram. "What's it for?"

"It's a time transmitter," Fatboy had answered with a smile. "We're going to send the winning Lotto numbers back to ourselves in the past and win the Lotto."

"Yeah, right!" Goony had just given one of those big droopy grins and got on with his work.

It had been three days of intensive work. Rebecca helped analyze the plans, and Fatboy helped solder components into place. Tane just stayed out of the way and made lots of tea and coffee.

Now, nearly at the last day of the year, the Chronophone was a waterproof aluminum box the size of a briefcase sitting in the garage. It was more than just a transmitter, according to Rebecca. Built into it was a radio receiver, which received the signals they would transmit from the submarine and re-transmitted them through the gamma-rays bursts.

"Don't we take it with us in the *Möbius*?" Tane asked.

"No. It needs a much more powerful aerial than the small one on the buoy," Rebecca explained.

The signal they transmitted, she told them, was not the one that would be received back in the past. It was a disruptor signal, which would disrupt the gamma-ray burst that was already on its way to Earth from the depths of the galaxy and imprint their message on the radiation of the burst. That burst of radiation would somehow seep through the quantum foam, through the fabric of time itself, into the past.

The signal from the Chronophone wouldn't even reach the gamma-ray burst for another two years. It was a hard concept to grasp. They sent a signal to the future, which ended up in the past.

By far, the hardest part of building the Chronophone was the location of the transmitter, when they had finally de-ciphered the schematics and worked out where that was. On the plan it showed just a tall, thin spike, with what looked like a satellite dish at the top, a serial number, and some coordinates.

As usual, it was Tane who had put two and two together.

"It's the Skytower. The top of that thing is stuffed with satellite dishes of all shapes and sizes. I think we're supposed to connect the Chronophone to one of those dishes, one with this serial number, and aim it at these coordinates."

"I hope the owner of the dish doesn't mind," Fatboy had said.

"Tough," had been Rebecca's answer. "We have no choice."

Tane steered the *Möbius* through a cloud of sludge, whirled up by a passing freighter from the bottom of the harbor. There had been no danger of collision, but the murky water was unsettling all the same.

Rebecca was intently watching a readout on one of the control panels. "We're getting close," she said.

The next batch of messages had proved quite informative. It was a series of numbers, each with an exactly specified time. It was Rebecca who figured it out.

"This is the final piece of the puzzle," she said. "I was expecting this."

"What is it?" Fatboy asked.

"It's the timings. Each message has to be sent at an exact time, to hit the gamma-ray burst at the right moment and end up in the past at the right moment."

The tail end of the last message had been interesting, too.

```
GPS,-36,50.999,174,49.876
```

GPS map coordinates, Rebecca had recognized at once, and a detailed map of Auckland had shown the spot defined by those coordinates to be on the edge of Rangitoto, a large island volcano, long extinct, that dominated the view from the shoreline of most of Auckland.

They were on their way to that spot now, while Fatboy and Goony continued working on the Chronophone.

It was daylight, but time was considered to be more important than discretion. The unspoken question was always, Had they wasted too much time before they had made their move on Motukiekie? If they had been earlier, *could they have stopped the Chimera Project in time?*

"What's in front of us?" Rebecca asked. "We are almost right on the coordinates."

The GPS readout on the control panel flashed red numbers in the dim light of the cockpit.

"Nothing yet," Tane said. "The seabed is starting to slope up. We must be just about at Rangitoto by now. There's . . . oh crap!"

A cliff face reared up suddenly in front of the *Möbius*. Tane flicked the craft into reverse for a moment, slowing the craft quickly, and they coasted up to the wall of rock.

"Just nudge a bit to your right," Rebecca murmured, and Tane complied, drifting a little in that direction.

"Nothing," he said.

"Try going down," Rebecca suggested.

"We're just about on the seafloor," Tane said.

"Then try going up."

A few yards higher up the cliff face, it became immediately apparent what the GPS coordinates were for. The wide mouth of a cave, almost oval, except on the left where a section had broken away from the top and made a mound on the bottom rim of the cave. It was well big enough for the *Möbius*.

"Want to take a look inside?" Tane asked, not waiting for an answer.

He touched a few buttons on the control panel, and the interior of the cave lit up like a cathedral in the glow of the underwater spotlights of the *Möbius*. The cave was huge.

"Probably a volcanic vent," Rebecca said, her voice full of wonder. "It could go on, or down, for miles."

Tane remembered stories of underground water channels that ran between Rangitoto Island and Lake Pupuke, just inland from Takapuna beach, and wondered if this was anything to do with that.

The cave was filled with marine life. A haze of tiny silver fish filtered past the glass dome of the driver's bubble.

"This is it," he said, maneuvering the craft around inside the underwater cavity in the side of the mountain. "This is our hideout. This is where we tuck ourselves away from whatever hell is coming for the rest of the human race, and wait until it is safe to emerge."

Rebecca nodded, examining the roof of the cave through the dome. "If we set her down close to the entrance, we'll be able to run the buoy up outside the cave to the surface. We can suck down as much air as we want and stay here indefinitely, if need be."

"I hope it's not that long," Tane said quietly. *Indefinitely* sounded like too long a time to be living in a tiny tin tube on the floor of an underwater cave. "We can bring in supplies, food, diesel, whatever, in airtight drums and stack it up on the cave floor."

"I think we're going to get mightily sick of tinned ham and peaches," Rebecca said, trying to make light of it, but the darkening circles under her eyes wiped away any trace of humor.

"God, I hope we're wrong about all this," Tane said. But he had a terrible feeling that they were right.

An Unnatural Disaster

The TV was on for the news. The news was not good. In fact, the more they heard, the more frightening it all became.

Tane held the remote and unconsciously kept turning the volume up, until it became painful, then would turn it back down to a reasonable level, only to start all over again.

They were watching a press conference. A room full of eager reporters. A thick bush of microphones sprouting from a wooden podium labeled with HYATT OREWA.

A tall, gaunt American entered and stepped up to the podium, closely followed by a woman, scarcely half his size.

"That's him!" Rebecca caught her breath.

"Who?" Fatboy asked.

"The leader of the soldiers on the island."

A graphic came up at the lower left corner of the screen identifying the speaker as Dr. Anthony Crowe of USABRF.

Just the sight of him was enough to make Tane's heart race.

The woman stood next to Crowe. She would need a stool to reach the microphones, Tane thought, then wondered why he was thinking about such stupid details when the fate of the world was at stake. Her name was Dr. Lucy Southwell, according to the subtitles.

A large map of the upper north island was pinned to a board behind them.

Crowe wore a military uniform, but wore it casually, as if the uniform was not a symbol of pride for him, the way it was for many Americans. His face was as long and craggy as a cliff face and showed no expression; in fact, his face might as well be made of stone for all the emotion that showed on it.

Southwell pointed to the map. "The *Horouta* is a delivery boat. Operates out of Russell, here. She makes a regular weekly supply drop at Motukiekie. Just a small boat, with a skipper and one crewman. Four days ago, she was discovered, beached in Kaingahoa Bay, about forty miles east of Motukiekie. The throttle was wide open, and the engine was still running. There was no sign of the crew."

"Odd," murmured Fatboy.

Southwell continued, "A coast guard vessel was sent to investigate. Six-man crew. It didn't return."

"Odder still," Tane said.

Southwell drew a circle on the map. "An airforce Orion was dispatched to search for the missing coast guard cutter. It covered roughly this area here, which was as far as the cutter could have traveled in the time. It overflew Motukiekie but was unable to see anything due to a dense fog. By this time, the local police were involved and wisely decided that it was time to call in the experts.

"I work for the Biological Hazard Containment Unit, a

part of our Ministry of Agriculture and Fisheries. A team of three colleagues of mine—two men, one woman—was sent in, in full biohazard suits and in constant radio contact with a command unit based in Russell. Naturally, at this stage, our fear was of some . . ." She clearly didn't want to say it. ". . . biological agent that had been released on the island. They . . . um . . ."

"They disappeared," Crowe intervened. "Their biosuits were found on the island when we went there to investigate."

"What about Whangarei?" a female reporter was asking. "Fifty thousand people. They can't just have disappeared."

"Actually, ma'am, that's exactly what seems to have happened," was Crowe's reply.

Strange how Americans called women "ma'am." It was such a British expression.

Another stupid thought!

"Disappeared to where?" the reporter persisted.

"We have no information on that at this time."

"Do you anticipate finding them alive?"

Crowe replied without emotion, "No, ma'am, we do not."

The room grew suddenly, unnaturally silent.

Southwell broke the silence. "Civil defense are evacuating everyone in the projected path of the fog and are preparing an evacuation plan for Auckland, should that become necessary. I must stress that there is no need for panic. Any evacuation will be completed in plenty of time; we are asking residents to remain calm and at home until we make an announcement."

"Yeah, right," Fatboy muttered. "Fifty thousand people missing, but don't panic!"

Southwell wore a rather drab, olive blouse and a staid gray skirt. She dressed older than her years. Her hair was pulled back in a loose ponytail, held together with a butter-fly band.

"Is there any chance that a breeze will push this toxic fog out to sea?" a man asked.

"Toxic fog." Tane sounded the words out loud.

"The movement of the fog does not appear to be governed by the direction of the wind." Crowe answered the question, and the room grew completely silent again for a second or two as people tried to work out how that could be.

"Toxic fog," Tane said again, blankly. Rebecca was staring at him with a horrified expression, but he ignored her and concentrated on the television.

"If the toxic fog continues on its present course and at its present speed, when do you anticipate it will hit Auckland?" the same man asked.

Crowe answered, "It's hard to be accurate. The fog does not seem to move at a constant speed. It did not move from Whangarei at all for two and a half days. I would say we have about a week."

The questions were coming from all over the room now.

"Is it true that the fog is growing in size?"

"Yes. Substantially."

"By how much exactly?"

Crowe looked as if he would rather avoid answering that one, Tane thought. He turned the television louder.

"On our satellite photos, the fog was roughly circular and only a few hundred yards across when it entered Whangarei. It now measures several miles across."

Rebecca said, "Several miles! That means it has grown by a factor of twenty or thirty times since it rolled into Whangarei. Or even more!"

Someone asked, "How many survivors are there?"

"Currently three. The youngest is a boy of four."

"And what about the reports of snowmen in the fog?"

"We believe these sightings to be of people wearing bio-hazard suits, like this one." Crowe motioned to his side, and an assistant wheeled in an inflated silver suit on a trolley. It looked more than anything like a space suit, although the faceplate was narrower, not as spherical as a NASA space suit.

Southwell moved around the front of the suit and placed her hand on it.

She said, "This is a UN-issue biohazard suit. It is silver but reflective. Surrounded by white mist, this would appear white also."

A tall reporter whom Tane recognized from the TV3 news stood up and raised a hand, asking, "So there are men or women, inside the toxic fog, wearing protective suits. Can we assume that these people are responsible for the fog?"

"That would be a reasonable assumption," Crowe answered as coolly as before.

"Then it would be another reasonable assumption that these people are terrorists. Bioterrorists," the TV3 man said.

"Yes. Possibly. Probably. Yes."

"Has there been any kind of demand or ultimatum?" someone else asked.

"No."

There was a strange, stunned silence from the pack of reporters. Crowe stood impassively, waiting for the next question.

"So it is terrorists," Fatboy said calmly.

"Maybe," Rebecca said noncommittally.

"Why?" Fatboy asked. "Why here in New Zealand? What have we ever done to deserve this? What have we done to offend anyone?"

"What if . . ." Tane started, then paused, thinking for a second. "What if it's a demonstration? What if their plan is to choose a small isolated country, release their toxic fog, and wipe the country clean? Everybody, gone."

"Why would they do that?" Fatboy asked.

"Think about it. What kind of ransom could you demand then? From Australia, Britain, or the USA. They'd say, 'Remember New Zealand. Land of four million people. Now just feral sheep and possums. You're next if you don't pay up.'"

"How do you plan to stop the fog from reaching Auckland?" a reporter finally asked on the television.

Crowe answered slowly. "The answer to that is in two parts. Firstly, we have taken samples of the fog, and we are analyzing it to see what we are dealing with. We hope to find a way of neutralizing it before it gets to Auckland. Secondly is the matter of dealing with the terrorists, with the"—he almost smiled, Tane thought—"snowmen. We have set up a line of defense just north of Orewa. We have taken the high ground of the Waiwera hills and will be aiming to prevent either the fog or the terrorists from proceeding beyond that point."

"Who will be manning that defensive line?" It was an anonymous voice from somewhere in the crowd of reporters.

"My own men, from the U.S. Army Bioterrorism Response Force, along with your Special Air Service and units of your regular army. All will be outfitted with biohazard suits like this one. Eighty of the New Zealand Army Light Armored Vehicles will be deployed along the line, leaving twenty-five in reserve. As you no doubt know, these vehicles are also protected against chemical and biological agents."

"That's a lot of firepower," somebody said.

Crowe nodded. "In addition, we will have air-strike capability from FA18 Super Hornets flying off the USS *Abraham Lincoln*, which will be within striking distance within three days. Whatever, whoever, is causing this, we will stop them at the Waiwera hills."

"What about the children?" the TV3 man asked. "The ones you have been looking for, from the island."

"We're still looking," Crowe said noncommittally. "We think they may have some information that will help us."

Someone shouted out, "What kind of information?" but Crowe ignored it.

When the press conference finished, Tane turned the sound down but left the television on, in case there were any more developments.

They all sat in silence for a while, until Tane finally spoke.

He said again, "Remember New Zealand, land of four million people. . . ."

FTBY DNT GO

Fatboy went around to Goony's house to pick up a pair of overalls, and while he was gone, Rebecca came and sat next to Tane. She put her hand on his arm.

"What have we got ourselves into?" she asked.

Tane didn't answer. There was no answer to give.

He covered her hand with his own, and she leaned forward, touching her forehead to his.

"We'll always be mates," she said. "Whatever happens."

"I hope so," Tane said.

Rebecca leaned back a little and nodded. "I know so. I just wanted to make sure you knew too."

"I never doubted it," Tane lied, thinking about the argument on the submarine and feeling more and more guilty about it.

"Friends forever," she said, and sat with him silently for a while before moving off into the kitchen to get herself a drink, leaving Tane with such a warm feeling that it was as if she was still sitting next to him.

Friends forever. Friends since forever.

The feeling was still there when Fatboy came back with a pair of clean, white overalls, emblazoned with *Telstra-Clear* across the front and back.

"The genuine article," Fatboy said proudly. "Goony once worked for them."

Tane asked, "Didn't he ask any questions about why you wanted them?"

Fatboy nodded. "He did. The answer was a thousand bucks."

Tane laughed.

"When do we do it?" Rebecca asked. "When do we install the Chronophone?"

"Security is going to be a real problem," Fatboy said. "It's a casino, so they have tight security anyway. These days with terrorist alerts all the time, they are going to look pretty suspiciously at anyone wandering around the Skytower with a suitcase."

"Even in your lovely new overalls?" Tane asked.

"Even in my overalls."

The satellite dish they were going to use belonged to Telstra-Clear.

Tane had carefully stenciled the name of the company on the side of the aluminium briefcase also, so it would look like a toolbox.

"Are you sure you should be doing this alone?" Rebecca asked. "Wouldn't it be safer with two?"

Fatboy shook his head. "We talked about this already. Neither of you looks old enough to be a Telstra-Clear technician."

In some ways, Tane wished he was going. This was the

climax of the creation of the Chronophone, the greatest invention since the telephone, or the airplane, or maybe just the greatest invention ever. And he, Tane Williams, had thought of the idea that had started it all. And nobody knew. Maybe nobody would ever know. It seemed wrong not to be there at the critical moment.

In other ways, though, he was glad he was not going. Fatboy would have to take an elevator over two hundred yards straight up, to the main observation deck, then another elevator up another fifty yards to the Sky Deck. Then it was a climb up the internal ladders to the crow's nest, a tiny platform on the *outside* of the Skytower, three hundred yards high. But even that wasn't the end of it. The Telstra-Clear satellite dish, one of many atop the tower, was another fifteen yards above the crow's nest, accessible only via a ladder up the side of the topmost spike of the tower.

He would have to do all this lugging a heavy metal suitcase. It would take steady nerves and a fair bit of strength.

"Better get on with it," Fatboy said determinedly. Tane sensed that he was more nervous about the climb than he was letting on.

"Good luck," he said as Fatboy climbed into the overalls.

"Final test?" Rebecca suggested.

"Suppose we'd better," Fatboy replied.

They had been testing and testing the Chronophone. The last thing they wanted was for it to fail, once it was high above the ground.

"I'll do it." Tane disappeared into Rebecca's room, where her laptop was sitting on a small study desk.

He opened the small program that Rebecca had written and typed in "good luck Fatboy," then clicked SEND.

The small radio transmitter attached to the laptop would

now be sending the message to the receiver built into the Chronophone. Inside the case, a small digital readout would be displaying the characters he had just typed, as it encoded it into the gamma-ray disruptor signal. Right now, that was as far as the signal would go. It needed the big satellite dish on the Skytower to be able to transmit the signal to the gamma-ray bursts.

There was no "Okay" from the kitchen to acknowledge the receipt of the message, so he tried again. "Don't look down," he typed, and sent it.

Still silence from the kitchen, which was a little odd. All the previous tests had worked fine.

He was just about to wander out to see for himself what the problem was, when a flashing light caught his eye on the side of the screen.

Another message!

Rebecca's software now checked the NASA site hourly for new BATSE messages and automatically decoded them.

He clicked on the flashing light and it opened the BATSE message window. As usual, it was a cryptic jumble of letters and numbers that they would have to try and figure out as quickly as they could.

```
FTBYDNTGO.WTRBLSTMPS.DSVLETHM.
SLTABS.DNTABSRB.
```

There were still some parts of previous messages that they hadn't fully understood.

WTRWKS for example.

He printed a couple of copies of the message on the inkjet, to show it to the others, and as he was doing so, the first nine characters caught his eye.

FTBYDNTGO.

He caught his breath and tried to make any other inter-
pretation from it, other than the obvious. FTBY DNT GO.
Fatboy don't go!

"Oh crap!" He grabbed the printout, knocking the chair
over in his haste to get out to the kitchen. The second copy
whirred swiftly out of the printer behind him.

He rushed down the short hallway and in through the
swing door.

The Chronophone was open on the kitchen table, and
even from the doorway he could read the words DON'T LOOK
DOWN visible on the display.

Fatboy couldn't see them, though. Neither could Rebecca.
He had his arms around her, and she had her arms around
him, lost in each other's world. As Tane entered, her lips
met his.

Friends forever!

Any remnants of the earlier warm feeling died a sudden
cold, jagged death. His breath caught in his throat, and a
black rage that he hadn't known existed inside him welled up
from deep within his belly. He forced it back down and
coughed, loudly. They both looked up, startled.

"What is it, Tane?" Rebecca asked in alarm, taking a
quick step away from Fatboy.

Tane stared at them, breathing heavily through his nose.

"What is it?" Fatboy asked.

He looked at them both for a moment longer. "Nothing," he said tightly. There was a ringing in his ears and spots
dancing across his vision. He folded the piece of paper dis-
creetly behind his back and slipped it casually into a pocket.
"Nothing." He laughed. "I thought the Chronophone had

stopped working, because I didn't hear anything from you two, but I see that it's all okay." He gestured at the message on the readout.

Fatboy looked at the message and laughed.

Rebecca just looked at Tane, in a rather strange way, and said, "We were just saying goodbye."

"Yep," Tane said, "I could see."

10

CANDID CAMERA

When Fatboy left, Tane and Rebecca busied themselves with the supply barge. They called it a barge, but it was
really more of a cage. A large plastic-coated wire box with
floats attached.

When loaded with supplies, it was just buoyant enough
for the *Möbius* to tow, without dragging the little submarine
to the bottom or floating up to the surface.

Fully loaded, it had room for twelve crates.

The crates themselves were watertight plastic boxes,
with a rubber seal around the rim, purchased from a local
plastics shop. They would not be able to withstand pressure,
but they were being stored in shallow water, so that wasn't a
problem.

This was the last load. There were already over a hundred
crates stacked neatly in rows on the bottom of Rangitoto Cave,
as they had come to call it. By Rebecca's careful calculations,

there was enough food and fresh water there to last four people for over a year, or six people for at least nine months. Rebecca's mum didn't know it, but she had a berth booked on the submarine. So did Tane's mum and dad, but they didn't know it either.

How do you explain to your parents that the country you live in is about to be devastated and that the only hope of survival is to live in a submarine in an underwater cave for the conceivable future?

This last load was probably the most important. Oxygen cylinders and Sofnolime cartridges. The oxygen cylinders replenished the air in the sub, and the Sofnolime cartridges removed the carbon dioxide that they breathed out.

While they had the air hose up to the surface, they wouldn't use either, but they had planned for a long period of time when they would not be able to draw in air from above the waves.

They would only do that when they were sure the air was safe and clean, and there was no real way of knowing that, so they planned for at least the first few months to be entirely sealed off from the rest of the world.

They worked as a team in the small wooden boatshed but said little. Rebecca loaded the cylinders and cartridges into the plastic boxes, and Tane stacked them onto the barge. He wanted to talk but found that there was little to say. There was a strangeness about Rebecca that hadn't been there before he had walked in on them in the kitchen. It was as if she had something to say but was afraid to.

He thought about showing Rebecca the message, but was too embarrassed. Instead, he tried to ring Fatboy after a while, feeling guilty about letting him go, when the message said not to. Maybe it wasn't too late. But Fatboy's phone rang and rang, then went to the answering service.

It took them over an hour to load up the barge. There were a few spare cylinders that would not fit in the last few plastic crates, so they just loaded them on board the *Möbius*. You never knew when you might need them.

Rebecca flopped, exhausted, into one of the lawn chairs in the backyard of the house and stared silently out over the water toward the city. Tane looked around to make sure they had everything and noticed the laptop still sitting on the outdoor table.

He packed it up and took it down to the *Möbius*, holding it carefully as he negotiated the wooden staircases that led down to the boatshed.

Halfway back up the staircase he heard the phone ring. He hurried to the top in case it was Fatboy. Rebecca was waiting for him, the phone in her hand.

"It's for you," she said.

"Who is it?"

"I don't know." She shrugged.

So it wasn't Fatboy.

Tane put the phone to his ear but heard only the *pip, pip, pip* of a disconnected line.

They walked back to the house together silently, uncomfortably. Rebecca's mum popped her head out of the open window of her room.

"There you are!" she called. "I've been looking everywhere for you!"

"Are you okay, Mum?" Rebecca called back, but her mother interrupted her.

"You're on the TV! You and Tane and um . . . Tane's brother."

Tane looked at Rebecca. Surely she meant the police sketches. But there hadn't been a picture of Fatboy.

Simultaneously, they broke into a run, hurtling through the ranch slider of the lounge to the big TV in the corner.

No more indentikits. The police now had photos. Photos of all three of them. Not sharp, but clear and easily recognizable.

"Where the hell did they get those from?" Rebecca breathed.

"I don't . . . wait," Tane said. Something about the background of the photos was familiar. Suddenly he got it. The painting on the wall behind them. It was *Tuatara Dawn.*

"Oh crap, they're from the security cameras on Motukiekie," Tane said. "We should have thought of that. They have gone back through the old security tapes! Crap!"

"We've got to warn Fatboy!" Rebecca shrieked. "With that *moko,* they'll recognize him in a second. We've got to stop him!"

"I think we're already too late," Tane said. "We've got to get out of here now!"

Crap! Why had he let Fatboy go off without telling him about the message?

"No! We've got to warn him!" Rebecca said, charging down the hallway to her room. "If he doesn't install the Chronophone, there won't even be a Chronophone. Or a Lotto ticket. Or a submarine!"

She grabbed her cell phone off the desk and started to dial, but stopped abruptly. She remained stuck in the doorway as if transfixed by the frame.

Tane caught up with her and stood beside her.

The second copy of the Chronophone message was

still on the printer. In his haste and anger, he had forgotten about it.

"There's a new message," Rebecca said in bewilderment. "Why didn't you tell us?"

"I . . ."

She scanned quickly through the string of letters, then came back to the words at the start.

"Fatboy don't go," she read out slowly. She turned to face him. "Oh my God! You already knew."

She stared at him, her face just a few inches away from his.

"You knew!"

There was nothing to say.

"You knew and you said nothing. You've destroyed it all. You let Fatboy go, despite the warning. Tane!" She screamed his name out suddenly, from close range. Tane recoiled and tried to think of anything that would lessen what he had done.

"This was because you saw me and him together, wasn't it?" Rebecca said slowly. "You were going to tell us and then you saw us, and then you didn't. You stupid . . ."

Her legs suddenly seemed unsteady, and she took two short steps and collapsed onto the side of her bed.

"Tane," she said softly, "I just broke up with Fatboy. I told you, I was just saying goodbye."

"Oh, Rebecca," Tane breathed. "I'm sorry, I'm so sorry . . ."

She blocked her ears like a child. "I don't want to hear it!" she screamed. "I don't want to hear it!" She took a long breath and continued, more calmly, "Tane, I've known you all my life, and it turns out that I don't know you at all."

He moved toward her, his arms held out.

"Get away from me!" she screamed, and that was when the roof fell in.

There was a huge flash and an enormous crack of thunder that pulverized his brain. The windows were gone, smoke was swirling around in the draft from outside, and there were men everywhere. Men in black uniforms with black masks and black guns.

In a daze, he saw them dive on top of Rebecca, forcing her facedown onto the bed, her knees on the floor. He thought she might have screamed, but he couldn't be sure. Then the men had him, too, banging his face down onto the carpet, twisting his arms behind him.

The smoke danced around his head, and spots danced around his eyes from the pain of his arms, twisted so high he thought they must already be broken. Rebecca was screaming and someone else was screaming and it was him.

Then everything turned to black.

ZETA

Tane watched the chimpanzee, watching him. There were two chimpanzees, actually, but only one was watching him. The other was watching Rebecca. His was called Z2. At least that was what it said on the cage. Rebecca's was Z1.

Z1 was the younger of the two, as far as Tane could tell, but he was no expert at guessing the age of chimpanzees. It was just the wise, almost serene expression in the eyes of Z2 and the way she sat, erectly, regally, with her hands clasped together in her lap. Hers was the face of a sad clown.

Z1 had a more mischievous expression. Impish, if you could call a chimpanzee "impish." Perhaps that would make it "chimpish," Tane thought.

The cages were set up near the center of what should have been the central restaurant of a fancy new hotel, the Hyatt Kingsgate in the seaside town of Orewa, except that the chairs and tables were stacked against the walls.

Not all the chairs and tables. The two chimpanzee cages rested heavily on the polished wooden surface of a couple of tables. Other tables were full of test tubes and petri dishes, being worked on by men in black space suits with open faceplates.

In the very center of the restaurant, three tables supported a long glass tank of some kind, covered with white tablecloths.

Rebecca and Tane sat quietly. The soldiers who had brought them here had not exactly encouraged talking, but Tane suspected that Rebecca would not have had a lot to say to him if it had been allowed. Nothing nice anyway.

They had been brought here half an hour ago. The troopers who had raided their house in West Harbor had brought them directly here, sat them down, and left them in the care of these other men, in the black space suits.

Where was Rebecca's mum? he wondered. *Had she been arrested also?*

The troopers at the house had been New Zealanders. SAS, Tane guessed. But these were not. The murmured conversations all had an American burr to them. Anyway, he recognized the uniforms, the space suits. These were the men they had met on the island.

They waited, and watched the chimps. The chimps watched them back until eventually they tired of that and started watching each other and playing with the newspaper that lined the bottoms of their cages.

Eventually, a door opened and a tall man entered, talking into a mobile phone. Tane recognized him immediately. The leader of the soldiers: Dr. Anthony Crowe.

Two other soldiers entered behind Dr. Crowe. Between them they held the defiant shape of Harley Rawhiri Williams.

Fatboy. His arms, like those of Tane and Rebecca, were fastened behind his back by a plastic tie, but his chin jutted staunchly. He walked with his usual swagger, and he still wore his hat. The scientist they had seen on the television, Dr. Lucy Southwell, followed.

Dr. Crowe pocketed his mobile phone and stopped in front of Rebecca and Tane. He opened his mouth to speak, but Fatboy spoke first.

"Sorry, guys," he said.

Tane glanced involuntarily at Rebecca. Would she tell? Let Fatboy know what he had done? She didn't get the chance.

"Found your voice at last," Crowe said amicably. "That's two more words than I've heard out of you the entire time I've known you. Sit down."

He motioned to the other two soldiers, who sat Fatboy down next to Rebecca.

Crowe pulled up a chair, turned it backward, and straddled it, facing them, resting his arms on the chair back.

He pulled Rebecca's notebook from a pocket on his leg and thumbed through it, frowning. Eventually, he closed it and put it back in his leg pocket.

He looked at them for a few moments, then said, with a glance at Southwell, "Cut them loose."

An even taller man with a mop of curly hair and a Texan accent said, "You sure, Stony?"

Crowe nodded. "These kids aren't terrorists. I'd stake my life on it. Him, I wasn't sure about"—he jerked his head at Fatboy—"but these two, definitely not."

The Texan produced a pair of cutters and motioned them to lean forward, so he could reach behind and cut the plastic ties.

"Just promise me you won't go jumping overboard again," Crowe said with something that approached a quick smile.

"Can't promise anything," Rebecca said.

"Well, if you must," he sighed, "but we're two stories up, and I think you'll find the landing a bit harder this time."

"How did you find us?" she asked.

"Fingerprints," Crowe answered.

"From the air bottles?"

Fatboy said, "There was a roadblock at the end of the street. I didn't even have time to call and warn you."

Rebecca glared at Crowe. He picked at something in a tooth with his tongue and stared back at her. Southwell pulled up a chair and sat next to him. After a while, Crowe asked, "Who are you? And what were you doing on the island? Why were you at the research lab?"

"You wouldn't believe me if I told you."

"You have no idea what I would believe. Especially today. Especially here."

Tane could see Rebecca thinking. He wondered if she would tell the full truth. They might not believe all of it. Which would make them not believe any of it.

Rebecca must have thought the same, because she just said, "We were trying to stop the Chimera Project."

"Why?"

Why! He hadn't said *what*, Tane realized. So he knew about the Chimera Project.

"Because we believed that bad things would come of it, if it was allowed to proceed. That there might be a man-made disaster."

"Do you think this is that man-made disaster?" Crowe asked, waving a hand toward the north.

"Do you?"

He pursed his lips a moment before answering. "I think we have a bunch of bioterrorists loose with some new weapon. What that has to do with Professor Green, I couldn't say. So tell me why you were so worried about the project. Tell me how you knew about the project."

"We met Professor Green on the island a few weeks earlier," Rebecca said truthfully, then lied, "She told us all about it."

Crowe considered that for a few moments.

"Do you believe them?" Southwell asked.

Crowe looked around. "It fits the facts. The fact that they arrived on the island after everyone had disappeared."

He turned back to Rebecca. "I sure would like to know how a bunch of kids could afford that dinky little submarine, though."

"We won the Lotto," Rebecca said evenly. "Where's the sub now?"

Southwell answered, "It's safe. Don't worry about it. We towed it to the naval base at Devonport."

Crowe said, "So you won the lottery and decided to spend your winnings on a submarine, then used it to sneak onto an island and try to break into a genetics lab?"

"Yes. That pretty much sums it up."

"And the cryptic messages in the notebook?"

"Our plans. We wrote them in code in case the notebook got lost."

Good call, Tane thought. The cryptic messages would look like code to an outsider.

"And I'm sure there's a very glib explanation for the strange transmitter in the aluminum briefcase."

"Sure," Rebecca said easily. "We were going to connect

it to a mast at the Skytower. It uses gamma rays, which transmit through water. It lets us connect to the Internet, even when we are submerged." She smiled. "Check our e-mail, you know."

It almost seemed believable.

Crowe thought it over. "Gamma rays, huh?" He seemed uncertain. "There are some holes in what you're telling me. Some damn big holes. But overall, I'll buy it."

He took out the notebook and handed it to her. "Seems we got off on the wrong foot. I'm Stony Crowe, from the U.S. Army Bioterrorism Response Force."

"Rebecca Richards." She took the book tentatively, as if there might be a trap of some kind in it.

"Harley Williams," Fatboy said.

"Tane Williams," Tane said in turn.

Lucy Southwell introduced herself.

"Well, seeing as you know so much about the Chimera Project," Crowe said, "perhaps you could enlighten us a little. We've been through Professor Green's notes, but there's nothing to indicate any kind of a problem or how it could be used by terrorists."

Tane started to protest that they knew absolutely nothing about the Chimera Project, but Rebecca shot him a warning glance. An icy-cold warning glance.

"Happy to help," she said.

"Did Professor Green mention anything to you about macroscopic pathogens or bacterial clusters?"

She hadn't. Tane had never heard of either. Rebecca evidently had, though, as she said, "That's impossible."

"So you are familiar with the concept, the theory, of macroscopic pathogens."

"No," Rebecca said, as if it were a stupid question, "but I know what a pathogen is, and I know what *macroscopic* means. But that's impossible. Surely!"

Tane had no idea what *macroscopic* meant. He tried to work it out.

Crowe said, "Just because something is beyond the realm of what we already know doesn't make it impossible. You'd better come and look at this."

He stood and led them toward the long glass tank, still covered, in the center of the room.

They stood around the tank as he reached out and pulled off the cover in a single movement. The tank was filled with thick, impenetrable fog. Thick rubber gloves were embedded into the sides of the tank at intervals down its sides.

"You got a sample of the mist," Rebecca said. "Have you analyzed it?"

"Mmmm." Crowe seemed distracted. "Inconclusive results as yet. But that's not what I wanted to show you."

Tane looked deeply into the mist. Was there something moving around in there?

"What, then?" Rebecca asked.

"This."

Crowe placed one hand on the side of the glass tank, then tapped the glass with his free hand. There was a low whistling noise from within the tank, and suddenly, from out of the mist, a shape materialized, flying at high speed toward the palm of his hand. Tane, Rebecca, and Fatboy jumped, and even Crowe flinched involuntarily as the shape slammed into the side of the tank. He withdrew his hand.

"What the hell is that?" Fatboy asked. Tane just stared, openmouthed.

"We call them *jellyfish*," Crowe said. "They seem to be attracted by vibrations. Either movement or sound."

Tane could see where the name had come from, although this creature was far smaller than any jellyfish he had ever seen in the ocean. It was about the size of a large bumblebee, a bulbous shape made of a gelatinous, translucent material. The main body seemed to be in three parts, forming a Y shape, with a mass of thin fibrous tentacles trailing underneath.

"You caught that in the fog?" Rebecca asked.

Crowe shook his head. "Nope. We just sucked up a sample of the fog and released it into this tank, to help us study it. There were no jellyfish in it then."

"Then how . . . ?"

"They just formed, out of the mist. Little dense patches at first that gradually got bigger."

"Holy crap," said Fatboy.

Rebecca said incredulously, "You're not trying to tell me that that is a macroscopic pathogen."

"What on earth is a macroscopic pathogen?" Tane asked.

Crowe looked appraisingly at him. "A pathogen is an organism that attacks another larger organism. Like bacteria or a virus attacks the human body. All the pathogens we know of are microscopic. Too small to be seen with the naked eye."

Southwell added, "*Macroscopic* means large enough to be seen without a microscope."

Rebecca scoffed, "You're not trying to tell me that this creature is some kind of giant virus!"

Crowe almost smiled, just a brief twitch at the corners of his mouth. "A giant virus? No. Viruses are subcellular. Smaller than a human cell. They have to be. They crawl into cells to attack them. No, not a giant virus."

The small jellyfish-like creature drifted slowly away from the wall of the tank, losing definition gradually in the mist.

Crowe continued, "I attended a lecture a few years ago. At Oxford. A Doctor Hans Heinrich was the lecturer, a highly respected immunologist. He hypothesized the existence of macroscopic pathogens. Not viruses, but bacterial clusters."

He paused and looked around the little group. "Bacteria are single-celled organisms. But if you grow a whole lot of them together, then they form a colony, or cluster together, in what we call a *biofilm*. And a bacterial cluster can show characteristics quite different from those of a single bacteria. They exchange chemical signals between cells, and the cluster itself can grow into a quite specific shape. We see wave patterns, towers, and other structures. Dr. Heinrich suggested the existence of bacterial clusters that behaved as a single organism. Perhaps as large as a grain of salt. Thousands of individual bacteria, acting in concert. A single macroscopic pathogen. Invading the body, then overwhelming its defenses by the sheer volume of the bacterial cells released. To the best of our knowledge, that is what we have here."

Fatboy mumbled, "It's a bit bigger than a grain of salt."

Rebecca said, "You're not trying to tell us that these terrorists, these 'snowmen' in the fog, have developed bacterial clusters that are trained to attack humans."

Crowe shook his head. "They're not 'trained' to attack humans any more than a cold virus is 'trained' to attack us. It's just what they are. It's what they do. But we can't find any reference to bacterial clusters, or anything even remotely connected to it, anywhere in Green's journals. That is where I was hoping you might have a little more inside knowledge."

One of the other soldiers approached and said quietly, although for little purpose, as they could still hear every word, "We are ready for the test now, Doctor."

"Then get on with it," Crowe said.

"Z1 or Z2?"

Crowe shrugged. "Whichever."

"They are living creatures. Why do you call them by numbers?" Rebecca asked. "Why not give them names?"

"They're not pets," Crowe replied curtly. "Pets have names. These are lab animals."

The Texan opened one of the animal cages and the older-looking chimp, Z2, jumped out with a squeal of delight and began tousling the tall man's hair.

He smiled and Tane laughed.

"She's got character." Rebecca smiled. "I'll name her for you." She thought for a moment. "Z-two, zeto . . ."

"Zeta," supplied Tane.

Rebecca looked at him for a moment, before accepting it.

"Zeta," she said. "Hi, Zeta!"

Zeta looked over at her and held out a hand as if she would like to jump onto Rebecca, but the Texan held the animal firmly.

Crowe did not find it funny. "They're not pets," he repeated.

"Makes it harder to stick electrodes in their brains and vivisect them, doesn't it," Rebecca said with a little-girl innocence completely at odds with her words. "How about the other one, Z-one?"

"Xena," suggested Tane.

"Zeta and Xena," Rebecca declared. "And what little test

have we got lined up for you today, Zeta?" She held out a hand to Zeta, who patted it and looked up at her with big, sad clown eyes.

"We're going to put her in the tank," Crowe said flatly, to Rebecca's look of horror.

The end of the tank was a separate box, sealed off from the rest of the tank by a glass door with thick rubber seals.

They let Zeta climb in the box, which she did willingly, trustingly, and then sealed the lid above her. In the main compartment of the tank, there were whistling, swishing noises as the jellyfish, agitated, swept around in circles in the mist.

Zeta jumped a little and turned around and around inside the small area, but otherwise didn't seem too concerned about being shut in a glass box.

"You can't!" Rebecca said, again and again. "You can't put her in the tank with that thing!"

Southwell, looking quite uncomfortable, tried to explain. "She'll give us very valuable data. Chimps are our closest cousins."

Manderson contributed, "Genetically, they are ninety-nine percent the same as humans."

"Don't flatter yourself," Rebecca muttered, but the insult went straight over Manderson's curly head.

Crowe said, "We need to know what these pathogens can do to us."

"And you need to sacrifice an innocent animal to find out?"

"It's just one chimp," Crowe said with a look of annoyance. "Fifty thousand human beings got 'sacrificed' in Whangarei. And there'll be more if we can't figure out what is going on."

With a nod from Crowe, Manderson released the seals and Zeta's compartment flooded with the fog.

"No!" shrieked Rebecca. She pressed her fingers against the glass by Zeta's head. Zeta looked at her and gave her a big clown smile. The other USABRF men gathered around to watch.

Zeta seemed bemused by the fog at first, as it started to fill her chamber, then a little confused as it thickened around her. The jellyfish whistled around in the thick of the fog, avoiding the thin vapor at the other end.

"They can't exist outside of the fog," Crowe murmured, watching intently. "They can't move, they can't live. It's their nutrition and their locomotion."

One jellyfish flashed down the side of the tank near them. By now the fog had spread evenly between the two partitions. The jellyfish whirled around Zeta, then disappeared back into the fog.

That was all. Nothing else happened.

After a while, Zeta went for a walk. Tane held his breath and could hear from the sharp intake of air from Rebecca that she was doing the same.

Zeta wandered through the main tank, comically trying to wave the fog away from in front of her eyes. She found one of the jellyfish, drifting at about her eye level, and Tane winced as she stretched out a hand toward it.

The jellyfish remained motionless. She even batted at it with her hand, swatting it like a fly, but without effect.

"It's not interested in her," Southwell said with a puzzled look.

"Okay, that's long enough," Crowe said.

"Go, Zeta!" Rebecca yelled in a mixture of delight and

relief, hopping from one leg to the other and punching the air. "You go, girl!"

Zeta screeched and danced happily inside the cage, a little two-legged, two-armed Irish jig. Tane and Fatboy laughed, but Crowe just shook his head.

They reversed the procedure with the small compartment at the end of the tank, sealing off the main section before pumping in air and extracting the fog.

"Are you going to let her out?" Rebecca asked.

"She may be contaminated," Crowe replied, then, a little too quickly, said, "Dr. Southwell, would you show them the journals?"

Southwell led them to the far side of the room, where a series of notebooks were spread out on a table.

"Professor Green's notes," she said. "Do you know much about what they were researching?"

"Tell me," Rebecca said. "Vicky told us it was rhinoviruses."

"Actually, it was rhinoviruses they were researching. They did a small amount of work on NLVs, but only for a short time, to confirm some aspect of their main research. They were researching conserved antigens. That's common structures within the viruses that can—"

"She told us about that too," Rebecca interrupted. "How much do you know about the Chimera Project?"

Southwell said, "Conserved antigens proved to be elusive. Our immune systems just kept getting fooled by the changing shapes of the viruses. It was a dead end."

"So?"

"Professor Green recently gained health department approval to experiment on the other side of the equation."

"The human side of the equation?"

"Yes. They were playing around with bone marrow, where antibodies are produced, genetically engineering our immune systems to try to produce a generic antibody."

"An antibody that would recognize any kind of virus."

"Any kind of rhinovirus. That was the field they were concentrating on."

"And how," Rebecca asked, a little skeptically, "do you start to create a generic antibody?"

"The scope of the project approval was quite specific. They were genetically splicing together different kinds of antibodies, creating a . . ." She trailed off, seemingly unwilling to finish the sentence.

"A chimera." Rebecca finished it for her. "Is that it? Is there anything else you can tell me?"

Southwell shook her head. "Nothing. Professor Green had not yet submitted a report on the results of the research. All we have is her notes." She indicated the table again. "Would you mind having a look through? Tell us if anything sticks out."

"Of course," Rebecca said, and picked up the first journal.

Tane idly leafed through one. Rebecca was the only one with a hope of understanding them, but it was interesting to see the clearly handwritten notes, dates, and formulas that the late Professor Green had written. Vicky's handwriting was small, neat and verbose, flowing on, page after page. Tane idly wondered why she hadn't just typed up her notes on a computer.

Fatboy was the first to notice, glancing across at the other side of the room. "What are they doing?" he wondered.

Tane looked across, and Rebecca also. Two of the men had their hands in the gloves in the sides of the compartment.

One was holding Zeta while the other ran a needle into her arm.

Zeta didn't like it; she screeched and snarled at the men.

"They'll be taking a blood sample," Rebecca said. "To see if the fog had any effect on her."

She looked back at the journal she was reading, only to look up again a second later to check on Zeta.

The man with the syringe had withdrawn it, but it was empty. With a frown, Rebecca walked across the room to the tank. Zeta looked sadly, imploringly, at her from inside the glass.

"What are you doing?" she asked. "You're taking a blood sample, right?"

Crowe was there now. "Miss Richards, this is our work. I'd like you to let us get on with it."

"That was a blood sample, right?"

Inside the tank, Zeta began to shiver. She sat down suddenly and looked up at Rebecca like a frightened child. The top lip of her clownish mouth drew up into a sneer.

Southwell put her arm around Rebecca's shoulders and tried to steer her away. She shook the arm away violently.

"What have you done to her?"

Zeta slumped against the side of the tank, her eyes open. Her breathing was ragged, heavy. She looked up at Rebecca one last time; then her eyes just glazed over and remained open. Her chest was still.

Crowe took Rebecca's arm this time, firmly, and drew her away from the tank.

Rebecca cried, "You killed her! What are you going to do, dissect her to see if the fog has affected her?"

Crowe said nothing.

"You are! You monsters!"

"Monsters?" Crowe hissed, the stony façade cracking for the first time. "Monsters!" He grabbed Rebecca by the back of the neck and pressed her face against the glass of the large tank. There was a whistle and a flash of white fog, and two of the jellyfish smashed into the glass, just a few thin fractions of an inch away from her eyes and mouth. She screamed. Tane jumped forward, and Fatboy was with him, but strong arms gripped their elbows, pinning them.

"There are your monsters! We don't have time to wait and see how the animal is feeling in a month or so. We have just a few days before the fog hits Auckland. We need answers right now!"

"Murderer!" Rebecca whispered, sobbing, her lips crushed against the glass.

Manderson reached in with the rubber gloves and laid the body of the chimpanzee flat on the floor of the tank. In death, Zeta had found peace once again. The forced sneer was gone, and her face held its natural sad-clown expression.

Crowe looked at Rebecca with stony eyes. "I told you not to give it a name," he said.

XENA

Rebecca could move pretty quickly when she wanted to. The soldiers should have known that already. But they were all gathered around the tank.

Rebecca was at the cage, unsnicking the lock, and Z1—Xena—was in her arms before anybody realized what she was doing.

"Put the animal down," Crowe ordered, and he was clearly a man who was used to being obeyed.

Rebecca was a girl who was used to disobeying. "You've murdered one innocent creature today; you're not getting this one too."

Crowe moved toward her. Manderson and another soldier, Crawford, according to a badge on his helmet, moved slowly in behind her. She edged to her side. "Leave us alone!" she yelled.

"Leave her alone," Southwell said. "Let her calm down."

Crowe almost looked as if he were considering that for a moment, then he said, "No, we don't have the time. I had hoped that they might be useful in understanding Professor Green's work, but so far they've been just an obstruction."

He spoke to Crawford, behind Rebecca. "Take the animal off her and get all three of them back to Auckland." He turned to Southwell. "Get them charged with trespass or . . . something . . . so your police can keep them out of our hair."

Crawford nodded and circled around Rebecca to grab Xena. Manderson gripped her shoulders from behind, despite her shaking and struggling. Crawford put his hands under Xena's arms and began to pull. Rebecca held on tightly, and the chimpanzee, sensing the struggle, hugged her tightly back. Crawford was just trying to pry Rebecca's hands from around the chimp's back when Tane hit him broadside.

Fatboy had played rugby league in school and had a pretty tough reputation from years of tackling huge front-row forwards. Tane had never played rugby in his life. But he'd been to plenty of games to watch his brother play, and he hit Crawford in a textbook midriff tackle.

It cut him in half, knocking him to the floor and sliding both of them across the room toward the tables holding the tank. Crawford's back hit one of the table legs and the whole structure shuddered.

"Look out!" Crowe yelled.

Manderson, with incredible reactions and speed for a big man, was at the side of the tank before there was any danger of it falling, steadying it with two hands.

Crawford leaped up and angrily hauled Tane to his feet, his arm swinging back in a fist. Tane, facing the side of the tank, brought his hands up to protect himself and had just enough time to wonder, *Where are the jellyfish?* when Southwell said, "Something's happened in the fog tank, Stony."

Crawford's arm remained tense but his eyes were on the tank. Everybody's eyes were on the tank.

The fog was swirling. Not just quivering a little from the knock to the table leg, but twirling and swirling in broad patterns inside the tank.

"Where are the jellyfish?" Manderson asked in his slow Texan drawl, echoing Tane's thoughts. His hands were on the glass sides of the tank, but the jellyfish had not attacked.

A young-looking soldier, whose name badge read EVANS, said from the other side of the tank, "There's something new forming over here."

The chimpanzee was forgotten, Rebecca was forgotten, and Tane was forgotten. Crawford's arm dropped as the men crowded around the tank.

Tane moved to where he could see. It was a larger object, not really a definable shape at all, just a mass of a white substance, more visceral than the jellyfish, with a moist, diaphanous surface, like that of a slug.

"The fog is thinning," Crowe noted. "It is being formed out of the fog."

Tane watched as the shape grew a fraction of an inch or two in diameter in front of his eyes.

"Why now?" Crowe asked, as if he had been expecting this to happen sooner or later.

"The knock to the tank?" Crawford asked.

"No. Look at the size of it. It's been forming for quite a while," Manderson pointed out.

They all watched in silence for a few moments, but the shape grew no farther.

"It's run out of fog," Crowe decided after a while. "It needs more fog to grow. But why suddenly now? What has happened to trigger that growth?"

He sounded concerned.

"Do you want to run the same tests?" Crawford asked, glancing at Rebecca and Xena. Rebecca recoiled, taking a few steps backward and twisting Xena around behind her as if to protect her.

"I don't know," Crowe murmured, not taking his eyes off the glutinous shape. "Start with the human cell tests."

Rebecca was ignored and drew closer to the tank again, intrigued, as two of the soldiers put their hands in the thick rubber gloves on the side of the tank. The big white slug quivered, but did not move.

A small petri dish was introduced through an air lock at the end of the tank, and one of the soldiers opened it carefully inside.

The fog was a lot thinner now, and it was easier to see what was going on. Inside the petri dish were a few small objects that took Tane a moment or two to recognize. There were a few hairs, human he realized, and some nail clippings. Evans picked up a hair out of the dish and dropped it carefully onto the white shape.

It touched the surface of the blob and just disappeared. At first Tane thought it had sunk into the material, but then he realized that it hadn't. It had just "melted" on the surface.

The fingernail clippings followed, with exactly the same effect.

"Test the pH," Crowe said.

Evans tore open the plastic seal on a small cardboard

strip already placed inside the tank and touched it to the surface of the object. After a moment he said, "Neutral. Just slightly alkaline."

"So it's not an acid," Crowe said, deep in thought. "But it dissolves human cells."

"Like butter on a hot griddle," Manderson drawled.

Rebecca, Tane, and Fatboy might as well have been invisible, so little attention was paid to them.

The soldier-scientists spent the next hour running batteries of tests on the small white blob, but always, Tane thought, with inconclusive results. At least that was the impression he got from their expressions as they discussed, in highly scientific terms, the results of each test.

One thing was clear to Tane, though. This substance, whatever it was, was related to the disappearance of all those people on Motukiekie and Whangarei.

A fax machine set up on a table in a corner rang while the tests were going on, and Southwell went to check it. She came back with a concerned look on her face.

"Stony," she said, "the fog is moving much faster than we thought."

Crowe looked at the printout, a detailed weather satellite image of the area. His eyes opened wide. "Warkworth! We hadn't expected it to get that far south for another couple of days. It's accelerating! At this rate, it'll be here by tomorrow."

"Let's hope it doesn't get any faster," Manderson said slowly.

Tane, Rebecca, and Fatboy looked at each other in alarm.

"Had they completed the evacuation?" Crowe asked.

Southwell said, "Yes. Orewa also, and they're starting to evacuate Torbay, Albany, Greenhithe, and Helensville."

Those three towns represented the northernmost tip of Auckland. The fog was getting close to the homes of a million people.

"When were these taken?" Crowe asked, scanning the image for a date and time.

"This morning at first light."

"First light! Get back to the meteorological people. I need to know how far south it's come since then." He spun around to Manderson. "Where are the SAS and NZ Army units?"

"Base camp. Silverdale. Just down the road."

"Pull them back to Albany. We'll never have time to set up the defensive line at Waiwera before it gets there."

He looked back at the tank. "Damn! I was hoping for much more time than this. Get the equipment packed up, and get the men ready to evac. That fog is just up the road and heading this way. I don't want to still be standing around, running tests, when it gets here."

There was a flurry of activity as the soldiers worked to pack up their equipment, disappearing, probably down to the big black trailer units that Tane had seen parked outside.

Only the main tank remained, and some odds and ends of equipment, lined up by the door, when Crowe looked across at Xena, still perched in Rebecca's arms. Rebecca was sitting on a chair on the far side of the room having a long conversation with the chimp about the *Möbius* submarine. Xena seemed interested, interjecting occasionally with screeches and sudden gestures of her own. At one point, she started looking through Rebecca's hair, apparently looking for nits, but (fortunately) didn't find any.

Rebecca noticed Crowe's gaze and instinctively drew away.

"What do you want to do, Skipper?" Crawford said.

"Evacuate the kids back to Auckland. We'll put the chimp back in her cage and take her with us."

"Liar," Rebecca spat, "I know what you're going to do with her, and you're not getting her. You're going to put her in the tank with that white blob to see what it does to her. I'm not going to let you."

Crowe sighed tiredly. "Sort it out, Mandy."

The soldiers were all gone now, packing their trailers, except for Manderson and the young man, Evans. The tall Texan didn't waste time with threats of physical violence. He just reached under a table and brought out his weapon, one of the long, strangely rounded guns they had seen earlier.

"Hand over the animal, ma'am."

"Shoot me!" Rebecca shot back. "You big brave American GI. Just shoot me!"

"Don' wanna," the lanky Texan drawled. "Will if I have to."

Tane stood and moved next to Rebecca. She glanced at him, appreciating his presence, he thought. He sensed a movement behind him.

"Give me the chimp," Manderson asked politely.

"Give him the chimp," Crowe roared suddenly, and Xena screamed.

"Dr. Crowe!" Southwell pleaded.

"Leave her alone," Tane shouted. "Leave us alone!"

Manderson's rifle drifted toward Tane. For the first time in his life, Tane stared straight at the small black circle that was the mouth, the end of the barrel of a gun. Just a tiny amount of pressure on the trigger at the other end of the barrel was all it would take. Such a small movement of one finger, and . . . He shut his eyes.

He opened them again as he felt a hand push him to one side.

Fatboy was an imposing figure for a seventeen-year-old. Tall, strong, toughened by years of rugby league, and the cowboy hat added even more height. The *moko* seemed suddenly terrifying on the face of the warrior who now stepped in front of Tane. Fatboy's knees were bent, his back rigid, his chest puffed out. Tane had seen him act tough before, but this was something more. This was something deeper, something ancestral. Fatboy's eyes burned and his tongue stabbed at the soldiers. He smashed his hands into his chest.

"Ka mate! Ka mate! Ka ora! Ka ora!"

Fatboy faced the soldiers and their deadly weapons with the spirits of ancient warriors on his shoulders. Crowe and Manderson froze in the face of such ferocity. They had faced lethal viruses and terrorists with guns, they had faced hell, and they had faced death, but never before had they faced up to Fatboy and his *moko*.

Xena was still screaming, lips flared, jumping up and down on Rebecca's lap as Fatboy continued the *haka*.

"A upa . . . ne! ka upa . . . ne! A upane kaupane whiti te ra!"

"Leave us alone!" Tane yelled.

"Stony!" Southwell shouted.

Xena screamed again and broke free of Rebecca's grasp. She ran across the floor of the room on her hands and feet. Long drapes covered the windows and she lunged at them, tearing at the fabric. She screamed and screeched in alarm.

One of the drapes tore from its hooks, falling away from

the window even as the three soldiers froze, listening intently to their earpiece radios.

Tane didn't need to hear the message to know what was being said. Through the torn drape, fog whirled and swirled around outside the second-story windows of the hotel.

Then came the sound of gunshots.

SHAPES IN THE MIST

"Get them into biosuits," Crowe ordered, his face tense.

Gunfire sounded again from outside the hotel. A few sporadic shots, followed by long bursts of automatic fire.

Southwell wasted no time. She opened a suitcase from a small stack near the door and motioned to Tane and Fatboy to do the same.

"It's a pressurized suit," she said. "You'll feel it inflate when you seal the faceplate."

She put on her own suit, then helped Rebecca into hers. Tane and Fatboy imitated as best as they could. She showed them the earpiece radios and how to strap the throat mike around their necks.

"You want to talk, press here," she said, indicating a small button on the outside of the suit, near the neck. "But don't use the radio unless it's important."

She connected her air hose and closed her face mask with a click, then helped Tane with his.

The moment Tane plugged the small earpiece into his ear, he was suddenly immersed in the battle that was raging outside. A cacophony of orders, shouts, and cries of alarm. The gunfire was constant now.

Crawford's voice was recognizable. He seemed to be co-ordinating the battle outside.

"Don't mind the jellyfish," he was shouting, the voice tinny but surprisingly real in Tane's ear. "They can't get through the suits. Watch out for the big ones!"

The big ones! The big ones?

"Crowe, this is Crawford, I've—"

The voice was cut off suddenly amidst a sustained burst of gunfire.

All three of them were in their suits now, and Tane realized that Crowe was shouting at them.

"Get behind us. We're going down the main stairway. We need to make it to one of the trailers!"

Xena leapt into Rebecca's arms.

"Let me," Fatboy said, and Rebecca passed the chimp over gratefully. They had to move fast, and Fatboy's strength was going to be needed.

"Leave the chimp behind," Crowe ordered, but Fatboy ignored him.

The sounds of shouts and confusion intensified on the radio.

"Fall back, fall back to the trailers!" That was Crawford's voice again. "Try your sprayers. The bullets don't bother them; just cut straight through them!"

Cut through what?

"Crawford, this is Crowe. What's going on out there?"

They were already moving, out through the double doors of the restaurant and toward the main staircase. The fog had poured in through the main doors to the hotel, flowing over and around the reception desks and rolling up the staircase, creeping up the stairs, one by one.

"They're all over the place, Stony."

"Crawford! What are all over the place?"

"The . . . Oh my God! Oh my God!" Crawford's voice again, desperate, despairing. The voice cut off suddenly.

"Repeat that, Crawford!"

The radio remained silent, but from outside they could still hear the sounds of firing.

"What the hell is going on?" Crowe raced along the short passageway to the stairs, close on the heels of Evans. Manderson and Southwell followed, and the three kids raced behind her as quickly as they could in the bulky, armored biosuits that were far too large for Rebecca and Tane and were awkward to move in.

The fog was halfway up the long curved staircase and climbing rapidly. The first yard, maybe two, was soft and transparent, but then the fog intensified into a dense cloud.

Crowe turned to face them. "The trailers are outside the door to the left."

Even as he said it, they heard one of the truck engines start.

Crowe continued, "I don't know what we're heading into, but we'll try to deal with whatever it is. You kids head straight for the trailer. It's armored. Once we reach it, we'll head south, out of the fog. Are we clear?"

"Clear!" Tane and Fatboy said, but Rebecca drew in a sharp breath.

"Don't go mist," she said with a quiver of terror in her voice. "Don't go in the mist."

"DNT GO MST," Tane remembered, and realized the message had had nothing to do with Masterton at all. *Don't go in the mist.*

"It's our only way out," Crowe snapped. "We've got to go through the mist to get to the trailers."

"Don't go in the mist!" Rebecca screamed.

Crowe shook his head. "Evans, you're on point. Manderson, tail-end Charlie. Get moving, now!"

Rebecca didn't move. Tane was already three or four steps down, following Southwell who was following Crowe, when he realized that she was still on the top landing. The mist swirled around him, light at first but intensifying.

Evans, a couple of steps lower, disappeared into a cloud of the dense fog ahead.

"Stay close," Crowe ordered.

Manderson, realizing that Rebecca had not followed, retreated back up to the top landing and grabbed her by the arm. "Get moving," he shouted, pushing her down the stairs. She tripped and fell, sliding face-forward down past Tane and Fatboy, and stopping herself a step below Crowe. Her body half disappeared into the thicker fog ahead.

There was a sudden hissing sound, and Evans's voice came back to them, not in words, but in a strange strangled gurgle. Then silence.

There was a thud, and his weapon hit the stairs, the end of it just visible and protruding out from the fog.

Rebecca screamed and scrambled backward up the stairs, pushing herself up with her hands and feet.

"What is it, Rebecca?" Tane yelled. "What happened?"

"I didn't see," she screamed, turning and running back up the stairs. "He just disappeared!"

Tane turned and followed her, and realized that the others were with him. All of them.

They raced back into the restaurant. Silent now. The radio, too, was silent.

Crowe and Manderson turned in unison and slammed the double doors shut. Crowe used something on his weapon to coat a dense foam around the edges of each of the doors.

"What was that?" screamed Rebecca. "What's out there?"

"Calm down," Crowe shouted, not too calmly himself. "Calm down," he repeated with a bit more control. "Whatever it is, it can only survive in the fog. That foam will prevent the fog from getting in here."

Tane looked at the irregular pattern of the foam. It looked like gray-colored shaving cream. Or icing on some bizarre cake.

"What happened to Evans?" Manderson asked, checking the safety on his weapon.

"Don't know," Crowe said.

"Crowe, this is Miller," a voice on the radio said now.

"Go ahead, Miller. What is your status?"

"I have nine men with me, no injuries. We are in trailer two, heading south, out of the fog. What is your position?"

Crowe looked at Manderson before saying, "We are secure. We are in the forward command post. We have sealed the doors to prevent the fog from entering. We can probably hold out here for a while. What the hell is going on out there?"

"I wish I knew." The voice on the radio sounded frightened. "Some kind of . . . creature . . . I . . . don't know. But whatever they are, they are big, and they move fast, especially where the fog is thick."

Crowe said, "Okay, Miller. Keep moving. Get your-self clear."

"Roger that, Stony. We'll regroup, then come back for you."

The radio went silent once again.

"Nine men," Manderson drawled. "Plus Miller. Plus two of us."

He didn't need to say any more.

"Let's hope they made it to the other trailer," Crowe said without conviction. "Are there any other entrances to this room?"

"Fire escape."

Crowe and Manderson ran to the rear of the room to seal that door. They were just returning when Tane noticed a whisper of mist trickling in through a gap in the seal on the front doors.

"Dr. Crowe," he said urgently, pointing out the thin plume of steam.

Crowe nodded and moved forward to plug the gap with more foam.

He was only a few yards from the door when it exploded.

For just half a second, Tane thought he saw a vague white shape at the toughened glass of the door, as if some-thing had charged at the door through the fog on the other side. There was a hissing noise also, and then the entire door just shattered into tiny squares like the glass from a car wind-shield.

Pieces of glass smashed into his biosuit, and he thought for a moment that Crowe, who had been much closer, had been cut to shreds by the flying shards that enveloped him. But the biosuits were made of some toughened material, designed to stop bullets, and the glass fragments bounced harmlessly off.

Fog poured into the room.

"Get back!" Crowe yelled, running back and pushing Rebecca by the shoulder. "To the fire escape."

"What was that?" Manderson shouted. "That thing at the door."

Crowe had no answer. He just said, "Try your sprayer on them. Bullets don't work!"

"Water works," Tane said, without fully realizing what he had said. *Water works!*

Crowe looked at him without stopping. "What does that mean, son?"

"I don't know, but water works."

They hit the door to the fire escape and burst through it, scattering the gray foam that Crowe and Manderson had carefully sprayed there a moment ago.

It was a narrow concrete staircase, flight after flight of featureless stairs with a red metal railing.

The fog was lapping at the boots of the biosuits and rising up around their knees.

"Up," Crowe shouted, bounding up the stairs.

They couldn't exactly go down, Tane thought.

He took two steps and then stopped dead. Manderson, behind him, collided with him but didn't stop and brushed past.

Tane turned and ran back into the room.

"Tane!" His brother's voice. "Where are you going?"

"The Chronophone!" Tane called back. It was in a line of equipment by the double doors, waiting to be packed out to the trucks.

If he had stopped to think, given himself a chance to be afraid, he never would have done it. But he hadn't. So he did.

The fog was still thickening inside the room. The walls faded before his eyes as it intensified.

The jellyfish stayed in the dense fog, he remembered, and hoped the same was true for the *Big Ones*.

The Chronophone was where he remembered it, and he grabbed it with a snatch. It was heavier than he remembered and he stumbled but kept his feet.

The fog was alive, moving and scything around in broad patterns, and there were things in the center of those patterns.

From all around came strange hissing noises as whatever they were moved swiftly through the thickening fog.

The mist had risen up the stairwell also, but he cleared it in a single flight of stairs. The others were waiting for him, just out of the white clouds.

"Get moving," Crowe said in a gravelly voice, and that was all that anybody said.

The six of them, seven if you counted the chimp, flew up two flights of stairs and looked down from the next landing. Still the fog was rising up the narrow shaft.

"How high is this hotel?" Crowe asked.

Nobody knew the answer.

The next two flights of stairs were harder, but adrenaline gave them wings. Two more stories, though, and Tane could see that Rebecca was flagging. His own legs, unaccustomed to carrying the weight of the biosuit and the Chronophone, were rebelling also. Southwell seemed unaffected, and Fatboy, even with the weight of Xena, hardly seemed to have raised a sweat.

Looking down, Tane could see that the fog was swelling

up the narrow concrete shaft after them. Slowly, inexorably rising up the stairs.

If they couldn't get above it, Tane realized, it was the end of everything.

Two more stories and they came to the final flight of stairs. Above them a cold, hard concrete ceiling blocked their escape route.

Crowe looked down at the rising mist. "Through here," he said, flinging open the door to a rooftop area, where a few comfortable loungers skirted the edges of a long rectangular swimming pool. The afternoon sun burned into a light haze over the area, a thin spread of fog. Around them the rest of the world was white. They were a small concrete platform adrift in a sea of cloud.

"Are we high enough?" Tane asked. No one answered.

The mist around them began to intensify, rolling over the edges of the concrete parapets of the rooftop area and falling out of the doorway behind them.

"Miller, are you still there?" Crowe called.

"Roger that."

"We've had to DD. We are now on the roof of the hotel. We are in extreme, I say extreme, danger. We need evac now."

"Cannot help. I repeat, unable to assist. We have just cleared the fog and are proceeding south to the new command center at Albany. Will contact the Kiwis for you and see if there is anything they can do."

"Roger that." Crowe looked around grimly. He was hard to see, even in the full light of day, thanks to the thickening mist.

"What do we do now?" Southwell asked.

"Sit tight," Crowe said. "Sit tight and pray."

• • •

The jellyfish came first. Flying through the thickening fog. The harsh whistling sound they made was the first indication that something else, besides the six humans and the chimpanzee, was alive in the fog.

"Try not to move," Crowe said. "They are attracted to movement and sound."

Even as he said it, it was clear that it was useless. The biosuits themselves gave an audible click and a hiss with every breath they took.

It didn't take the jellyfish long to find them.

One landed on Tane's arm, and he watched it, horrified, yet fascinated for a second as it extended its long filaments and probed the black armor of the biosuit, trying to find an opening. The suit was strong enough to withstand it, though, and he flicked it away with a yelp of disgust.

It was back a second later, though, so he squashed it, flattening it with a sharp slap. It fell away into the mist.

The next one he squashed stayed there, stuck to his suit, but when he looked back at it a moment later, it was mostly gone. Dissolving, it seemed, back into the fog.

More came, though, and more still. He slapped at them, smashed them, shudders running through his body at the thought of the fine tentacles needling their way inside the suit. He looked at Rebecca's back and realized with a shock that her black biosuit had turned white. Her back was covered with the jellyfish, the odd Y shapes fitting into each other like pieces of a jigsaw puzzle. Smothering her.

He forgot his own creatures for a moment and began hammering on Rebecca's back, screaming wildly as the creatures went flying, unable to get a grip on the smooth surface of the suit.

"The jellyfish can't penetrate the biosuits," Crowe said calmly.

"It's not them I'm worried about," Fatboy muttered.

There was a swirling in the fog near the door to the fire escape, and Tane thought he glimpsed a white shape through the mist.

"Here they come," he breathed.

"The pool," Rebecca suddenly said. "Water works. Get in the pool!"

"Everybody in the pool," Crowe ordered. "Now!"

"What about Xena?" Rebecca asked, but a pair of hands cut short the argument, shoving her violently in the back, toppling her headfirst into the water. She didn't see who did it, but Tane did. It was Lucy Southwell.

Tane let himself over the side of the pool and splashed into the deep water. He sank like a stone and fought a rising panic, until he realized that he was in a fully self-contained suit, with its own oxygen supply. He hoped the metal case of the Chronophone really was watertight.

Fatboy was talking, but Tane could not hear him. Crowe motioned them all into the center of the pool and held out a hand. Manderson laid his hand on Crowe's, and after a slightly confused moment, the rest followed.

Crowe's voice sounded suddenly in Tane's ear. "The radio signals don't travel underwater. But if you touch one of the other biosuits, the signal will travel directly from one to the other."

"The entire suit acts as an aerial," Manderson explained.

"Still think it's terrorists, Dr. Crowe?" Rebecca asked, a little cynically.

Crowe ignored her.

"How do you know we'll be safe in here?" Fatboy asked.

Crowe replied immediately, "They can only survive and move in the mist. You kids were right. The fog can't penetrate the water, so the creatures can't either."

The suits were all black again. The jellyfish released their hold the moment they hit the water and floated to the surface. They bobbed around there for a little while, hundreds of them, and gradually disappeared.

It was left to Tane to ask the next obvious question as vague shapes moved around the sides of the pool and across the surface of the water above them. Large, whitish shapes, indistinct and blurred through the water of the pool.

"How much oxygen do these tanks have?" he asked. "How long can we stay down here?"

14

EPIPHANY

The water above Tane rippled with the passage of one of the—*what were they?*—above him. The sun, still high in the sky, diffused down through the opaque whiteness of the mist above, then softened and soothed further by the wash of the pool water into the dull brightness of a child's toy lamp.

When one of *them* passed over the surface of the water—never breaching the surface—the resulting ripples created undulating patterns over the light blue walls and floor of the pool.

Tane sat with his back to the pool wall and watched the soft light play over the faceplate of Rebecca's suit. Here under the water, the tinted faceplates turned to mirrors, preventing any glimpse of the face inside.

She could be smiling at him. She could be scowling. He had no way of knowing.

What were they? The *snowmen*. The human mind

always tries to rationalize things. To fit what it sees to what it already knows. To judge new experiences by previous experiences. Tane's mind wanted to believe that the creatures that now ruled the world above them were human, in some strange costume perhaps. But no matter how hard his mind tried to rationalize that, the image kept recurring of the shape at the door, just as it exploded into a million shards of glass. And human beings couldn't walk across water. Besides, he had a horrible feeling that they had seen one of these things being born. In the fog tank.

A darker shadow blocked the light for a moment by the edge of the pool. Xena. She had been wandering around the poolside since they had jumped in. Looking for them. Wondering when they would resurface. Rebecca hadn't mentioned Xena again. Fortunately, the snowmen were no more interested in Xena than the jellyfish had been.

Xena moved on, lurching around the poolside. She must be just about as confused as they were, Tane thought with an ironic inward laugh.

He looked around the bounds of their underwater prison. Rebecca sat opposite him, unmoving. Maybe even sleeping, although he doubted it. Southwell was next to her. Just to his right, Fatboy and Crowe were sitting next to each other against the end wall of the narrow pool, and Manderson had stretched out full length on the bottom of the pool, as if resting.

It was surprisingly comfortable, once you got used to the hiss and click of the oxygen valve. The water bore most of his weight, cushioning him in a soft cradle.

He checked his oxygen levels again. Half full. Crowe had said they had about four hours on a single tank, which was all they had.

Crowe touched him on the arm and his voice came over the radio.

"You went to a lot of trouble to save that suitcase, son."

Rebecca looked up, and Crowe motioned her to join in the conversation. Southwell did also, but Fatboy and Manderson remained where they were.

Crowe repeated his comment, then added, "These cryptic comments you keep making. 'Water works' and 'Don't go mist.' And the submarine. They're written down in that notebook of yours, aren't they? It seems that you know more than you are letting on."

"Tell him, Rebecca," Tane said, pressing his radio button. "It can't do any harm now."

After a moment, Rebecca's voice came through his earpiece. She said, "Do you remember telling us that we did not know what you might believe?"

"I remember saying something like that."

"Then would you believe me if I told you that we've been receiving messages from the future, warnings about what is going on now?"

Crowe said, "I remember Tane blurting something about that just before you jumped off my ship. Go on, convince me."

Rebecca said, "We discovered a way of deciphering messages embedded in bursts of gamma radiation, picked up by a NASA satellite."

"From whom, exactly?"

"From ourselves."

There was a brief silence. Then Crowe said, "Okay. It's a bit far-fetched so far, but under these circumstances . . . Carry on."

Rebecca explained, "Only so many characters can fit into a gamma-ray burst, so the messages have been extremely short and cryptic. But we figured out enough to buy the submarine, to try to stop the Chimera Project, and to end up in the mess we're in now."

Tane added, "We're not scoring too well at the moment."

"No," Crowe mused. "If it were true, and I'm not saying I believe you just yet, then it would raise some interesting complications. Have you heard of the grandfather paradox?"

"Oh God, don't start," Tane groaned. "You'll be building a Möbius strip soon."

"What?" Crowe asked, but got no answer.

"I've been thinking about the snowmen," Rebecca said.

So that was why she had been so still for so long.

She continued, "And I don't think they fit with your theory of bacterial clusters."

"Go on," said Crowe.

"And you surely don't still think we're dealing with terrorists?"

"Possibly not."

Rebecca lapsed back into silence.

A new voice joined the conversation, and Tane realized that Manderson had shifted one of his long legs across, touching Rebecca's and thus linking him in to the conversation.

Manderson said, "I might try sticking just my hand above water and seeing if I can pick up a signal. Let the others know where we are."

Crowe's helmet bobbed up and down in a nod. "Worth a try."

Manderson rolled himself into a sitting position, then squatted, tentatively raising a hand up into the air above the pool.

"Blue Three, this is . . ." He stopped talking and snatched his hand into the water again as fast ripples spread across the surface of the pool toward him. The light cascaded in waves over the sides of the pool as some kind of feeding frenzy took place above them.

The short flurry of activity died away as Manderson lay back down on the floor of the pool. "Won't be trying that again," he said.

"Any chance the fog will move on?" Tane asked.

"It's several miles wide and growing," Crowe answered. "It won't pass us by in time. We only have a couple of hours of air left."

"And then what?" Rebecca asked.

"You tell me," Crowe replied. "Ask your friends from the future."

Manderson asked, "How did they know that I was there? I'm in a biosuit; they can't smell me. They can't see me, except for my hand. They're not bothering Z1. How did they even know who or what I am?"

"Maybe they know what a human hand looks like," Crowe conjectured.

The words connected with some hidden memory in Tane's brain, and he said absently, "Shape recognition."

"What's that again?" Rebecca asked abruptly.

"Shape recognition," Tane repeated, wondering where he had heard the phrase before.

Rebecca removed her hand, cutting herself out of the conversation, and was still again, thinking.

Tane looked at his oxygen gauge. What would they do when the air ran out? Face the snowmen? Pray that the fog had moved on more quickly than they expected? The only thing to do now was wait it out. "Don't move too much," Crowe had said to them just after they had submerged. "It uses oxygen."

The tranquillity of the pool bottom was shattered suddenly with a huge splash, and Tane's heart leaped inside his chest as something plunged into the water at the shallow end of the pool. It was a snowman. It had to be a snowman. He cowered away from the shock wave that swept past him and fought the urge to surface. That would be fatal.

It wasn't a snowman. It was a rescue harness, attached to a long steel wire cable.

Crowe was at the harness in a second. He ignored it and grabbed the wire cable with his hand, using his free hand to key his radio.

It took Tane a moment to realize what he was doing. The steel cable acted as a huge aerial, taking the signal from Crowe's radio out above the water. He touched Crowe lightly on the ankle, to hear the conversation.

"Rescue helicopter, this is Dr. Crowe of the USABRF," Crowe said. "We are mighty glad to see you."

A New Zealand accent came back through the earpiece, terse and professional. "Dr. Crowe, how many in your party? Over."

"Six. How fast is your winch?"

"Two feet a second at full speed. Why do you ask? Over."

"Not fast enough. We will be attacked on the way up. I repeat, we will be under attack on the way up. You have to get us clear of the fog faster than that."

"We could climb as we winch. That would more than double the speed. Over."

"That'll have to do."

Crowe motioned Rebecca toward him and strapped her into the harness. He grabbed the wire again. "Crowe to rescue helicopter. Allow some slack in the line also. Then start climbing and winching at the same time. You'll whip us out of here like a slingshot."

"Roger that. Over."

"First person ready," Crowe said. "Take her away."

Rebecca grasped onto the harness tightly, as if she might fall out of it, although it was a secure-looking strap. Tane lifted a hand in a kind of goodbye wave, but she was already gone.

She was there one moment and not there the next as the whiplashing cable snatched her from the bottom of the pool like a tiny doll on the end of a bungee cord.

A moment or two later, the harness splashed back into the water, near Crowe. He pointed to Tane.

The harness felt snug and secure around his shoulders, but like Rebecca, he grasped it firmly. He had seen the speed of the whiplash and did not want to be jerked out of the harness by it. He clipped the handle of the Chronophone to a metal clip at his shoulder.

The cable above him tensed, and then suddenly the water was gone, fog rushing down past him. White shapes roared toward him, rising up with him, but then he was above the mist, hanging below a large black helicopter in the broad sunshine of a beautiful summer's day.

He wanted to scream with exhilaration. It had been a short but wild ride. He clambered over the side of the helicopter with a little help from a crewman as he was winched on board.

He looked down. The helicopter was hovering well clear of the fog. Being careful. Just as well, he thought. If you knew what was roaming around in there, though, you'd be a lot higher still.

Ten or twenty minutes later, they were leaving the fog-covered township of Orewa behind them, soaring high above the mist on the black blades of the chopper.

Crowe was leaning forward, busy on the radio, asking questions, and answering them as well. Their faceplates were open and the fresh air tasted great.

Crowe sat back after a few moments and his eyes were grim. Tane had heard why. Four of his men had disappeared when the mist had rolled in from the north.

"What about Xena?" he asked Fatboy.

"We'll go back for her later," he said carefully. "When the fog has cleared."

Tane wasn't sure if that was likely to happen or not, but he let it go. He didn't want to upset Rebecca any further.

She had been silent since they had been snatched off the rooftop, thinking, wordlessly working away inside her own mind. She looked up now, though, and said suddenly, "I know what they are."

All eyes were on her.

"I bought into the idea of bacterial clusters"—she was looking directly at Crowe—"of giant pathogens, because we didn't have any other ideas. But that didn't explain, that couldn't explain, the snowmen."

She paused, thinking, and Crowe took the opportunity to interject, "It's the best guess we've got. Until some more reasonable explanation is found. And I mean reasonable, not some fantastical story about—"

Rebecca was staring at him now, frowning, a look of realization slowly dawning on her face.

"You know, don't you? You don't want to admit it, but you know too."

Crowe interrupted, "I don't know what you're—"

"The moment that Tane said 'shape recognition.' That's when you realized. You couldn't *not* have known. You're an immunologist. Heck, I'm just a fourteen-year-old kid, so it took me a little longer to work it out, but you must have known straightaway."

Southwell seemed shocked. "Rebecca, are you saying what I think you're saying? My God, you'd better be wrong."

"They are bacterial clusters," Crowe insisted.

"They're not! And you know they're not." Rebecca was thinking furiously now. "The strange Y-shaped jellyfish. Those . . . *things* . . . in the fog. It's so obvious. You do know. I know you know."

"What the hell are you talking about?" Tane shouted. "What are they? What are the jellyfish if they're not bacterial clusters?"

Rebecca spoke distinctly, as the rotor blades of the helicopter changed pitch in preparation for landing.

"Antibodies," she said.

IMMUNITY

Manderson lowered his eyes and smiled quietly to himself. Crowe just sighed tiredly. Only Lucy Southwell looked kindly at Rebecca and said, "You know that's impossible, don't you?"

Manderson looked up with a bemused expression and said, "I suppose that would make the big ones, the snowmen, phagocytes of some kind."

"Macrophages," Rebecca said firmly. "Mother Nature's immune system. Now triggered by Dr. Vicky Green. Against the human race."

Southwell put a hand on her arm. "Rebecca, it's an imaginative idea but just not very likely. Antibodies are simple proteins. They're microscopic."

"I never said they were human antibodies," Rebecca said, and wouldn't say anything else until the helicopter had landed on the lined green surface of the main playing field at the North Harbor Sports Stadium in Albany.

• • •

The Command and Control Center was set up in a sponsors' lounge on the fourth floor of the stadium. Through huge plate-glass windows, the green rectangle of the rugby ground was now home to a number of helicopters and row upon row of armored fighting vehicles, preparing for battle.

Tane, Rebecca, and Fatboy were waiting to leave. Their transportation was coming up from the central city. All vehicles here apparently were already hard at work, transporting troops and equipment to build the defensive line.

"They are antibodies," Rebecca finally spoke again, in a small but determined voice. "Antibodies and macrophages. Accept it. You have to. You can't defeat what you can't understand."

Crowe glanced momentarily up from a detailed topographical map of the surrounding area that he and a grayhaired officer from the SAS had been poring over for about fifteen minutes, discussing something called kill zones, along with fields of fire and "claymores."

Crowe said without any further trace of humor, "Rebecca, even if that were possible, think about what you're saying. That would make us—human beings—pathogens. Antibodies attack pathogens."

"I know," Rebecca said softly.

Crowe shook his head and turned back to his work. An SAS trooper entered, saluted, and passed a note to the SAS officer.

Rebecca said, "We think of the Earth as a lump of rock, floating through space. Just a big stone, conveniently placed in a nice warm spot for us to grow on, like mold on cheese. But that's just a way of thinking about it. What if we thought of this planet in a different way. As a complex web of interrelated ecosystems, host to billions upon billions of smaller organisms." She paused. "Not all that unlike the human body when you think about it."

Crowe ignored her, sketching in a line of defendable positions on the map.

Manderson just sat quietly in the corner. Of all of them, only he seemed unfazed by what they had just been through.

A young soldier in the uniform of the regular New Zealand army came in with a stack of orders, which Crowe checked and the other man signed.

Through the window, Tane saw the first line of fighting vehicles began to move out.

Rebecca stood up and crossed to the map table. She leaned over it, her hands on the table, interrupting their work.

"You know what global warming is?" Rebecca asked calmly. "I do. The world has a fever. We are pathogens. Mother Nature is sick and the sickness is us!"

Crowe looked up at her through half-closed lids. Almost a display of emotion, Tane thought.

"I lost four men today," he said slowly. "I am not in the mood, and I don't have the time for your childish environmental fantasies. Get her out of here."

This last was to Manderson, who rose without question and moved behind Rebecca.

Rebecca didn't budge. She laughed, a little hysterically, which was unusual for her, but then again, it had been a very unusual day, Tane thought.

She said, "We don't inhabit a place: We infest it. We poison rivers; we pollute the skies and chop down the trees. We drill holes deep into the earth and suck out all the goodness. We are malignant and highly infectious."

Manderson grasped Rebecca by the arms, but Lucy Southwell intervened, drawing Rebecca away from the table. "What are you saying, Rebecca? That Professor Green somehow created an antidote to the human race?"

"No. I think these things have been there all along. Locked in our genes. Some kind of safety cutout. A self-destruct mechanism for the human species. I don't think Vicky Green invented them. I don't think she even discovered them. But by playing around with the building blocks of life, I think she finally triggered them against us."

Southwell said, "That's crazy, Rebecca. Listen to what you're saying. You're wrong."

She led Rebecca across to the large window and stared out at the bush-covered ridge in the distance and the blue skies above that.

Tane and Fatboy followed. After a while, Fatboy asked, "But what if she is right?"

"She's not," Southwell said. "I've studied this field my whole life. It's just not possible."

Somehow she sounded less sure than she had a moment ago.

Fatboy repeated his question. "But if she is right?"

Southwell sighed. "An antibody exists for only one purpose—to destroy an infection. An antibody has no conscience, no morals, no power to decide. It just does what it was created for. It binds to an infectious particle and disables it, to make it easier for a macrophage to absorb it and destroy it. That's all it does. If what you are saying is true, then that's it. That's the end of the human species."

"I know," Rebecca said. "And maybe it's all we deserve."

"For Christ's sake, get that child out of here!" Crowe shouted, shaking his head erratically from side to side. Even the stoic Manderson seemed shocked at the uncharacteristic display of emotion from his commanding officer.

He motioned to Tane and Fatboy, who didn't argue but pushed open the double doors to the lounge and began to walk along the short corridor to the wide concrete staircase. Fatboy took the Chronophone. Manderson followed to make sure they did as they were told, and Southwell helped Rebecca along behind them.

Rebecca was crying now, and Tane wanted to comfort her but wasn't sure that she'd want him to; besides, Lucy seemed to be doing that job.

They exited the building and moved slowly past one of the huge black trucks and trailers of the USABRF team. The snout of the truck was tucked into the lee of the building.

An army Land Rover pulled to a halt by a row of ticket gates, and a uniformed soldier got out expectantly. A young-looking blond girl in the uniform of the transport corps.

"Why won't he listen?" Rebecca asked between sobs. "What's wrong with him?"

Manderson spoke up then, and in the Texan's slow Southern drawl, Tane heard a whisper that maybe he wasn't quite so convinced that Rebecca was wrong.

"What d'ya think is wrong with him? The skipper has spent his entire life fighting against dangerous germs and nasty bugs." Manderson turned and spat some gum into a plastic rubbish bin by the back wheels of the big black truck.

"An' you just told him he is one!"

BEFORE THE STORM

Private Gemma Shaw drove quickly, expertly, without speaking, at a regulation sixty miles per hour, heading west on the Northwestern Motorway.

Tane wondered how fast she'd drive if one of *them* was behind her.

Convoys of trucks passed them on the other side of the motorway, great olive-green behemoths with huge jagged tires, long columns of them that stretched into the distance. But in their direction, the motorway was clear, at least until they got out of the Albany basin.

Private Shaw carefully braked and brought the army Land Rover to a halt.

Tane stared at the scene in front of him. Two hundred thousand people lived on the North Shore of Auckland City, and it seemed that all of them were jammed into little metal boxes down the four lanes ahead. There seemed to be no order to it. No careful lines of cars. It was just a jumble of multicolored pieces, as if someone had emptied a LEGO set down the motorway. The cars spilled from lane to lane, invading the shoulder and even the narrow grass of the median strip, rasping paint off their doors as they scraped along the median barriers. There were five and in some places even six cars squeezed into the narrow asphalt corridor.

There were family wagons, and sedans, and tradesmen's vans, stuffed to the gunnels with belongings and people. Every second vehicle seemed to be a big, square four-wheel drive, spewing black and brown diesel fumes from its exhaust. Motorcycles somehow found chinks in the solid metal armor of the roadway, weaving and winding their way through.

Just past Bush Road a late model Audi had been abandoned in the middle of the center lane. There was no way to get it off the road; instead, it was bulldozed along by the Toyota SUV behind. Whenever the Audi veered to the left or the right, a clip from a car in one of the side lanes steered it back into line. Already it was a wreck from the constant battering. And yet, with the relentless pressure of the traffic, it kept moving, as if it too wanted to escape the horror that was creeping across farmlands, through gullies, and down the highway, a few miles to the north.

Members of a North Shore evangelical church walked the length of the motorway, clambering over car bonnets when they had to, handing out muesli bars and bottled water and religious tracts. Voices were shouting and horns were blaring, and from at least one vehicle, now pushed to the side, a column of smoke rose out of the engine.

"How the hell are we going to get through that?" Fatboy asked in dismay.

"Won't be a problem, sir," Private Shaw said, and performed an extremely nonregulation U-turn in the middle of the motorway, driving the wrong way down the on-ramp, under the overpass, and back up the off-ramp on the other side of the motorway. There was a police roadblock on the off-ramp to prevent people from doing exactly what Shaw was doing. They needed the eastbound lanes clear for the convoys of trucks. The army vehicle and Shaw's ID got them through the roadblock without problem, though.

Shaw turned her headlights on full-beam, even though it was daylight, as a warning to the oncoming traffic.

They passed police cars at irregular intervals down the motorway, trying ineffectually to create some order out of the chaos.

They saw any number of minor nose-to-tail accidents, but the drivers did not even bother to stop. One car was scraping its front bumper along the roadway in front of it.

Not that they were moving far. A yard at a time if they were lucky.

Most of the cars were packed with belongings. Suitcases strapped onto roof racks, backseats stuffed with cardboard boxes and canvas bags. They passed one car with an elderly woman sitting in a kayak strapped onto a roof rack, wearing a bicycle helmet for protection. The car was driven by a middle-aged couple. There was no room in the backseat for the old lady because that was taken up by three ferocious-looking rottweilers.

"What are we going to do?" Tane asked. "When we get home?"

"Tell Mum and Dad what's going on," Fatboy said. "Then get over to Rebecca's house."

Rebecca's mum had been questioned and released, and was now back at the West Harbor house, according to Crowe.

They had tried phoning them from the stadium but got only a recorded voice telling them to try again later. The entire telephone system was overloaded across Auckland as a panicking population tried to contact friends or relatives.

Rebecca had stopped crying now, but there was a strange sadness about her. More than that, a sense that she didn't care anymore. That nothing mattered. It was like a wall around her, and even Fatboy didn't try to penetrate it.

Tane wondered if she was right. About the antibodies and macrophages. He had known her for the whole of his life, of her life, too, and she was seldom wrong about anything.

Yet Crowe had been so insistent.

"At the start, there would have been just one," Rebecca said, mostly to herself. "A small cloud of mist rising out of a test tube or a glass flask. Thickening. Growing. Maybe it was late at night. Maybe no one was there to see. Then, in the mist, a macrophage grew, and it waited. It waited for a pathogen. Maybe it was a night watchman or maybe a scientist working late."

She paused, and stared out the window for a while.

"And those cells became a resource. Food, if you like. And with them, the fog grew, and then maybe there were two of the macrophages. And the fog spread, creeping along corridors and under doorways, finding its next target, and then there were three or four of the creatures. By the morning, the mist covered the island and the people were gone."

"Don't think about it," Fatboy said. "It's upsetting you."

It wasn't just Rebecca it was upsetting.

Rebecca ignored him and continued, "Then the fog reached Whangarei, wiping out a few scattered farmhouses and small towns on the way. And there were fifty thousand people. Fifty thousand germs to be disinfected."

"What is she talking about?" Private Shaw was getting nervous.

Rebecca said, "It's going to reach Auckland soon, and most of a million people will still be here, and it will use their cells to grow. And it will grow. If fifty thousand people makes a fog several miles wide, then how much fog will a million human bodies make?"

"Rebecca, stop it now!" Fatboy said.

"Rebecca," Tane said.

She closed her eyes and shook her head gently. "Sorry, guys. Long day."

"A long, strange day," Fatboy agreed.

Tane said, "Crowe and the rest of those scientists know what they are doing. They don't think we are a disease, and I don't either."

Rebecca lapsed into a strange, moody silence and said nothing more.

"What about the Chronophone?" Tane asked.

They still had to install the device, currently cradled on Tane's lap.

"We'll do it later," Fatboy said. "It'll be easier to get into the city on the bike; we can just cut through all the traffic."

A radio beeped, and Private Shaw held it to her ear, giving their location and direction to someone on the other end before pulling over and stopping.

"What are you . . . ?" Fatboy began to ask, but his question was answered as another Land Rover appeared behind them, headlights flashing.

Big "Mandy" Manderson got out of the other vehicle. He was grinning widely. They got out to meet him.

"Managed to commandeer a vehicle," he said. "Got some good news for you."

"Really?" Rebecca said sardonically, understandably, considering the circumstances.

"In times like these, any good news is a blessing," Manderson said.

There was a movement behind him, and a small brown bundle clambered out through the passenger window, chattering and waving its hairy little arms.

"Xena!" Rebecca cried as the chimp ran across and leaped up at her.

"Just wandered out of the mist about twenty minutes ago," Manderson said. "God knows how she found her way back down through the hotel in the fog. Must have followed the main road south. Just pure luck, I guess."

Maybe, Tane thought, but animals had a strange instinct sometimes.

Rebecca hugged the chimp like a long-lost daughter, and Xena hugged her back.

"Hi, Xena," Tane said. She screeched joyfully at him, and he found himself strangely pleased to see the happy little chimp again.

"Please say thanks to Dr. Crowe for us," Rebecca said as Manderson climbed back in the Land Rover.

He smiled, and said, "Stony is a bit busy at the moment."

"You didn't tell him, did you." It was a statement, not a question.

Manderson smiled again and shook his head. Rebecca walked over before he could pull away, leaned in the window, and kissed him on the forehead, just below that unruly mop of curls.

"Thanks, Mandy," she said. "Is there any way of reaching you, if we need to? All the phone systems are out."

He reached into the rear of the vehicle and handed her a portable radio. "It's already set to the right frequency," he said. "Just holler if you need anything."

"I think you'll be too busy to worry about us." Rebecca smiled.

"You take care now," he said. "Go and hide somewhere nice and deep in that little submarine of yours."

Rebecca hugged Xena tightly as Manderson headed back up the motorway. Toward Albany.

Toward the fog.

KAITIAKITANGA

Private Shaw deposited them on the red gravel driveway of the house nestled into the bush, and said goodbye with a regulation wave.

Tane wondered where she was going to and hoped it was south, away from the fog.

The house was silent. The enveloping trees blocked the dwindling light of the fading sun, spreading longer finger-like shadows across the weatherboards and giving it a forlorn, moody appearance.

A note on the front door explained the silence. *Gone to Waitakere Marae.*

Like many others, his dad and mum had sought a place of refuge in uncertain times.

"I'll get the car." Tane unlocked the front door and opened the garage door for the others to enter. His mum's car, a bright red Volkswagen, occupied the left of the garage. There was a larger space for his dad's Jeep, but it was not there.

The spare keys to the VW were on the hook inside the pantry, and Tane tossed them to Fatboy.

Rebecca sat silently in the back, playing hand games with Xena.

"Do you think that Crowe and his men, and the army, will be able to hold back the fog?" Tane eventually asked the question that was on all of their minds.

"They don't know how," Rebecca answered, and there was something about the way she said it that made Tane turn around and look closely at her for a moment.

"Do you?" he asked.

Rebecca didn't answer, but she didn't deny it.

"Rebecca," Fatboy said gently, "is there a way to stop the antibodies? To defeat the macrophages?"

"I don't know," Rebecca said, shaking her head. "It's just something that was in one of the messages. I'm not sure."

"What!" Tane was flabbergasted. Xena put her hands over her eyes and peeked out from between her fingers.

Tane desperately tried to remember the content of the last message. Or was it something in an earlier message, one that they had failed to decipher?

Fatboy said, "Rebecca, try to remember. You are talking about the lives of hundreds of thousands, millions, maybe billions of people."

She was silent. Fatboy and Tane looked at each other in growing concern.

"Come on, Rebecca," Tane said lightly. "Let's be heroes and save the world!"

She just said, with a weariness that filled the small car

around them like a black shroud, "I think the world is doing a pretty good job of saving itself at the moment."

She said no more after that.

They came down out of the mountains and headed south toward the Marae.

The road they were traveling had been the scene of a battle. The aftermath was everywhere. A battle of desperate people, trying to force their way along one of the main feeder roads to the Northwestern Motorway. Earlier in the day, this road must have been jammed solid with cars. Broken-down or fuelless vehicles were shunted haphazardly onto the verges. A few sat in the center of the road, and they had to drive carefully around them. Most showed signs of damage.

When Rebecca finally spoke again, it was to say, "I'm hungry."

Tane realized then that they hadn't eaten all day.

"Want a Big Mac?" he asked, seeing a McDonald's sign ahead of them and trying to be funny.

She just sighed tiredly and said, "It won't be open."

Of course it wouldn't be open. That was the point of his joke, which didn't seem at all funny now.

The light was on, the great golden *M* glowing like an ancient tribal beacon down the road before them. The crew must have left in a hurry and forgotten to turn the sign off. There was no way it was going to be open.

It was open.

With an expression of disbelief, Fatboy pulled into the drive-through.

"Can I please take your order?" a bright young girl in a blue McDonald's uniform asked from behind the small window.

"A Big Mac," Fatboy said cautiously. "Two Big Macs. Combos. What are you having, Tane?"

"Same same."

"Make that three."

"Certainly, sir," the girl said cheerfully. Her tag said her name was Helen. "Would you like to upsize those to a super-combo?"

Fatboy stared blankly at her for a moment. "All right," he said.

She took his offered money and said, "Please drive on to the next window."

The young man at the next window handed them their food, and as they pulled out, Tane and Fatboy looked at each other in amazement.

The whole transaction had been so utterly commonplace that for a moment Tane wondered if he was dreaming the rest of it all, the fog, the antibodies, and that the normalcy, the *insanity* of the fast-food outlet was really the reality, in an insane world.

But they passed a number of boarded-up houses, eyes peering suspiciously out at them through gaps in the planks, and the nightmare proved to be real once again.

The world is doing a pretty good job of saving itself.

Even in these strangest and most desperate of times, some Maori protocol was observed. As a pakeha—a non-Maori—Rebecca needed permission from the tribal elders to enter the sacred ground of the Maori meeting ground. That duly came, although they dispensed with the traditional welcome. There was some discussion over Xena, but she, also, was eventually allowed to trot along beside Rebecca, holding her hand.

His father and mother were in the big meeting hall along with at least a hundred others of the tribe. Tane was acutely aware that Rebecca was the only pakeha there.

It was a tall, timbered, high-roofed hall, lined with traditional carvings, representations of their ancestors. It was dim inside, even under normal circumstances, but now the meager light of the white-hatted electric bulbs scattered around the ceiling was swallowed up by the black plastic sheeting that was taped around each of the windows.

It might stop the fog, Tane thought, but it wouldn't stop *them*.

His mother screamed when she saw them. A mixture of fear, delight, and relief. She hugged Tane, and his father hugged Fatboy just as fiercely. Then she hugged Fatboy and Tane's father embraced him. Both his parents were crying and trying to talk about visits from the police and the fog all at once. Then his mother hugged Rebecca, and after an initial hesitation Rebecca's arms crept around his mother and held on tightly for a surprisingly long time.

Xena scrambled over to a chair at the side of the hall. A group of children surrounded her, laughing and playing with her.

After a few moments, the outpouring of emotion started to get a bit uncomfortable for Tane, but it was still another ten minutes before he could get a word in.

Rebecca joined them then, and his dad made a small circle of chairs at one end of the hall for them to sit in.

The others ignored them, lost in their own soft conversations and dramas.

Over the next hour, as the twilight dripped away into darkness, they told his father and mother everything. They started with Lake Sunnyvale and left out nothing of importance up to their trip home with Private Shaw.

There was silence for a long while after that. The light from the bulbs skimmed across the faces of the carvings cleaving deep shadows out of the somber expressions.

Fatboy and Tane knew not to speak, and Rebecca seemed to have nothing to say.

His dad drew in a long slow breath after a while and looked deeply into each of their eyes in turn.

The silence lengthened until Tane broke it. "There are places for you on the submarine. You can hide out with us until the fog passes over."

His father looked at his mother, and Tane saw a small shake of the head pass between them. His father gestured around at the room. Children jumped and danced around the chimpanzee, with happy faces, unknowing of the terror that approached. A young couple with a newborn baby sat, just out of earshot, lost in each other and the child. Three old women, dressed in black with matching black headscarves, sat a few feet away, toothlessly chewing up every word.

"You would have us leave, and yet our family, our *whanau*, stay?" His father shook his head.

Tane said heavily, "Then you must run. The meeting hall won't protect you."

Fatboy said, "Get every car you can get, or buses if you can find them. Load everyone up and head south as fast and as far as you can."

"It's a sturdy old building," his father said doubtfully.

"We have seen these creatures up close," Tane said, struggling to stop himself from crying out in exasperation. "You have to run, or everyone here will die!"

His father closed his eyes. His mother reached out and took his hand in hers.

His father asked, "Can this thing be stopped? Now that it has started?"

Tane shook his head uncertainly, but Fatboy nodded.

"Rebecca thinks there may be a way," he said.

They all looked at her, her eyes on the floor, her shoulders hunched as if carrying a heavy load. She was, Tane thought. She had been carrying her burden for too long now.

"Maybe it's for the best. From a purely scientific point of view," she said, "once we humans are gone, this planet will be able to heal itself, and then when it is healthy once again, maybe in millions of years' time, the human race can start over. Like a forest fire, cleaning out the congestion and decay, so new life can sprout amid the ashes."

Tane started to argue, but his father held up a hand for silence. "You really believe we are a disease," he said.

Rebecca stared at the floor. "A biologist would describe us as a plague."

There was a piano against the far wall of the hall, near the entrance. Xena struggled for a moment with Rebecca to be let loose, and then ran across to the piano, with a crowd of children trailing her like the tail of a comet. She jumped up onto the seat and began to hammer tunelessly at the keys. She looked around as if expecting applause.

His father stood and crossed to Rebecca. He placed a hand under her chin and lifted her head up to meet his. "Maybe in this new age, what you say has some truth, but it was not always so."

"I know," Rebecca responded, a tear welling up in the corner of her eye.

His father watched her silently for a moment.

"Do you understand the meaning of 'Kaitiakitanga'?" he asked.

She shook her head. "Not really."

His father smiled. "You pakeha believe that land belongs to people. But we Maori believe that people belong to the land. We are *tangata whenua*—people of the land. It is our privilege, not our right, and with it comes a great responsibility: Kaitiakitanga."

All were silent now, watching his father. Tane found his eyes wandering around the carvings of the ancestors that guarded the walls of the meeting house. He had a very real sense that they were watching him back.

His father said, "For thousands of years, we Maori have guarded and protected our environment. Replenished and replaced what we used. But then the pakeha came to our land. We *kaitiaki* who should have stood up to the pakeha, who should have defended Papatuanuku—the Earth Mother—did not. Our voices fell silent."

"Then you agree," Rebecca said slowly. "Mankind must be destroyed before it destroys its host."

"No." His father's voice was soft, little more than the breath of an infant, and yet somehow carried such intensity that the carvings of the ancestors seemed to quiver and come to life, carrying his words to all corners of the room. "We are a part of nature, creatures of Papatuanuku. Greed and stupidity are the disease, not us."

The rest of the room had gathered around now, listening to the conversation.

"We can't go back!" Rebecca cried out against him. "You cannot reverse a mutation. Human beings can't go back to living in villages and farming *kumara*!"

"We cannot." His father smiled sadly. "But we can learn

to live with the trees and the lakes, the mountains and the seas, the fish and the animals, as family, as *whanau,* not as invaders, conquerors!"

There was a silence, and a breeze crept into the hall from outside, rustling the black plastic sheeting and reminding Tane that time was growing short.

"What can we do?" he asked quietly.

"What you know you must do," his father said, and repeated it. "What you know you must."

He sighed. "We live in a Western society, so we adopt Western ways, but we have never forgotten our culture."

"I have," Tane said painfully. "I have forgotten."

My people. My culture. My whakapapa.

His father was silent for a moment. "No, son. You are Tane Williams, son of Rangitira Williams, grandson of Hemi Te Awa of the great Tuhoe tribe of Aotearoa. You have not forgotten your *whakapapa,* because you cannot forget. You have merely closed your eyes for a moment. And now they are open." He placed a hand on Tane's shoulder. "You will face this challenge, find a way to defeat it, then show the rest of the world's people the way forward. The way of the *kaitiaki.*

"You will lead the people, all of the world's people, into a new age. Te Kenehi Tuarua—the second genesis. You must teach the ways of *kaitiakitanga* if the world is to survive. We must all become *kaitiaki.*"

He turned from Tane and addressed the room, "They call me a disease, but I am not. I am a child of the land. I am *tangata whenua.* I am a spiritual guardian of the Earth Mother. I am *kaitiaki!*"

There was a silence, and Tane felt that ancient spirits were repeating his father's words, whispering them to one another.

Fatboy rose and placed his hand on his father's arm. From an inside pocket in his jacket, he produced the *patu pounamu*, the greenstone club their parents had given each of them at Christmas. He pressed it against his heart. "Neither am I an illness. I am *tangata whenua*. I am *kaitiaki*."

There was a murmuring amongst the gathered crowd that subsided only when Tane rose, a little awkwardly, to his feet. He spoke quietly but his voice was clear.

"I, too, am *tangata whenua*. I am *kaitiaki*." The room seemed to fade into blackness around him, and he looked only into the face of his father.

"I am Maori."

NEW YEAR'S EVE

The first whispering tendrils of mist crept over the ridges of the Albany hills just after nine p.m., sifting down through the tree blanket or slithering down the main highway that cut through the bush of the hillside.

It was New Year's Eve. The last day of the year. Some said the last day of all years.

That might be true, Crowe thought, watching the mist creep toward him on the video monitor, if they couldn't stop it here and now.

The mist flowed up to and over the camera, a small metal box stuck in the middle of the highway, near the top of the hill, turning everything to white. He switched to another camera, about halfway up the hill, and saw the mist just starting to writhe around a corner of the highway, far ahead.

In addition to the ground cameras, they had three helicopters operating, well above the puffy cumulus top of the fog, feeding images back to the control center.

Crowe picked up a radio. "The fog has crossed the hill-top," he said tersely. "Time to light it up."

Around him, the control center, just three hundred feet behind their main defensive line, was buzzing with activity. NZ Army and SAS officers were barking orders, running here and there, answering phones and radios. The battle for Auckland was commencing.

Lucy Southwell's voice came back to him on the radio. She sounded scared but calm. "Stony, we've had a lot of problems trying to evacuate Auckland. We are still trying to get people out. You have got to stop that fog, or at least slow it down. If it keeps going at the rate it's going, hundreds of thousands of people are going to die!"

Crowe turned and looked at Manderson standing next to him but said nothing.

Manderson smiled. "Let's show these fluffy white teddy bears who they're messing with."

Flight Lieutenant John Ramirez was already in the cockpit of his FA18 Super Hornet fighter-bomber with the canopy sealed when the order came through his headset. He acknowledged immediately and gave a brief wave to the ground staff who were preparing for takeoff. The rest of his wing were already lowering their canopies and would follow him off the deck at intervals of just a few seconds.

The USS *Abraham Lincoln* was sailing a steady fifteen knots into the light breeze, to assist with the takeoffs. Once airborne, the flight to Auckland would take less than ten minutes.

On a hand signal from outside, he fired up his engines, turning night into day behind the jet, but held in place still by the steely grasp of the aircraft carrier.

All the planes had names. Some of the pilots named their planes after girls, like in the old bomber days. There was the *Mary-Lou* and the *Barbara-Ann*. Others gave their planes macho names, full of bravado, like *Sky Warrior* or *Grim Reaper*.

Ramirez's plane was *Deus ex Machina*. Most of his fellow pilots had no idea what it meant. Some thought it was Hispanic, like Ramirez. It wasn't Spanish, though; it was Greek. *Deus ex Machina*. The God from the Machine.

Ramirez had majored in literature. In the ancient Greek plays, the hero would often get himself into all sorts of drama and strife, only to have it all solved, just in the nick of time, by a god, who would be lowered onto the stage by an elaborate piece of equipment. The God from the Machine would intervene, just when all looked lost, and save the day for the hero.

That was his role, Ramirez felt, and he had named his plane for it. When ground troops were under threat, his wing of close ground-support fighter-bombers would be called in to save the day.

Today he had a mixture of high-explosive and incendiary napalm bombs attached under his wings. Someone, or something, was in for a very hot time in Auckland tonight.

The launch officer raised a hand above his head, then brought it sweeping down. Ramirez punched in his afterburners as the launch wire exploded forward, catapulting the fighter down the short runway of the carrier.

The acceleration rammed him back in his seat. It was a volatile adrenaline thrill that no roller-coaster ride could ever come close to simulating. He would miss it, he thought, when he was too old to fly and rotated off onto some boring desk job somewhere.

The edge of the carrier flashed past, and the plane dipped fractionally, then caught itself and he arced upward to the left. The other five planes of his wing were off the deck in quick succession, forming up on his wing tips. The six planes seemed as one as they banked around toward the dark coast ahead of them.

Tell me your troubles, Ramirez thought, *confess me your sins, for here comes the God from the Machine.*

Fatboy's motorcycle was still parked on the gray concrete pad by the side of the house, where he had left it that morning. Had it been just one day? Tane realized that it had. It seemed like an eternity of time had passed since Fatboy had set out with the Chronophone.

The house was in darkness, except, unsurprisingly, for the flickering blue glow from an upstairs window.

They had driven back from the Marae in his dad's Jeep Cherokee. The roads were increasingly impassable, and the sturdy four-wheel-drive Jeep seemed like a better bet if they had to go across fields or shoulder other vehicles out of the way.

Rebecca hadn't said a word the entire trip. She had just sat there, thinking. Tane felt that she was making a momentous decision and left her alone to make it.

His own mind was filled with the image of his mother and father, standing at the carved wooden gates of the Marae, facing the fear, facing an uncertain future, in the embrace of their people, their *whanau.* He wondered if he would ever see them again and thought that he would not.

They entered the house quietly, so as not to alarm Rebecca's mum.

Rebecca's room was unchanged from when they had left

it. The hole in the wall where the window used to be, the torn drapes, and the glass and wood splinters spread throughout the room. Even the paper was still on the printer.

```
FTBYDNTGO.WTRBLSTMPS.DSVLETHM.
SLTABS.DNTABSRB.
```

Rebecca looked at the message a long time, and finally sighed. "MPs, macrophages. ABs are antibodies."

"Water blast," Tane said. "High-pressure water."

"I think so," Rebecca said. "The macrophages are made of some kind of spongy tissue. Bullets don't affect them; they just punch straight through. But a pressurized jet of water would cut them to pieces and dissolve them."

"SLT?" Fatboy asked.

"My guess is salt," Rebecca replied. "I thought it meant that the antibodies can't absorb salt, but that makes no sense. But what we do know is that if you crush an antibody, it just gets absorbed back into the mist. Then the mist probably just makes a new one. So no matter how many you destroy, there are just as many attacking you a few minutes later."

"But salt stops them being absorbed," Tane worked out slowly.

"It's only a guess. But I suspect that salt, on that slimy surface, would alter the chemical structure of the creature, and that would stop it being absorbed."

Fatboy said, "So once you kill them, they stay dead!"

"Something like that."

Fatboy said, "We need to tell Crowe."

"What about the Chronophone?" Rebecca asked.

Tane asked, "What about the *Möbius*?"

"I can get back to the Skytower and install the

Chronophone," Fatboy said. "I'll be able to squeeze into the city on the bike."

"No," Rebecca said. "I think you should both go to the Skytower. That has to take priority. I'll try and raise Crowe on the portable radio."

"Do you think he'll listen?" Tane said.

She just shrugged.

There was a long drawn-out scream from the skies above them, rising, then dropping away as the sound passed overhead.

Xena screeched in fright and leaped into Rebecca's arms. Rebecca looked up. "What was that?"

"A jet," Tane said, "moving fast."

"More than one," Fatboy said. "Sounded like fighters."

"Oh crap," Tane breathed. "It's already started."

As if to confirm his analysis, a sound of distant thunder rolled in from the north. Through the smashed window, the skies lit up with brilliant flashes.

"They're bombing the hell out of something," Fatboy said.

"We're all out of time," Rebecca whispered. "We've got to get moving. We may already be too late."

"I'll get the Chronophone," Fatboy said. "Tane, find me a backpack of some kind to put it in. Rebecca, you've got to take the Jeep. Get to the Devonport Navy Base, find the submarine. I don't imagine it will be difficult to spot. Bring it across the harbor and we'll meet you down by the waterfront, at, say, the end of Princes Wharf. That's easy to find from the sea. On the way, try to raise Crowe on the radio."

"What about Mum?" Rebecca asked quietly.

"Take her with you. You can explain about her new home on the way."

Her new home. A little tin tube on the floor of the ocean.

Fatboy raced out to the Jeep to get the Chronophone and Rebecca disappeared upstairs.

Tane opened a few cupboards, trying to remember where he had seen Rebecca's schoolbag, a black backpack.

He had found it by the time Fatboy came in with the silver briefcase.

"Have we got time to run a test?" Tane asked.

"No. Where's Rebecca?"

"Still upstairs with her mum," Tane replied.

"Go and hurry them up. She's got to get moving."

Before he could move, he heard Rebecca's voice, shrieking from above them.

Tane bounded up the stairs and down the hallway to Rebecca's mother's room. The door was wide open.

The television was on. Helicopter camera shots showed the fog creeping over the top of the Albany hills. The view cut to the black silhouettes of warplanes streaking overhead, just visible in the moonlight, then back to the hillside. Massive explosions rocked the camera, and the whole hillside shook in front of their eyes. Rivers of fire exploded in the treetops as breathless reporters tried to explain in voice-overs what was happening.

"Mum!" Rebecca shrieked once again. "You have to come with us. Now!"

"Don't be silly," her mother replied calmly, her eyes glued to the images of fire and fog. "This is the news. This is important."

Tane looked out the window. The sky to the north was ablaze, massive tongues of flames leaping up into the black air from the conflagration on the ground. There were more flashes, more thunder, and he saw the silver flash of a jet caught for a second in the moonlight.

Rebecca turned to Tane in anguish. "She won't come!"

"I'll get Fatboy," Tane said calmly. "We'll carry her out."

Rebecca had one last try. "Mum, if you stay here, you will die!"

"Ssshh," her mum said irritably. "I can't hear what they're saying."

"I'll get Fatboy," Tane said again, turning to go.

"No." Rebecca's hand was on his arm. "No. We don't have the time."

Her legs seemed to be unsteady, and Tane put his arm around her shoulders to support her.

She slowly backed out of the room, one small footstep after another, her eyes never leaving her mother, washed in the soft light from the television set.

Tane, by her side, had no words of comfort.

Rebecca said again, her voice just starting to crack, "We don't have the time."

THE BATTLE FOR
AUCKLAND

Tane rode on the back of Fatboy's motorcycle with the cool night breeze on his face and the touch of Rebecca on his lips.

She had been strangely calm as they had come down the stairs from her mother's room. Strangely accepting.

Fatboy had given him the backpack containing the Chronophone and handed him a spare helmet, but before he could put it on, Rebecca had been in his arms, her hands around his neck.

She wasn't crying. In fact, she had seemed stronger, more determined than before. She had spoken quietly, her lips right next to his ear. "What I said this morning, about not knowing you, it wasn't true. I wanted to hurt you. I was angry."

After a moment's hesitation, Tane had put his hands on her arms.

He'd said, "You were right to be angry. I was stupid."

"You weren't stupid; you were hurt. I knew that and I should have accepted it."

Tane had started to say something, but she had put a finger on his lips to hush him.

She'd said, "I've known you all my life. I've always known you. I will always know you. But I'm not strong."

Tane began, "You're the strongest—"

She hushed him again and said, "I'm not strong. But you make me strong."

Then her lips had brushed in passing against his, and the engine of the Jeep had roared and she was gone.

Tane had looked up a little guiltily at Fatboy, but there was no anger on his brother's face, just a quiet smile.

I will always know you.

For the first time, right then, it had occurred to Tane that he might never see her again.

The engine of the Harley gave its usual throaty chuckle, and Fatboy swerved in between two deserted cars and up the motorway on-ramp, heading toward the city.

The motorway was clogged with cars, all of them deserted. The owners, unable to go forward or backward, had simply left their vehicles and their belongings and either started walking south or had gone back to their homes.

Fatboy had to pick his path carefully. The cars ramming their way down the motorway had not kept in nice straight lanes but had zigged and zagged all over the road.

A couple of times they found themselves in a dead end in the maze of vehicles and had to get off and push the heavy bike backward in order to try a different route.

It was eleven o'clock by the time they made it as far as spaghetti junction—the main motorway interchange.

The going was easier after that. Most of the traffic was

heading south. Heading back north into the city, there were fewer cars. Bigger gaps. They made good time up between the lines of abandoned vehicles.

Not entirely abandoned.

From more than a couple of cars, frightened faces stared out at them as they glided past. Either not knowing what to do or too afraid to do it, or both.

As they got closer, they could see several small fires burning in the city center.

Once they were off the motorway and into the city, the avalanche of abandoned cars disappeared. This was the northern side of the city. Anyone in their right minds was on the southern side, trying to get on the Southern Motorway.

As they came off the flyover onto Nelson Street, a gang of drunken youths in a brand-new Mercedes convertible swung out of the darkness and tried to sideswipe them.

A skinny kid standing up on the backseat threw a bottle at them, but it just shattered on the road behind them.

Fatboy calmly accelerated away from them, swerving around abandoned vehicles, the side pegs scraping on the ground. The Mercedes engine roared as it gave chase.

A bus was parked sideways across the road at the intersection with Victoria Street, and two cars were tangled together in a smash on the other side of it. Fatboy gunned the bike through the gap, and Tane heard a satisfying screech of brakes behind them as the driver of the Mercedes realized his car couldn't fit where the bike could.

A small block of shops was burning fiercely just across the road from the Skytower, the flames brighter than the surrounding streetlights, burning back the darkness of the central city street. Looters, or vandals, Tane thought. It seemed that antibodies and macrophages were not the only dangers in Auckland city this night.

Left unattended, the fire would quickly spread to nearby buildings, and the whole city center could soon be ablaze. A massive funeral pyre for Auckland. But even as they swung around the corner by the entrance to the Skytower casino, they could see red flashing lights arriving from the opposite direction and a fire engine rolled smoothly to a stop in the middle of the road. It was a pumper, with a roof-mounted water nozzle. The crew quickly and efficiently set to work.

Fatboy pulled the Harley up outside the main doors to the casino. The huge glass doors were shut, and a quick shake by Tane ascertained that they were locked as well.

The casino never shut. But it was shut now. Inside, only the massive water feature, a thin sheet of water cascading two stories down a sheer glass plate, showed any signs of life. The lights that never went out, were out. The gaming rooms above them were silent.

Tane got back on and Fatboy gunned the bike past the busy fire crew, around the corner, and down the concrete ramp into the underground car park.

The barrier arms were down, but the Harley squeezed past, just, and Fatboy kicked down the stand of the bike right outside the main elevators.

"We have to go up to the lobby," he said, "then down the escalator to the base of the Skytower itself."

"I hope the elevators are still working," Tane said.

And they were.

The radio produced nothing but static.

Manderson had said it was tuned to the right frequency, but when she pressed the CALL button and released it, all she got was a loud squawk. Had they knocked the frequency knob somehow? She desperately tried every setting on the radio as she drove, her eyes flicking between the road and the radio. What she had to tell them would help; it might even turn the battle. But only if they had enough time to use the information.

It was slow going. It wasn't far to the naval base, as the crow flies, and if she'd had a boat, she could have cut straight across the harbor and been there in a matter of minutes.

But traveling by road meant heading north and then cutting back east through Greenhithe and Albany. And that proved to be a circuitous maze of blocked roads.

She played with the knobs on the radio as she maneuvered the Jeep through the constricted streets, and by the time she had reached the motorway overpass, she had managed to get through to the command center.

It was Manderson who answered the radio. "I thought I told you to hide away somewhere nice and deep," he drawled.

Rebecca stopped on the overpass and looked north toward the upper harbor highway. Along its length, Rebecca could see lights moving, vehicles, and soldiers with flashlights. There was no second line of defense. The line was just too long. It stretched from the beach at Mairangi Bay along through Albany and Greenhithe, all the way out to West Harbor.

If the line was breached, then Auckland was lost.

A flight of jets screamed just over her head, and the hillside in the distance, already blazing, flared like the sun for a brief second. A shock wave rattled the car windows a moment later. In that flash, though, she saw the reason for all the activity around her. The terror of Auckland.

In the flash of the incendiary bombs, she saw the long white cloud of the fog, stretching down the hillside, engulfing the North Harbor stadium and rolling forward toward them.

"I have to talk to Stony," she said urgently.

"He's busy," Manderson said. "If we don't stop this fog, or at least slow it down for a few hours, Auckland is going to become the biggest catastrophe the world has ever seen."

"I can help," Rebecca insisted.

"He really is too busy. We've had lab results come in on the chemical composition of the fog, so there's a lot of pressure to come up with some answers."

Rebecca could see that arguing was just going to waste a lot of time and produce no result. She said instead, "You can't shoot them. The . . . creatures."

"We know," Manderson said curtly.

"You can't shoot them and you can't blow them up."

"Not true. We've been knocking the stuffing out of those things for the last half hour. Claymore mines, rockets, mortars, you name it, we're chucking it at them."

"Hasn't stopped them coming, though, has it," Rebecca remarked.

"What are you saying?"

"You blow them up and the fog just reclaims them. They just get absorbed back, and the fog starts building another one. All you're doing is slowing them down."

There was a silence on the other end of the radio as Manderson thought about that. "You got a solution, or just a problem."

Rebecca said, "You need water, and lots of it. Water blasters. Fire hoses, if you can get them. They're soft. High-pressure water will cut right through them, and the water dissolves the material they're made of. It'll just run away into storm water drains and out into the ocean. That's the other thing. Salt. Spray salt, or even salt water on them and it alters the chemical structure of their bodies. Antib . . . the small ones as well as the big ones."

Manderson smiled and said, "You call them what you like. Are you sure about this?"

"Pretty much. Have you got any better suggestions?"

Mandy just said, "You just get somewhere safe. I'll get your information to the boss. He'll listen to me."

Rebecca said, "I hope so."

Tane and Fatboy emerged from the top of the last flight of stairs and stumbled out onto the observation deck of the Skytower. The tower elevators had been locked down. Protected by touch-pad security panels to which they did not know the combinations. The alternative was the stairs, and even that door had been locked, but a set of chairs had made a worthwhile battering ram, and they had been up the first flight in record time.

By the time they had reached the twentieth flight, the vigor was gone and it had just become a long hard slog. Made harder by the thought that this was just the start of the journey up to the peak of the tower. Fatboy took the heavy Chronophone, for which Tane was incredibly grateful. Even on the motorcycle, it had cut into his shoulders through the narrow nylon straps of Rebecca's schoolbag. Climbing twenty stories with that weight on your back seemed impossible, yet Fatboy carried it indefatigably.

From the observation deck, they could see the entire central city, the darkness, the scattered fires burning in vacant buildings. Here and there, the lights of a car roamed the urban wasteland.

In the north, across the harbor and behind a dark ridge in the distance, the furious fires of technology were burning against the inexorable forces of Mother Nature. The low clouds were punctuated again and again by the thunderclaps of bombs.

The moon was rising in the sky now, and from the height of the Skytower they could see the fog itself, smothering the hillside north of Albany. It stretched as far to the east, toward the east coast beaches, and as far to the west, toward West Harbor and Kumeu, as they could see.

It took them a while to find the next set of stairs, leading from the observation deck up to the Sky Deck, the upper observation deck. That door, fortunately, was not locked.

Tane offered to take the Chronophone up the next section, and to his surprise, Fatboy agreed. It must have been taking more out of him than Tane had thought. He hadn't complained, though.

The next ten flights of stairs were far more grueling with the weight on his back crushing down on his knees and his leg muscles with every step until finally they came out onto the Sky Deck.

Another door. Locked. Fatboy had brought a screwdriver and forced the lock with that. Tane shone a flashlight up inside the shaft. A metal ladder led straight upward.

The many flights of stairs had been lit by emergency lighting. Here there was none. The only light inside the narrow shaft was the dull glow of moonlight through the open door at the bottom of the ladders and from Tane's flashlight.

Fatboy lifted the backpack from his shoulders, and Tane breathed a small sigh of relief.

He gripped the ladder tightly. At least the staircases had been safe. Here it would take only one missed rung from one tired leg, and he would be lying at the bottom of the shaft with broken bones, or worse.

Above him Fatboy seemed as tireless as ever. Hand, foot, hand, foot. There seemed to be no end to the succession of metal rungs.

There was. But that only proved to be a small landing, and the start of the next ladder, on the opposite side of the shaft.

The sides of the Skytower were squeezing in on them all the time now as they neared the top.

Tane tried not to think too much of the last section. That would be the hardest. That was up another ladder. On the *outside* of the tower.

LINE OF FIRE

Ramirez looked down at the path of destruction from the height of his FA18 Super Hornet. The line of burning trees, scrub, even some houses, extended from the coast into the far distance. It was a line of golden fire, eating a ragged path across this darkened country.

Six wings of Tomcats, some thirty-six planes in all, had worked for hours to create the flaming barrier. A fence of fire to keep the deadly fog trapped on one side.

It hadn't worked entirely. The fog rolled up to and over the burning hilltop. But it did have some effect. To the north of the line of fire, he could see dense banks of fog rolled up into tight blankets, painted in silver by the light of the moon. To the south, the fog was a light haze, and streetlights and some buildings were vaguely visible through the light gauze curtain.

To the south of that were the busy lights and black shapes of the men and machinery of the defensive line. He wished them luck and even said a quick prayer for them. He was glad to be in the embracing seat of the *Deus ex Machina*, not dug into a hole in the dirt, waiting for the battle to arrive.

They had been ordered to stand off and to ascend, and now he saw why.

A river of dots showed up on his radar scope to the south, and when he sought visual confirmation, the moonlight showed a squadron of small aircraft approaching. They were just silver dots in the sky, too small to make out any features, but he knew what they would be from the radio traffic.

Just about every crop duster in the whole of the Waikato farming district, south of Auckland.

The fog was merely a few hundred yards from their line, Crowe realized. The massive searchlights mounted on the ridge behind him illuminated the front edge of the mist, making eerie patterns in the shifting clouds, in the darkness.

The moon helped, too, frosting the top of the mist and giving it a half-light glow.

Where the hell were those fire trucks?

Troopers had been dispatched to every fire station in the vicinity with orders to bring every machine they could find.

A smart supply sergeant had suggested a water blaster import company in West Auckland, and a small convoy of army supply trucks had been dispatched there immediately.

The first fire appliance arrived even as he was asking the question. A few more fire trucks, blood-red in the moonlight, were close on the heels of the first, and Crowe barked orders, positioning the trucks at intervals down the highway. They seemed few and far between.

A convoy of water tankers crested Sunset Ridge and made their way carefully down toward his position. Crowe swung up onto the running board of the first truck as it drew up near him.

"Seawater? You have a tank full of seawater?"

The trooper nodded. Crowe didn't ask where they had found the trucks and didn't much care. He jumped down and showed the trooper, with hand signals, where to go.

An explosion sounded, just over the highway. Then another, and another. The fog was getting closer and so were the blasts of the claymore mines as the creatures passed in front of their sensors. A new sound now. A low buzz from the sky. Many moving stars to the south. That would be the crop dusters, loaded, not with fertilizers or herbicides, but with water.

Salt. Water. Salt water. If they survived this long night, he was going to see that that girl got some kind of medal. They could make her the prime minister if they wanted; he'd support it. If she was right about the water, and the salt, then that might just turn the battle in their favor.

He hoped she was right. She could be right. It made scientific sense. But then, when you thought too hard about it, so did her explanation for the jellyfish and the snowmen. Certainly they had not yet come up with any other explanation for them. He shook his head violently, trying to shake out the ideas. Four of his men were dead. He wasn't going to let her call them germs.

• • •

Rebecca was less than ten miles from Devonport when she realized that she was not going to be able to get through. Devonport was at the end of a long peninsula, stretching from the North Shore like a finger pointing across the harbor. The road had clearly clogged up early in the day, and both sides of it were choked solid with empty vehicles.

She had avoided the motorway and come down the coast, on Beach Road. There had been fewer abandoned cars and blockages along that route, but here at Takapuna there was no way through. The center of the town was a tangled web of metal.

She stopped in the middle of the road, alongside a shiny silver Porsche sports car. A large theater complex, the Bruce Mason Center, lay to her right. To her left, a series of tall towers, apartment blocks, dominated the smaller shops and terraced houses on the other side of the street and the side roads.

Lights were on in many of the apartments. People who had been unable to escape and had decided to just wait it out.

The upper two floors were alive with light. People congregating as high as they could, she thought, hoping to get above the fog.

"What do I do now, Xena?" she asked the chimp, who was curled up, apparently sleeping, on the passenger seat. "And why aren't you wearing your safety belt?"

Xena said nothing.

She couldn't get through. But she had to get through. If she couldn't, then Tane and Fatboy would be stranded on the waterfront as the fog rolled down from the north.

There was a chance that Crowe and the army would stop it, but she didn't want to count on that.

To her left, a side road led down to the Takapuna boat ramp and onto Takapuna Beach.

The beach!

She spun the wheel of the Cherokee and bulldozed the expensive little Porsche out of the way. Rubber shrieked and metal crunched, and sparks began flying off something underneath the car, but then it was to one side and she was flying down the side road.

A trailer-sailer had been abandoned at the bottom of the boat ramp, but the nose of the Jeep turned that into matchsticks. The big tires dug into the sand, and she was moving once again toward Devonport. Toward the navy base and the *Möbius*. Toward sanctuary.

The tide was out and the hard-packed sand above the waterline made for easier going than the soft white sand at the top of the beach.

Rebecca kept her speed as fast as she dared on the beach, in the dark, not wanting to run into any driftwood or rocks, partially buried in the sand, that might damage the big tires, or throw the Jeep off balance.

Jeeps were made for this kind of driving, though, and it was almost a cruise until she got to the end of the beach and the rocky point that separated Takapuna Beach from the next bay beyond.

She gingerly let the wheels of the Cherokee pick their way up through the rocks, hoping that the Jeep's clearance would be high enough to pass over some of the larger rocks between her wheels.

There were harsh scraping sounds from underneath, but she kept moving forward. Then she was up over the crest of the point and bouncing over boulders down toward the sand on the other side.

• • •

Tane surveyed the battle from the ladder above the crow's nest, a sturdy ring of metal around the outside of the Skytower; it seemed to Tane no more wide or stable than a tightrope.

The countryside was alight. The fire was spreading, and the fog disappeared in those brightly burning patches. But all around the flames the whiteness gathered, moving always southward.

Looking to the south, they could still see long lines of taillights of thousands of cars, buses, and army trucks, jammed in a desperate race to get out of the city.

They hadn't counted on the wind. It was gusting now, in from the sea, not in a steady breeze that they could counter by leaning into, but in irregular puffs, sudden gusts that wrenched at their hands and tried to knock them from the ladder.

Technicians did climb this ladder. But they did so on calm days, with safety harnesses. Tane and Fatboy had no harnesses. And this was not calm. Or even daytime.

Already they were ten yards above the crow's nest. Around them now was a forest of satellite dishes and aerials, some large, some small.

Tane went up the ladder, shining a torch on the serial numbers stenciled in large black letters on the base of each dish. Fatboy was fastening the Chronophone to the metal grid of the crow's nest by winding some strong wire through loops built into the corners of the case.

The wind tore at him again, and he lost the grip of one hand, clutching desperately with his other hand and winding one knee around the ladder until the gust subsided.

He looked down and saw Fatboy spread-eagled over the

top of the Chronophone. He got up, though, and nodded to show he was okay.

A few yards more and Tane found the dish they were looking for. It was massive. He didn't need to check the number; he had memorized that long ago.

"How the hell are we going to realign that monster?" he shouted over another gust of wind.

"No worries." Fatboy climbed up to him and passed him the end of a black cable. An identical cable was already plugged into the base of the satellite dish. Tane tried to unplug it, then realized that there was a round silver ring that had to be unscrewed first.

He let the original cable hang loose from its fastenings on the side of the tower and plugged their cable in its place, tightening up the silver ring until he could tighten it no more.

Fatboy was just below him now, and Tane swung to the side, hooking his leg around, hanging off the thin edge of a narrow metal ladder, hundreds of yards above the ground, to let his brother past.

Fatboy produced a ratchet wrench from a pocket in his leather jacket and fitted it onto a nut on the base of the dish.

"Watch the numbers," he shouted, the wind whipping his words out into the void around them.

The dish was calibrated. There were two adjustment bolts—one to control up and down, and one for left and right.

Tane looked down at the coordinates written on the back of his hand and watched as the mouth of the dish began to climb skyward.

"That's it!" he called when the red line matched perfectly with the correct white line.

Fatboy moved the wrench to the other bolt, almost dropped it, but regathered it in time, and began to turn.

"Try the other way," Tane yelled.

The dish began to align itself.

They were almost home.

FATEFUL LIGHTNING

Manderson's tall frame jutted out from the foxhole to his right. Next to him, a fire crew, outfitted in biosuits, manned a couple of hoses in front of their truck. The rest of Crowe's men were spread along the side of the highway to his left. He had asked for volunteers from the Green, Orange, and Yellow Teams, and forty of the forty-eight members of those teams had flown in since the Christmas Day disaster, joining Red and Blue Teams, now dug in along the highway.

Already the streetlamps along the highway were clouded. They were on the edge of the mist.

Crowe raised his weapon. Not his usual XM8, but a common industrial water blaster. The gas-powered engine throbbed away behind him.

He made sure the setting was on its highest power and tried a short burst. The jet of water shot clear across the highway. Up and down the line, there were occasional bursts as other troopers tried out theirs.

Overhead, the tiny shapes of the crop dusters circled, waiting for instructions from the command center.

Crowe didn't want to use them, possibly his most potent weapon, until he was sure of his targets.

The streetlights disappeared into the thickening fog, yellow halos forming around the bright stars of the bulbs. The mist lapped at the edge of his foxhole, then drifted slowly down into it, wrapping around his legs and waist as he knelt in the shallow dugout.

The fear seemed to be a part of the mist. It was palpable, so real that he thought he would choke on it. He wanted to turn, jump out of the hole, and run for his life back down the motorway toward the city.

There was something about the mist that went beyond the usual fear of going into combat. It held the fear of the unknown, and something else, too. It was impossible to describe. It was as if, not just his mind, but his very body was afraid of the mist. As if the cells that formed the structures of his being were quivering at the approach of the creeping fog.

But he could not run. This was it. This was the moment of truth for Auckland, and possibly for the human race. Right here. Right now.

Crowe knew that if he was feeling the terror, then the rest of his men, and the Kiwis ready to fight alongside them, would be feeling it, too.

A voice sounded in his earpiece, Manderson's voice. He turned. His friend was singing. The song was an old one. Once the stirring hymn that had led the soldiers of the North against the Confederates in the American Civil War and later the battle cry of U.S. soldiers in the First and Second World Wars: "The Battle Hymn of the Republic."

"Mine eyes have seen the glory of the coming of the Lord. He is trampling out the vintage where the grapes of wrath are stored. He hath loosed the fateful lightning of His terrible swift sword. His truth is marching on."

Other voices were joining in now, from up and down the line. First the rest of the USABRF agents in their black combat biosuits. Then a few hesitant Kiwi accents.

He switched on his throat mike and added his voice to the chorus.

"Glory, glory! Hallelujah! Glory, glory! Hallelujah! Glory, glory! Hallelujah! His truth is marching on."

The fog swirled up around them, and the first jellyfish struck out of the darkness before the chorus had finished. The hymn trailed off into a ragged end as the men slapped at the creatures, whose tentacles were writhing into the fabric of the biosuits.

They came straight out of the dark fog. No searching, no seeking. Guided missiles locked onto their targets, arrowing through the mist, their fine tentacles trailing behind them.

Men hammered at them, squashing them, wrenching them off the arms and bodies of their biosuits. The air was suddenly thick with the swarming creatures.

Crowe twisted the nozzle of his water blaster around to "spray" and pulled the trigger, aiming in the air above them. Five or six of the jellyfish dropped out of the air and began squirming on the ground in front of him. The surface, the skin, if that was what it was, of the creatures was fizzing and bubbling. That was the salt, Crowe realized.

"Take that, you bloodsuckers!" Manderson cried to his right.

Crowe tried another spray and sent an instruction to the crews of the fire engines.

More of the jellyfish dropped to the ground, and he saw the fire crew to his right raise one of their nozzles. A curtain of salty water appeared in front of them. A mist of their own.

The jellyfish were dropping and fizzing by the hundreds, perhaps thousands. The roadway in front of them was covered in them, wriggling for a few moments, then lying still.

The ones he had sprayed earlier were still there, he noted. The outer surface had hardened, calcified into a pale white shell. *They had not absorbed back into the mist!*

"Here they come!" someone called in his earpiece, and he strained his eyes to see the first of the snowmen lumbering out of the fog toward them. The noise they made was no longer a hiss. Here in the thinned-out mist, they moved more slowly and the sound was like that of wind around a house on a stormy night.

At first he saw just a few, gradually solidifying out of the mist. Then more appeared behind them; and more behind them. Suddenly they seemed to be everywhere, marching across the gray asphalt toward them.

"My God!" Manderson murmured.

"Water blasters hold till they are closer," Crowe ordered. "Hose crews, fire at will."

The fire hoses to his right swelled and burst forth in two heavy streams of seawater. Long wet arms that reached through the fog across the highway to the hordes of creatures that approached.

Where the high-pressure water struck, the snowmen exploded, great globs of their substance flying into the air.

Crowe watched as the closest of the creatures were all but cut in half by the saltwater jets from the fire hoses.

And yet still they marched forward.

Crowe keyed his throat mike. "Bring in the dusters, right down the highway. Right over our heads."

There was a roar above him as the first plane made its low-level run, just above the fog, and the mist intensified as the salty sea spray drifted down around and in front of them.

Clouds of jellyfish dropped down through the mist, piling up on the highway, but the snowmen still marched forward. Their skin, too, was shriveling and bubbling with the salt, but it did not halt them.

The fire hoses were sweeping back and forth, ripping the creatures to shreds, but the fire crews were spread too thinly.

"Water blasters, pick your targets," Crowe yelled. "Make it count!"

More tankers were already on their way, but the water was still a limited supply. Thank God, or thank Rebecca, for the salt, which prevented the fog from reclaiming its own.

A white, sluglike creature lurched toward him. Crowe sighted along the barrel of the black plastic and metal rod of the water blaster and squeezed the trigger.

The jet of water shot out, and he directed it across the chest of the creature. It punched a hole straight through the spongy material, and Crowe sawed the blade of water back and forth, cutting the creature into pieces. Manderson was doing the same.

This close, and in the lighter mist, Crowe finally came face to face with the enemy. He could see why the first to sight them had referred to them as snowmen. They looked like puffed-up human beings, inflated somehow from within, and covered in a white, gelatinous substance. They had faces, he realized. Almost human, with mouths, noses, and even eyes, but all formed from the same white spongy substance. The eyeballs, the eyelids, were white. The eyelids did not blink. The terror that had welled up in him before intensified, but he stood his ground.

He cut another couple of the creatures down, taking the legs off one and slicing through the neck of another.

The creatures dropped.

The jet from the fire hose swept across in front of him then, and the ragged line of snowmen faltered for the first time. Crowe hacked at the creatures with the blast of water from his weapon and found he was whooping with exhilaration.

They were winning. The line was holding!

"The mist is thickening," Manderson called, next to him.

"Get those fighters in here," Crowe shouted. "Close support. Light up the other side of the road, see if we can thin out the mist a little."

The fog was indeed thickening, he realized, and the creatures were starting to move faster. He ripped another couple apart. The mass of the creatures' flesh was filling the roadway. Overhead, the crop dusters swooped, covering the bodies of the creatures with brine, shriveling and fizzing.

Across the highway, lightning flashed and he ducked down into his foxhole for a moment as the shock wave of multiple explosions shook the ground around them.

Lucy Southwell's voice on the radio then, from the command center, three hundred feet behind the line.

"Crowe, this is Lucy. The evacuation is nearly complete, but we've lost all contact with the easternmost sections of the line."

"My God!" Manderson said for the second time that night, only this time it sounded like a prayer.

SILENCE IN THE MIST

Ramirez pulled up and watched below him as the last of his air-to-ground missiles impacted on the grassy strip, not even a hundred yards from where the troops cowered in their foxholes on the other side of the highway.

Now that was precision flying and precision targeting.

The crop dusters had left now, having exhausted their tanks. His aircraft were also out of bombs and missiles and were already heading back to the carrier to re-arm.

Ramirez alone remained over the battleground, circling, to feed information back to the carrier and to the troops on the ground.

The line was holding here at Albany, he saw, and also out to the west. But the east coast suburb of Mairangi Bay had been long swallowed by the dense white cloud, which had outskirted the defensive line, floating slowly out to sea and back in again behind it.

The frigates *Te Mana* and *Te Kaha* had been positioned

in the bay, against just such an eventuality, he knew, but the *Te Mana* was now resting, listing over, on the sands of Mairangi Bay beach, and the *Te Kaha* was slowly grinding itself to pieces on the rocks of the head land. There was no movement on board either vessel.

The fog, apart from the holdup at Albany and farther west, was pouring down the east coast of the North Shore, spreading out behind the defense force at Albany and chewing its way across the affluent suburbs of Castor Bay, Campbells Bay, Milford, and on to Takapuna and Devonport.

He risked a low pass over the highway, trying to see the troops on the ground, but the mist was too dense.

Rebecca pulled up off the sand onto the grassy verge alongside Cheltenham Beach and thought she was lucky to have made it.

Some of the rocky promontories between the bays had been almost impassable. If it were not for the low tide, it would have been impossible.

She gunned the engine up past the navy training center and around onto the main road. Glancing to her right at the intersection, she realized with horror that the mist was barely a few hundred yards away and crawling rapidly forward along the road.

Only a few cars blocked the road here, and she swung from side to side, weaving in and out of them, the fog, omnipresent in her rearview mirror.

The final stretch, alongside the Devonport Golf Club, was clear.

Xena had woken now, if she had actually been asleep and not just resting. She was quiet, though, watching Rebecca drive with wise eyes.

Rebecca skirted the base of Mount Victoria on the long looping road and accelerated down the deserted main street of Devonport.

At the wharf, she turned right, heading along the breakwater toward the naval base.

The barriers were down at the entrance to the base, which didn't surprise her. What did surprise her, and perhaps shouldn't have, was the armed guard who stepped out of the security booth and waved her to a halt, the pistol held ready for use in his right hand.

"No admittance," the guard said, not at all calmly. "This is a military area."

Another guard stepped out of the booth then, and he had an automatic rifle held at the ready.

"I have to get through," Rebecca said urgently. "I have orders from Doctor Crowe and Doctor Lucy Southwell."

"No admittance," the guard repeated.

"Get out of here," the other guard growled.

Xena screeched, alarming the guards, who had not noticed her until then.

"What the hell?" the first guard said, looking at Xena.

"Oh hell!" The second guard said, looking where Xena and Rebecca were looking.

The fog was rolling rapidly down the slope toward the sea, swallowing building after building as it came.

Two more of the nightmarish white creatures hurled themselves out of the ever-thickening fog. Crowe cut a diagonal slash across them with the jet from his water blaster and they fell.

The crop dusters were gone now. So, too, were the fighter-bombers. The girl had been right. She had been right about the salt and the water, and everything else she had advised or suggested.

Another snowman reared up in front of them, but Manderson cut it open at the neck before Crowe could pull the trigger on his weapon.

Was it possible that she was right about the creatures?

The twin fire hoses next to them were silent now, and Crowe glanced across to see why. Had the water run out?

Where the crew had been, two men to a hose, four of the white sluglike creatures stood silently. Absorbing. Digesting.

"Stony," Manderson said urgently, looking behind them.

Crowe turned. The fog had come up behind them. It was closing in on their position as he watched. The front of the cloud was alive with antibodies, and behind them moved the dense shapes of the macrophages.

"Stony, we did it," Manderson began, with a quiet resignation in his voice. "We held out long enough . . ." But there was a hissing noise from the front, and Mandy disappeared, replaced by one of *them*. The white-lidded eyes stared unblinkingly at Crowe from where Manderson had crouched.

Crowe screamed and turned his water blaster onto the macrophage. It tore a jagged line across the creature, and the remains of Manderson's suit spilled out, hanging loosely out of the torn white flesh.

The fog was thickening all around them now. He looked to the left and right, but if any of his men were left, they were invisible in the fog. He tapped his microphone and called his team, but got only silence in return.

An antibody struck the faceplate of his helmet, covering his eyes. Crowe screamed again and slapped it away. He strode forward into the mist, shaking his head violently, erratically, from side to side. The hose of the water blaster pulled him back, tried to stop him, and he wrenched at it, felt something give, then strode forward again.

The barrel of the device, disconnected and useless in his hands, swung around as he aimed the empty weapon at the whiter-than-white shapes that appeared around him.

"Mine eyes have seen the glory of the coming of the Lord. He is trampling out the vintage where the grapes of wrath are stored."

His voice filled the suit, and he unsealed and flipped up his face mask to let the words out into the fog.

"Glory, glory! Hallelujah!"

And then there was silence in the mist.

THE GOD FROM
THE MACHINE

It was faster going down the ladders, but there were still a lot of rungs. The staircases, too, were faster; they bounded down them in the dim light of the emergency lamps, two, three, even four steps at a time.

But it still seemed to take them a long time to get down to the main observation deck.

Tane found the entrance to the many flights of stairs leading down the main shaft of the Skytower, but Fatboy said, "Wait."

He checked himself and backed up to where Fatboy was staring out of the huge toughened glass windows of the observation deck.

His heart began to pound and blood rushed to his ears with a thrumming sound. His legs felt unsteady and he leaned against a handrail for support. The world around them had turned to white.

Auckland was awash in a sea of mist. The entire city had disappeared. All they could see in the cold glow of moonlight was the top of a cotton wool cloud. Way below them, the fog flashed on and off, a dim red color, and Tane remembered the fire engine parked in the middle of the road.

"Did we give them enough time?" he asked, looking to the south.

"I think we did," Fatboy said.

"What about us?" Tane asked in a small, quivering voice.

"We're too late," Fatboy said steadily. "There's no way out. It's over for us now." He turned and looked at Tane. "But not for Rebecca. If she made it to the submarine, then she can still make it to the underwater cave. She can still send the messages."

"Not for Rebecca." Tane's voice was a distant echo. Rebecca alone would endure life in the submarine as the rest of the world disappeared above her. Rebecca alone would send the messages back to the past.

The messages!

"The messages were signed 'TR,' " Tane protested feebly. " 'Tane and Rebecca.' Not just 'R'!"

Fatboy was quiet for a moment, staring out at the cloud. "If you were Rebecca, alone in a submarine, sending messages to the past, to herself and to you," he said slowly, "how would you sign them off?"

Tane realized with a cold heart that he was right. He looked at his brother and said nothing. He just looked, and Fatboy looked back at him without awkwardness. How wrong he had been, Tane thought, not to trust him from the beginning.

Fatboy said, "You and Rebecca—"

"Good mates," Tane said quickly.

Fatboy laughed. "She likes you, Tane. She really likes you. More than just good mates."

"No, really. We're just . . . what did she say?"

"Nothing," Fatboy said. "I doubt she would. But I could tell."

"You're wrong," Tane said.

"No, I'm right." Fatboy shook his head. "But it would have been wrong for me not to tell you now. Now that . . ." His voice trailed off, and his eyes drifted back to the rising fog around them.

"You always looked out for me," Tane said. "I should have—"

"You shouldn't have done anything different," Fatboy said. "I knew where you were coming from."

But this time Fatboy wouldn't be able to look out for him. Nor would he be able to look out for Fatboy. There was nothing anyone could do.

Tane looked at his brother and held out his hand. It was strange, but it seemed like the right thing to do. Fatboy took it and shook it, but then pulled him closer and pressed his nose and forehead to Tane's. Three times he pressed in the traditional *hongi*. Once for the person, once for the ancestors, and once for life in the world.

The *hongi* was a greeting, but this, they knew, was a goodbye.

They descended into the stairwell, into the shaft of the tower.

"Get out of the way!" Rebecca screamed, and jammed the Jeep into gear.

It smashed into the barrier pole with a crunch and the sound of broken glass.

"Stop!" the first guard shouted, but he seemed uncertain, and his pistol wavered between Rebecca and the oncoming fog.

The barrier pole didn't break; it was metal and just bent a little.

Rebecca thrust the car into reverse and backed off a few yards.

"Stop!" the other guard shouted now, raising his weapon.

She ignored him and stomped on the accelerator. The Jeep rammed forward and the metal bar bent a little more. She kept her foot down hard and the tires began to smoke, the end of the Jeep sliding around as the bar prevented her progress.

There was a crack of a gun, and the windshield shattered. Xena and Rebecca screamed in unison.

She dived across the seat of the Jeep, catching the door handle on her first try and falling out of the door of the vehicle. She grabbed Xena by the hand and slung her up around her neck, running toward the edge of the breakwater, instinctively putting the Jeep in between herself and the guards to give herself time to get some distance before they could fire again.

It helped for only a few seconds. There was another crack then and a whistle past her ear. Xena squealed again.

Rebecca raced down the road leading into the small cluster of buildings that was the naval base. Old, weatherboarded buildings with tin roofs, dating from the 1940s or earlier.

There were no more shots, and when she glanced back, she saw why. The guard hut and the Jeep were shrouded in mist, and where the second guard had been, the white shape of a macrophage stood silently, motionless.

The first guard was lying on the ground, screaming noiselessly, with a dozen antibodies covering his arms, legs, and face.

The fog was rolling in over the dark buildings to her right, but she had no option except to follow the road.

And there it was. Moored to the side of a long jetty. The familiar, bulbous, warm-yellow shape of the *Möbius*. It was barely a hundred yards away, out along the jetty.

The fog clouded around her and she stumbled, tripped and fell, Xena rolling away from her across the tar-seal with a squawk.

Rebecca tried to get back up, but her leg didn't seem to be working properly. Confused, she looked down to see a glutinous shape, with short fibrous tentacles, latched onto her thigh.

She screamed in fear, and then screamed again in pain as the sting of the needlelike fibers reached her shocked brain.

Somehow she hauled herself to her feet and hopped forward, dragging the useless leg behind her.

"Come on, Xena!" she called, but the little chimpanzee just sat there, quivering with fright, and looked at her.

There was a stinging in her left arm now as two of the antibodies attached themselves to it; then her arm, too, went numb and useless.

"You come if you want to," she yelled at the chimp. "I ain't waiting for you!"

She had no chance of making the submarine—she knew that now—but if she could just make the edge of the jetty and the waters of the harbor . . .

She collapsed again, just a yard or so from the edge, from safety, and looked down at another antibody digging its way into the shin of her good leg.

"Get off me!" she screamed, and crawled forward as best as she could with one good arm and only a little movement in her right leg.

The fog swirled around her, and a shape moved in front of her. She raised her head to see a macrophage, tall and white in the early light before the dawn, standing between her and the ocean. Waiting for her.

"Leave me alone!" she screamed, and crawled forward another few inches.

The shadow of the creature approached, and Rebecca screamed one last time, except the scream wasn't hers. It wasn't her voice; it wasn't even a human voice. There was a blur of brown hair and the sensation of small feet on her back, and Xena leaped up from her shoulders straight at the macrophage, clutching around its neck, bending it backward, overbalancing, and then there was no macrophage in front of her, only a rising spout of seawater, and it seemed to be minutes later that she heard the splash.

"Xena!" she cried as the fog continued to make ghastly, ghostly patterns all around her.

The voice of his flight controller sounded in his headset, and Ramirez pulled his jet around in a tight bank. As far as he could see, there was only fog.

"Roger that," Ramirez replied. They wanted one last low-level pass to visually confirm the status of the ground troops.

He circled around once again and descended. Beginning his run from the north. Toward the tall spire of the Skytower, jutting up through the clouds in the distance in front of him.

He dropped down out of the sky and skimmed across the

top of the mist like a stone skipping across water. He tried to peer down through the fog, but it had thickened and was now impenetrable.

He shook his head and keyed his radio to call base, but the words never left his mouth. The fog itself seemed to rear up in front of his aircraft.

The world went white, and there were banging noises against the cockpit and the body of the plane.

He hauled back on the stick and lifted the jet out of the rising mist, but it was already too late. There was a cough from his right wing and the jet flamed out. Something had been sucked through the engine. The left engine went two seconds later.

"Mayday, Mayday, Mayday," Flight Lieutenant Ramirez said urgently, but with professional calm, into his radio, "I have a double flameout. I am about to eject."

He kept the stick back, gaining as much height as he could, and then punched out of the cockpit with the two-handled ejection lever. The ejector seat kicked like a horse, and the jet hurtled onward in the sky, pilotless, toward the dark tower in the distance.

Ramirez's parachute opened with a grab on the back of his spine that wrenched at his insides. He felt sure he had broken something. But it didn't matter. By the time the parachute had floated gently to the earth, the harness and the flight suit were empty.

HOBSON STREET

The shaft was clear of mist. Free from antibodies and macrophages. They descended slowly, step by step, then faster.

Fatboy wore his full motorcycle leathers, but Tane had on just jeans and the fashionable leather jacket he had bought with Rebecca on their Lotto spending spree, a hundred and fifty years ago.

He thought the leather might be strong enough to keep out the antibodies, but he wasn't sure about the jeans.

At the very base of the tower, they had stowed their helmets, both full-face. It felt comforting to slide it on. It was at least some protection.

They emerged into a silent world at the top of the long staircase. The main foyer of the casino. The huge, weather-proof glass doors of the casino remained shut. Keeping the world, and the fog, at bay.

Fatboy moved toward the elevators but Tane put a hand on his arm.

"We'll never make it on the Harley," he whispered. "We need some protection from *them.*"

"What are you thinking?" Fatboy asked.

Tane nodded toward the huge glass doors of the foyer. Even as he did so, a shadow moved through the mist outside, silhouetted by the flashing red lights of the fire engine farther down the street.

They crouched hurriedly down inside the circular security desk near the casino entrance.

"The fire truck?" Fatboy asked with a frown. "They'll see us coming for miles."

"It's big and strong," Tane said. "And from here to Princes Wharf is all downhill, straight down Hobson Street."

Fatboy nodded his agreement. "It's worth a go."

More shapes moved past the doorway in stark contrast to his hopes. There was a sudden bang from one of the glass panels, and they both instinctively looked up but saw nothing.

Then came another loud bang, this time accompanied by the sound of cracking glass.

"I hope Rebecca is waiting for us when we get there," Tane said.

Fatboy smiled tightly in the mist. "How are we going to reach the fire truck?"

Outside, the intermittent red flash seemed like a bait to lure them out into the clutches of the macrophages.

"I say we make a run for it," Fatboy said. "Make a break for the fire truck, try to get inside before they can get to us."

"We'll never make it," Tane said doubtfully.

"Can't stay here forever," Fatboy countered.

Tane nodded. "Okay, but I think I need something a bit thicker than just a pair of jeans covering my legs if we're going out there."

He glanced around the foyer. There was a long reception counter on one side. A concierge desk in the center and on the other side a large café and a gift/souvenir shop. That seemed the most likely.

The shop door was locked, but the window surrendered easily to a blow from a trash bin, and they picked their way gingerly through the broken glass.

"A few plastic tikis are not going to keep those things away," Fatboy said.

There were baseball caps with New Zealand symbols, scarves, belts, woolen beanies, and T-shirts on a clothing rack in the center of the room. Tane was experimenting with the T-shirts, wrapping them thickly around his legs, when Fatboy said, "Over here."

Piled in a corner of the shop were sheepskin rugs, thick, woolly, and whiter than white. A popular souvenir for tourists of a country with 80 million sheep. Tane ran his fingers over the thick leather backing and nodded. "That should do it."

He wrapped a thick sheepskin around each leg, strapping them on with expensive leather belts. Another went around his midriff.

He pulled up the collar of his leather jacket and then tied a thick woolen scarf around his neck for further protection. A pair of leather gloves covered his hands.

"How do I look?" he asked.

"Baa," Fatboy replied.

Tane stopped what he was doing and considered that. He took another large sheepskin and draped it around his shoulders, fastening the corners around his neck with a large metal safety pin.

"Shape recognition," he said. "The antibodies recognize shapes. Remember Dr. Green's diagram with the circles and triangles and stalks? If we can change our shapes, then maybe they won't recognize us."

A moment or two later, Fatboy also was covered in fluffy sheepskins. If nothing else, they reasoned, it was more protection against the creatures.

They looked at each other for a long moment, then both burst out laughing, despite, or perhaps because of, the danger they faced.

The banging and crashing was constant now, from the toughened glass of the entranceway, and the ominous cracking noises were getting louder.

"We can't go that way," Fatboy said. "Maybe if we go back down in the elevator and come out through the car park on the side of the—"

Two of the huge glass panels shattered simultaneously, and fog poured into the atrium of the casino. With it came a terrible hissing sound, and the front of the fog came alive in front of them. Antibodies, hundreds of them, and behind them the larger shapes of macrophages.

"Get back," Fatboy yelled, spinning around and racing back into the interior of the casino.

Tane risked a glance backward. The casino was already full of a light mist, and it was thickening with every second. The macrophages were following them, but slowly, as if moving through water.

"They've slowed down," he shouted. "They can't move as fast where the fog is thin."

Tane looked over at the central row of elevators. The doors were open on the one they had used earlier.

They ran to it and Tane pressed the button for the first parking level. Nothing happened.

"Oh crap!" he said.

Outside the lift, the macrophages turned the corner of the central lift well and floated toward them, almost as if in slow motion.

Tane jammed his finger on the button again, and Fatboy stabbed at the CLOSE DOORS button.

The white shapes moved closer, blocking their exit. Tane cowered into the back of the elevator, holding his arms in front of him as if that would somehow protect him against *them*. Fatboy pulled himself up to his full height, folded his arms, and faced the approaching creatures. The closest of the creatures was just about at the doors of the lift when they slid smoothly shut.

The doors opened again with a *ping* on a misty, murky, gray concrete parking level. Only a small stream of fog flowed slowly down the ramps from the upper levels and was swiftly dealt with by the heavy air conditioners, used to dealing with car exhaust fumes.

"This way," Fatboy called, pointing to a sign marked EXIT.

It was an eerie feeling running through the underground mist. A broken fluorescent light flickered nearby, bleakly strobing the thin vapor. Their running footsteps echoed off the hard walls of the parking level.

Tane expected antibodies or macrophages to come flying out of the mist at any moment, but none materialized. Here on the parking levels, the mist was simply too thin for them.

They ran up a long sloping ramp, and then another, toward a sign marked HOBSON STREET EXIT.

The exit proved to be a curving lane, taking them up and out into the thicker fog of the open air.

"Crawl, don't walk," Tane said with a sudden flash of inspiration. "We have to change our shapes as much as possible. And move slowly. Crowe said they can feel movement in the fog."

They dropped to their hands and knees and moved with languorous, careful movements, trying not to disturb the thickening fog. They bypassed the payment booths and barriers at the far end of the lane, to find themselves on the pavement outside.

The fire engine was barely fifty yards away, in the middle of the intersection, the twin red flashing lights at the front and rear of the machine the only thing they could see of it. There was no sign of the crew, but Tane had not expected there to be. In the distance, a dog was barking madly.

The city street itself might as well not have existed, for all they could make of it.

Tane touched his helmet to Fatboy's and whispered, "Don't speak if you can help it. They are attracted to sound as well."

From near the fire engine, there came a hissing sound, growing in intensity. Tane froze and saw Fatboy do the same. He drew a cross over the faceplate of his helmet, which Fatboy could just see in the thick fog. *Don't even breathe.*

Two macrophages flew past them, moving fast, not stopping. They seemed not to sense Tane and Fatboy, motionless, on all fours, on the pavement at the top of the ramp. There was a whistling sound and a swirling in the air around them and a handful of antibodies drifted by.

Tane waited until the sounds had faded before tapping Fatboy lightly on the shoulder.

They stopped once more on the way to the fire engine, when a macrophage hissed to a halt right in front of them. Tane was sure it had seen them, and what it was waiting for he couldn't imagine. He shut his eyes and held his breath, waiting. What was it like, he wondered, to be ingested by one of the creatures? Did it hurt, or was it all too quick? He slowly opened his eyes, still waiting for obliteration; however, after a few moments, it slid away with a gradually increasing hiss.

Tane peered around the corner of the casino, trying to detect if there were any macrophages waiting by the machine. If there were any, he could not tell. They were invisible in the thick fog, and if they were not moving, they were silent.

The dog started barking again, very close by, although he could not see it.

There were hissing noises from the same direction, and the barking grew louder. The dog was quite safe, Tane thought bitterly. It was *human* cells the macrophages were out to destroy.

He crawled a yard forward, then another, and suddenly there was a low shape running through the fog at him, barking madly. The dog stopped a yard away and growled viciously, snarling at him with its lips drawn back and teeth bared. He reared back and upward in an instinctive reaction.

Suddenly there were hissing noises converging on them from three different directions.

"Run for it!" Fatboy cried, jumping to his feet.

The door closest to them was open.

Tane was in through the door first and heard Fatboy slamming it behind him. The driver's window was down, and he groped for the handle in the dark and fog. His hand latched on to something and he wound it furiously. The window closed.

There was a bang from the door they had just dived through, but the metal and toughened glass held. He caught a glimpse of a bloated white shape outside but forced his attention back to what he was doing.

Through the front windshield three or four of the creatures were approaching.

"Drive!" Fatboy shouted, grabbing at controls on the passenger side.

Drive? How? He had never driven a fire engine, or any kind of truck, before in his life. But then, neither had Fatboy. He found a key on the front dashboard, not on the steering column, and turned it. The engine roared into life.

Gearshift, where was the gearshift? The truck was automatic, he realized, and pulled the lever into DRIVE.

He found the handbrake and stomped on the gas pedal. The truck lifted and surged forward. There was a hard bang from the front of the machine, and two of the approaching macrophages disappeared, parts of their bodies flying out to the sides of the windshield. He spun the wheel to head down Hobson Street, toward the wharves. It was a one-way street, and they were going the wrong way, but that thought barely registered.

The thick wool of the sheepskins that covered him were smothered by antibodies, each Y-shaped creature fitting snugly into the next, more and more of them, covering him like a hideous patchwork quilt. A few landed on his helmet visor, and he brushed those away but ignored the rest.

There were more bangs now, from both sides of the truck.

"Got it!" Fatboy shouted, hitting a button and grabbing at a large joystick. A jet of water shot out from over their heads. Fatboy wrenched at the joystick and the stream shifted in front of the truck. "Go for it," Fatboy yelled.

Tane was. His foot was on the floor, and the big red engine accelerated smoothly.

A group of macrophages reared up out of the mist in front of them, and Fatboy swept the water across them, slicing them into pieces.

The crashing noises were all around the truck now, from the roof as well.

A side window behind them shattered, and the main windshield cracked as a macrophage slammed into it, the body crushing itself against the toughened glass, before flying away to the side.

The Mercedes convertible they had seen earlier was parked haphazardly, sideways across the street. Its nose was a crumpled mess, rammed into a parked car.

Tane hit it near the rear end, and it spun around and up into the air, over the parked car, and landed on its roof on the pavement.

Fatboy swept the jet of water from side to side and in front of them, clearing a path through the charging macrophages.

They flew across the Fanshawe Street intersection, colliding with, and demolishing, a traffic light. It barely slowed them down.

Tane held the engine straight on course, across the overpass, and gunned the engine again as the Tepid Baths slipped past below to his left.

A gust of sea breeze, the same sea breeze that had nearly knocked him off the tip of the Skytower, swept in from the harbor, lifting and pushing back the fog for a moment.

In that tiny window of time, Tane saw their doom.

They would never make it to Princes Wharf, he realized. They would never make it to the sea.

In front of them, blocking their path, revealed just for a moment by the rising curtain of fog, dimly lit by the long line of streetlights, were macrophages. Row upon ragged row. Column upon column. Spread across Quay Street and out through the entranceway to the wharves. Thousands of them. At the same location where he and Rebecca had once congregated with hundreds of people to march for the whales, now the macrophages were massed to march against the human race.

Not even the charging fire engine would be able to cut a path through that number of the creatures.

"Tane!" Fatboy shouted, and Tane spun his head to see the white face of a macrophage inside the truck, just a yard from his own. On Fatboy's side of the machine, the rear door had lost the battle with the macrophages and, now just a twisted mess of metal, hung pathetically from a single hinge.

Tane screamed, and the fire engine veered toward the concrete base of the overpass.

It all seemed to happen in slow motion. One moment the creature was moving toward him, and the next Fatboy was there, a shiny object in his raised hand.

Tane couldn't understand what it was for a second, and then it flashed down at the macrophage, slicing into its flesh. The *patu pounamu*, the greenstone club, slashing again and again at the creature.

It fell backward, and Fatboy thrust forward at it, the club a blur. He was shouting and chanting in Maori now, the blood of the warrior surging through his veins.

But the creature thrust forward again, its white flesh engulfing Fatboy's arm. He grunted a terrible, hollow sound, and the club dropped to the floor.

The truck veered into the concrete wall, sparks flying from the tortured metal. Tane wrenched his eyes back onto the road for a second, hauling at the wheel to keep the truck from smashing into the dirty gray concrete bridge support.

He looked back to see the creature, and Fatboy, disappearing out through the door of the machine.

Fatboy's voice, despairing but somehow undefeated, "Save the world, Tane!"

Then he was gone.

"Harley!" Tane screamed.

There was no time to grieve, no time to even accept the full enormity of the disaster that had just occurred. That would have to come later. There was a thunderclap above him, and he looked out through the shattered passenger window, through the thinned-out fog, to see a jet fighter aircraft clip the side of a skyscraper and plunge toward the ground in front of him.

The wreckage of the jet exploded along Quay Street in front of him, and there was no time to brake or take evasive action as the burning jet fuel and torn chunks of metal carved a long straight fiery scar across the city center.

The concussion blew out the window of the fire engine, and only Tane's instinctive reaction, ducking down behind the dashboard, saved him from being smeared over the back wall.

There was a wall of flames around him now, a barrier of fire, but then that was past, too, and he realized that the massive, fiery explosion had shattered the ranks of the macrophages, hundreds of them disintegrating in a single instant, many more being blown across the edge of the long wharf and into the ocean, where they shriveled and oozed. The seawater turned white.

Others disappeared under the thundering wheels of the fire truck, now out of control and tearing across the side of the wharf.

A small café, tables and chairs already scattered by the explosion, erupted under the charge of the fire engine. The truck veered to the left, but the metal safety railing coaxed it back onto a straight course.

Dazed, clinging to the doorframe, Tane could only watch as cafés, restaurants, and apartments flashed by the driver's window. The safety railing at the very end of the wharf was fast approaching.

The remaining macrophages were attacking now, flinging themselves at the broken body of the fire engine.

One reared up under the windshield and clambered over the edge of shattered glass and twisted rubber, reaching out toward Tane; then there was a thunderous crash, and Tane flew forward into the dashboard, blood pouring from his head, and the macrophage flew outward, spinning backward in midair as it fell toward the ocean.

Tane was almost aware of the safety rail shattering under the impact of the crash and the momentum of the fire engine, and then there was a strange silence, with just the screaming of the high revving engine and the ocean rushing up to meet the cabin of the truck.

THE DREAM

Images came in gasping blurs.

The sudden rush of water into the cabin. He remembered that, he thought. Or was it just his imagination creating dreams and tricking him into thinking that it was memory?

Like Fatboy's voice as the creature dragged him—no, that wasn't right, as *he thrust the creature*—out through the shattered door of the fire engine. Had that been real?

He thought he remembered the swirl of mud as the front of the truck nose-dived into the soft bottom of the ocean, at the end of the wharf. The patterns that appeared in the brown-gray whirls, the faces that tried to speak to him but just spiraled away into the water.

He remembered seeing the *Möbius*. The crazy yellow doll-like shape of the little submarine.

Giddy arses blown will tea-coffee a waste-bin.

He didn't remember swimming, or latching on to the top of the sub, or finding the escape hatch and climbing inside.

He didn't remember any of that, and yet he must have done all of that, for his next coherent memory was that of Rebecca, weeping, one arm around his neck, the other hanging limply by her side.

And the stupid grinning face of that damn monkey.

TE KENEHI TUARUA

Tane turned the outside lights on for a while to watch the fish at play, twittering around beneath the ceiling of the cave. They fascinated him.

It had been three days.

Three days since the wild ride down Hobson Street in the runaway fire engine. Three days since his brother had given up his own life for his. Three days since the end of the world.

No, not the end of the world. Just the beginning of the end of mankind.

There were millions, billions, of life-forms on the planet Earth, this tiny rock hurtling around the sun. But the human species was the one that had overstepped the mark. Pushed the boundaries a little too much. Tried to conquer and dominate that which could be neither conquered nor dominated.

Pride cometh before a fall, they said, and mankind certainly had had pride. Building monuments and civilizations that they thought would last forever, yet were just a pinprick in the long roll of fabric that was the history of the planet.

Three days, and he had spent most of them sleeping, according to Rebecca, who had somehow cared for him, despite grievous injuries of her own. Concussion, she thought, but she wasn't a doctor, so who could really know.

She wasn't a doctor, and neither was Tane. There soon would be no more doctors. Nor lawyers, nor stockbrokers, nor movie stars, nor presidents.

The view from the periscope camera was always the same. Endless banks of white fog, stretching in all directions.

By now it might have covered the whole of the country. Perhaps already made its start toward Australia. The Pacific Islands, and on to the coast of South America.

They'd try to stop it. They might even get better and better at fighting it. But it was too big. Too hungry. And there wasn't enough time.

There was good news, though. Rebecca's arm had regained a little bit of movement. She still couldn't walk, but she could feel her toes again, so that indicated that her system was slowly recovering from the tentacles of the antibodies.

Not Fatboy, though. There was no coming back from what had got him.

Rebecca smiled up at Tane from the bunk as he entered with a can of Diet Coke.

"There you go," he said, handing it to her one good arm. "Ready for some exercise?"

"What do you have in mind?" Rebecca smiled.

"I thought a little aerobics, maybe followed by some kickboxing, and a little mountain biking to round it all off."

She laughed.

Tane said, "Or we could just do the stretching exercises, like yesterday."

Xena flipped herself down from the topmost bunk as Tane grasped Rebecca's right ankle and bent her knee, pushing her ankle up to her backside. He held it there for a moment, then repeated the process on the other leg.

"Progress," he said cheerfully. "You were helping a bit that time. I could feel it."

She smiled again. "Every day it gets a little better. I don't think it's a permanent thing."

"Thank God."

"Indeed."

He stretched and bent her right leg a few more times.

Rebecca said wistfully, "I had my whole life mapped out, you know. Ever since I was twelve. I knew what university I wanted to go to, what I was going to major in. Where I was going to work. Everything like that. But life kept changing things. First my dad died. But after a while I thought I could cope with that and still stick to my plans. Then there was that thing with Mum. But I was on top of that, too, I thought."

Tane thought he caught a glimpse of a tear, but nothing more.

She said, "Then all this happened. Now nothing is the same. Nothing is ever going to be the same."

Tane changed legs. "Not me. I didn't know where I'd be, one year ahead. Most of the time I didn't know where I'd be one day ahead. But whatever I expected to come from my life, I sure as hell didn't expect to be sitting on the bottom of a cave in the Hauraki Gulf in a yellow submarine, drinking Diet Coke during the apocalypse."

Xena grabbed the can out of Rebecca's hand and wandered off toward the cockpit, chattering happily. She had quite a taste for it, they had discovered.

A brightly colored school of fish surrounded the porthole for a moment, as if fascinated by what they saw inside. Here, we are the goldfish bowl, Tane thought, but didn't say it out loud. It took a bit of getting used to, this life under the sea.

"Did we save them?" Rebecca asked. "Do you think?"

Tane smiled and took her hand. "I think we bought them a little time. We slowed down the fog enough to let them evacuate Auckland. But the fog won't stay still. It'll keep moving south, and so will the . . ." He paused, searching for the word.

"Refugees," Rebecca contributed, and she was right, but it seemed an odd word to be using for the population of Auckland.

"And pretty soon they'll run out of room to run."

Rebecca clasped her other hand over his and he felt the tension in her grasp.

"Is there any way to stop it? If only we—"

"I thought we agreed never to say 'if only.' " Tane forced a smile.

"Yeah, but if only—"

"If only this, if only that. If only we'd done things a little differently, we might have stopped the Chimera Project. You can never say 'if only.' "

"I know."

Tane closed his eyes for a moment, trying to get it out of his head. *If only* . . .

He looked up to see Rebecca smiling at him.

Tane fingered the *patu pounamu* hanging from a cord

around his neck. He hadn't remembered grabbing it, but Rebecca had apparently had to prize it out of his fingers after she had got him on board.

"You think we're supposed to start over?" Tane asked.

She nodded. "I think so. Once it is all over and the clouds of fog have slowly dissipated. Maybe months, maybe years from now. I think we get a new beginning. This time we will do it like your father said, as family with the world around us, not as conquerors of it."

He took her hand and held it, thinking about her words.

He tried to imagine it but a flood of images kept intruding. Fatboy in the door of the fire engine. His mother and father waving goodbye at the entrance to the Marae. Rebecca's mother, watching events on her television that were unfolding outside her window.

Xena sat in the corner of the cabin and slurped at her Coke and grinned at him.

"No," he said finally.

"No?" Rebecca's eyes were wide, questioning.

"Too many people died," Tane said. "Too many people died."

"But Kaitiakitanga," Rebecca protested. "Building a new race, teaching them to live in peace with the planet . . ."

"All of that I agree with," Tane said. "The teachings of the ancestors, the responsibility, the guardianship of all that lies around us. Kaitiakitanga."

He clasped her hand in both of his.

She said nothing, but he didn't need her to.

"You asked if there was any way to stop it, and I think there is. Nobody has to die."

"Nobody has to die." She twisted the words around in her mouth. "What do you mean?"

"The only way to stop it is to stop it from starting."

"Stop it from starting?"

She looked at him blankly and he asked, "Where's that notebook of yours with all the messages in it?"

"It's in my pocket. Why?"

"Those aren't the messages we're going to send."

She caught her breath, catching on to his meaning. "We change the messages!"

"Nobody has to die," Tane said. "If we change the messages, we can change the past."

"If we change the past," Rebecca breathed, "we change the future!"

"Our present." Tane smiled. "We can change our *now*."

"Then nobody has to die. Not Fatboy, not your mum and dad, my mum. Not even Zeta."

"Not even Zeta." Tane smiled. "I'm not sure about Grandad, though."

Rebecca laughed, and said, "Just when I was getting used to the idea of being stuck in a submarine with you for the rest of my life."

Tane laughed, but then his face grew serious. "But we can't make the same mistakes we did last time."

He paused and looked her straight in the eye before continuing. "So this time . . . let's get it right."

27

THE BEGINNING

THEY TOOK ALL THE TREES
PUT 'EM IN A TREE MUSEUM
AND THEY CHARGED THE PEOPLE
A DOLLAR AND A HALF JUST TO SEE 'EM.
DON'T IT ALWAYS SEEM TO GO
THAT YOU DON'T KNOW WHAT YOU'VE GOT
TILL IT'S GONE
THEY PAVED PARADISE
AND PUT UP A PARKING LOT.

—JONI MITCHELL, "BIG YELLOW TAXI"

The saving of the world started quietly enough for Tane Williams and Rebecca Richards, lying on their backs on a wooden platform on Lake Sunnyvale. Which wasn't really a lake at all.

Sunnyvale School was set in a small valley. A nice little suburban valley. A hundred years ago, it had been a nice little swamp where Pukeko and Black Stilts had competed for the best nesting positions, and croakless native frogs had snared insects with their flicking tongues. But now it was a nice little suburban valley, surrounded by nice little homes belonging to nice little homeowners who painted their fences and paid their taxes and never gave any thought to the fact that when it rained, all the water that ran through their properties also ran through the properties below, and the properties below those, and so on until it reached the lowest point of the valley floor. Which happened to be Sunnyvale School.

As a consequence, Sunnyvale School had to have very good drainage. When it rained hard, as it often did in the west of Auckland, an awful lot of that rain made its way down from the hillsides surrounding the school and ended up on the playing fields and netball courts of the small but cheerful school.

The stars above shone down with a piercing intensity that penetrated the haze of lights from the suburban homes around the valley. The moon, too, was lurking about, turning the weathered wood of the small platform to silver. From an open window in a house somewhere on the surrounding slopes, an old Joni Mitchell folk song reached out plaintively across the water to them.

Tane and Rebecca lay on their backs on the small wooden platform in the center of the two main playing fields and looked up at the stars, for the rain had stopped many hours ago, and the night was clear and beautiful. . . .

ACKNOWLEDGMENTS

Many thanks to Mere Whaanga, who provided great wisdom and advice on the cultural aspects of this story, and to Dr. Roger Booth, associate professor of immunology and health psychology at the University of Auckland, whose vivid descriptions of the immune system at work provided the basis for much of the science in this book and made a technical and complex subject highly entertaining. Thanks also to Creative New Zealand for their generous funding, which allowed me time to work on this book.

Here's an excerpt from Brian Falkner's next book—

BRAIN JACK!

DIRTY TRICKS
(DONE DIRT CHEAP)

On Friday, on his way to school, Sam Wilson brought the United States of America to its knees.

He didn't mean to. He was actually just trying to score a free headset for his computer, and in any case the words "to its knees" were the *New York Times*'s, not his (and a gross exaggeration, in Sam's view). Not as bad, though, as the *Washington Post*. Their headline writers must have been on a coffee binge because they got even more excited and screamed

National Disaster

in size-40 type.

Anyway, it was only for two or three days, and it really wasn't a disaster at all. At least not compared to what was still to come.

On that Friday morning, the 25th, as soon as he realized he was awake, Sam swung his long legs over the end of the bed that had been too small for him since he was twelve and a half. At the age of fourteen, nearly fifteen, he felt like Gulliver in the land of the little people, or Goldilocks sleeping in Baby Bear's bed.

He stretched, touching the low ceiling with his fingertips, feeling his muscles unknot and his back crack as he worked the cramped sleeping position out of his system. As he did so, his toe nudged something on the floor.

A book.

He picked it up, a school library book that he had been reading the night before. Nothing to involve the intellect or the emotions, just a trashy adventure story. Something to distract his brain long enough for him to get to sleep. It must have fallen off the bed during the night, and when it had landed, one of the pages had folded and creased. He smoothed the page back into place and ran a thumbnail down the crease to flatten it out before placing the book, neatly, on his study desk next to his computer.

The desk itself was tidy, as was the rest of the small bedroom, but if you had told Sam that the bedroom of a normal teenage boy would not have shoes lined up in a row *inside* the closet, or that a normal teenage boy's room would have clothes strewn across the floor, posters of rock bands on the walls, and some kind of sports equipment, maybe a baseball bat or a football, leaning against the door in such a way that you had to move it to get in, Sam would have looked at you rather strangely and probably wouldn't have been quite sure whether to believe you.

Why would you keep a room in such a condition? he might ask.

He made his bed, stripping the bedclothes and the top sheet, before straightening the bottom sheet, retucking the ends in and folding the sides down around them to create a perfect forty-five-degree crease.

He checked his watch (it was 6:50 and set precisely to the second, using the atomic clock in France). It was also the precise time he had intended to be awake, and out of bed, ready for action.

There was no alarm clock in the room. Nor on his watch. His computer could have set an alarm for him, but he had never needed one.

If, the night before, he told himself to wake up at 6:45 a.m. and repeated it to himself once or twice, then 6:45 a.m. was the time he would wake up. Not before, and not after, and regardless of the season or the amount of light outside his bedroom window. (Not much, since they had built that new apartment block on the other side of West 38th St.)

His laptop was already in his schoolbag, as was everything else he needed for school, plus everything he needed for his other, not-to-be-talked-about activity, long ago planned for this morning.

From a drawer in his desk, he took a small bottle of PVA glue. A white, thick liquid that dried clear and rubbery. He poured a little into a small plastic container and dabbed the ends of his fingers into it, making sure they were well and truly coated.

They took a few minutes to dry, and he waved his hands around in the air to hasten the process. *Look, Ma, no fingerprints.*

He grabbed a muesli bar and a banana for breakfast from the kitchen and quietly made his way down the hallway, past his parents' room, past the room they still called Louise's room, to the door of the apartment. He was moving silently down the dark, peeling corridor of their apartment block toward the stairs (the lifts hadn't worked for years) long before his parents even thought about stirring from whatever night world they were currently visiting.

He cut down 38th St. and turned right at 7th Ave. to avoid beggars' row along Broadway, even though it was shorter. Left at 32nd took him onto the Avenue of the Americas, which was crowded—jostling, bustling, shortness-of-breath crowded—at this time of the morning, but he was used to that, and it was still the safest street in the whole of Manhattan.

There were two dogs fighting on the corner of Sixth and Broadway outside a gaudily colored shop that sold Asian trinkets for two bucks a pop. The Korean owner of the shop came out with a broomstick and shouted indecipherably at the dogs, who completely ignored him. They just didn't care, Sam thought, or maybe just didn't understand Korean.

He crossed at the light to avoid the dogs and glanced up as the dark shadow of a police helicopter slid across the street. His breath caught in his chest for a moment, but the chopper didn't slow, just a routine patrol. It weaved smoothly between the monoliths of downtown New York, the side gunner spotlighted in a brilliant orange burst of early-morning sun.

He entered the café at 7:43 a.m. Precisely. The table he wanted was in use, but the smartly dressed businessman was just draining the last of his cappuccino, so Sam loitered by the door for a moment, pretending to read the chalkboard breakfast menu, until the man left.

He ordered a chai latte from the surly, mono-browed server and waited for it to arrive before opening his schoolbag. His bag of tricks. Dirty tricks.

The café was long and narrow, with tables spread right along the wall. His table was at the back of the café, deep in the heart of the building, beside a large, leafy potted plant with an interlaced trunk. The position was carefully chosen.

Opening the schoolbag was both exciting and terrifying at once. It was crossing a line, he knew that. It was the start of something, like strapping yourself into a roller coaster. No, more like a Special Forces soldier going behind enemy lines, or a spy setting out on a dangerous mission, depending on their skill, wits, and fast reactions to stay alive.

The bag had a zipper that went all the way around, and he had to open it fully to pull out his laptop. From the front pocket he took a parabolic aerial, unfolding the wings and embedding it at the base of the potted plant, behind the ornate interlaced trunk (it had to be man-made, but how did they do things like that?). The aerial slotted neatly behind the trunk of the tree, the latticework parabolic wings protruding from either side, but still not very obvious to the casual viewer.

The laptop had finished booting up, and he took a deep breath and looked around before starting.

The café was about three-quarters full: mostly dark-suited businessmen and -women. The occasional arty Greenwich Village type, slumming it with the suits.

A man in his twenties with a completely shaven head and a spider's-web tattoo crawling up the back of his neck was seated with a stern-looking, matronly woman, possibly his mother, in a severe gray woolen dress.

A small group of Japanese at a table by the door, most likely tourists, were busy taking photos of each other with their cell phones, looking at them, and laughing.

The waitress placed the tea in front of him with a thump. "Place" was the wrong word. She *plonked* the tea in front of him, so that some spilled over into the saucer. He smiled at her anyway, just to be polite, but she just scowled before turning her back and heading to the counter. What a *plonker*, he thought.

He switched his gaze to his laptop and opened his wireless connection manager. A red light on the front panel flickered orange, then changed to green as it picked up signals from wireless networks nearby. Green like a traffic light. Green for go.

The panel on his laptop showed seventeen networks in all: The café's own, free network for patrons was the strongest signal. The others came from all around and above him, gigabytes of data flying through the air of the café. Personal, confidential, private data, broadcast by people with utter faith in the security of their wireless networks.

Nor was that faith totally unjustified. With intrusion detection and high-level encryption, it would take a very special person to hack into that data. An expert. A genius. A devil. All of the above, some would say.

Someone like Sam.

He ignored sixteen of the signals. There was only one that interested him, an indistinct signal from a wireless access point on the other side of the old brick wall next to him, probably quite close by. The interference from the bricks, and other building materials in the wall, degraded the signal until it was as thin as a ghost, and only the most powerful of aerials would pick it up.

The parabolic aerial he was aiming in that direction was directional, with a built-in signal booster. He casually reached down and turned it slightly, back and forth, gauging the angle where the signal was the strongest. Only one bar out of five on the signal meter, even with the signal amplifier, but that one bar was enough.

Hacking the wireless access point was the easiest part. "Wireless security" was a contradiction in terms. Like "military intelligence" or "jumbo shrimp." He simply transmitted a generic disconnect signal, dropping the other station off the network. Lost and alone, it immediately began bleating, like some abandoned kitten mewling for its mother.

Sam intercepted the reconnect signal and broadcast it from his laptop. Less than a second later, he was part of the network. Dirty tricks. Done dirt cheap.

Now came the hard part.

"Softly, softly," he murmured to himself, well below the range of hearing of anyone in the café. Then, with another quick glance around at the other patrons, he crawled into the network, into the electronic world on the other side of the wall.